I0818001

ISLA'S GAME

DS ALBIE EDWARDS SERIES BOOK 2

KIMBERLEY SHEAD

This book is a work of fiction. Names, characters, places, and incidents either are products the author's imagination or are used factiously. Any resemblance to actual persons, living or dead, events, or locales are entirely coincidental.

Editing by Josiah Davis

Book cover by The Cover Collection

For my parents Jim and Chris DeRose
Thank you for everything :)

1

Esther MacDonald had no complaints. If questioned, she would say that she loved her life. She knew that perhaps she hadn't been dealt the best hand, but she was alive and was responsible for the life of her most precious possession, her son.

A gush of cool air spluttered and spewed from the car's heater and hit her smack in the face when she turned the key—a simultaneous wake up call for herself and the car. Esther's frantic fingers fiddled with dials until air swept upwards to smother the frost curtain that covered the windscreen like intricate webs constructed from spider's silk threads. As the frost blotches cleared, she leaned across the dashboard and switched on the radio. Mellow tunes filled the car. Classics that played on repeat at this ungodly hour each morning. Esther pulled away from the curb knowing that most sane people were tucked up in bed and that from the following Monday she would join the millions of people who worked regular hours.

Cleaning had not been her first employment choice. However, as a cleaner in a school, other doors had opened for her. Ambition was a dirty word to Esther. She denied the desire to better herself and laughed at the thought of having a life plan. In fact, she believed life was something that happened to her, and until she saw otherwise, nothing would change her mind. Everything she did involved hard work and commitment. She was scared of neither, and as a result knew she would succeed—if not for herself then for Dillon. Dillon, just the thought of his chubby hand gripped around her finger and his cute giggle when she picked him up brought a smile to her face. Yes, she would succeed for Dillon.

Not one to notice her surroundings, especially before sunrise, Esther began her daily journey on auto pilot, passing few cars on the way. She passed a sign on her left, Kent: The Garden of England', a quote she questioned often. Kent covered an extensive area, and not all parts were as idyllic as the quote made them sound. She indicated left and took the next slip road to leave the A2. Esther approached the roundabout with care, but kept her foot on the accelerator knowing that vehicles were scarce at that time of the morning. She turned the corner at speed, slammed her foot on the brake, and swerved to avoid a stationary car. At the last moment, she slowed the car as it spun towards the central reservation. Her hands gripped the steering wheel, her arms outstretched but her elbows locked. Esther's entire body braced and her back pressed into the shape of the driver's seat. The screech of the brakes and the scream that left her mouth drowned out the mellow tunes and whir of the heater until she ground to a halt. Then her heart slowed while the whir from the heater worked to soothe her hysteria.

Through the partial haze of the misted rear-view mirror, a metallic-grey car sat squat at least two feet out from the side of the curb. The doors were spread like elephants ears. The driver's side hung from its hinges. Esther smoothed her hair back from her face with shaking fingers. A screech of car wheels and the extended beep of a horn brought her to her senses. She turned the key in the ignition and manoeuvred her VW Beetle to the curb-side in front of the stationary car she'd hit.

Esther sat and waited until her pulse mimicked the melody that escaped from the radio and filled the silence. Decision made, after a moments hesitation, she opened the door. She placed her feet on the road, then at the last minute leaned backwards into the car to retrieve her large leather handbag from the foot well. She turned and faced the car she'd collided with, then scanned the surroundings for the owner. To her right was an overgrown wooded area, to her left tarmac. It seemed absurd to Esther that although she was only seconds away from a major road, the dominant noise came from morning birdsong rather than traffic which she knew would intensify over the next few hours. Since pulling over, she'd seen only two cars. Neither had slowed nor shown any inclination to stop. So much for human kindness, she thought, perhaps that doesn't kick in until later in the day. The hint of a smile slipped her pale face as quickly as it had appeared. She took several tentative steps towards the grey car and wrapped her black cardigan around her midriff to counteract the chill that ran down her spine from feeling open and exposed. With each step she took, Esther's senses heightened, and the icy air brushed her delicate skin. The cool metal of the car door frame numbed her palm on contact. She bent forward and peered inside. The interior was spotless. There were no personal items in immediate sight. She struggled to release the glove compartment to no avail. The storage area in her car that was crammed with maps, CDs, and rubbish was empty.

A rustle from behind startled Esther.

"Ow." She rubbed the top of her head and cursed where it had hit the door frame. Another rustle had her spinning around on her heels in time to see a figure stumble from the trees and head straight towards her. Startled, Esther attempted to assess the situation. The woman's arms flapped, her face distorted, her eyes wide, frantic. Esther's instant reaction was reflected terror as the woman lunged at her like a rabid animal, her arms flayed, and she grabbed out at Esther with fingers bent like claws. Esther took in her mud caked primrose dress, gouged scratches seeped thick. Crimson blood, clotted brown as it mixed with dirt and grime, meshed on her arms and legs. Her bulbous eyes protruded from a dirt smeared ghostly face. They brought terror to her heart long before a piercing cry left the girl's mouth.

"He's coming."

Esther froze.

"Help me. He's coming,"

Esther hesitated for just a moment before she grasped the girls clammy hand and dragged her to the VW. They both jumped inside. The girl turned her upper torso and leaned one arm on the top of the passenger's seat, eyes wide and body shaking. Tension seeped from every pore of this woman. It was contagious. Esther fumbled with her keys, and with the third attempt the engine turned over. Esther panicked as she realised shock had taken away her ability to remember how to drive. As quick as the routine had disappeared, so it came back within reaching distance once she put the car into gear without stalling. The further they drove, the more aware she was of the tension in her muscles and urged herself to relax. She looked at her passenger, now slumped in the front seat with her eyes closed. Her face resembled a pale mask left out in the elements. She sighed, turned on the heater and switched on the radio, until she felt comfortable again.

What next? It was too early to take her to the police station, she decided, although she had no idea if this was true. What she was sure about was that reaching her work place meant safety for them both.

Esther wriggled her bottom into the apex of the car seat and forced her shoulders back, giving her five foot body an inch more height. Movement from the backseat was so swift, although she caught a flicker in the rear-view mirror. Not quick enough to dodge a cool gloved hand wrap around her neck before her brain registered. She smelt leather and aniseed as she struggled to breathe. Her hands gripped the steering wheel, and her rigid body bucked. Cool metal imprinted the side of her neck.

"I wouldn't struggle," a deep velvet voice whispered in her ear. The type that could put you to sleep with a bedtime story. He forced her body further back, the springs in the chair uncomfortable against her skin.

"Our aim is to keep you alive but obviously that depends on how good you are at following instructions. Keep driving straight ahead, I'll tell you when to turn."

The voice was soothing, which contradicted the scenario that played out now, with her as a major character. Something he'd said petrified her more than anything else. He'd said "our". Esther turned her head to the left, and in an instant she realised her worst fears. Her ally, the petrified youthful girl, was no longer feigning sleep. Instead her gaze penetrated Esther, and she wore a smile like a trophy on her grubby face.

2

An incoming text flashed on the screen as Albie leaned over to retrieve his phone.

"Damn." He scanned ten messages, all from Eva. Next came the ring of the intercom. He jumped from seated, lifted the intercom, and buzzed her up, then unlocked the front door and left it ajar. Why bother to talk to her? He would get a mouthful, regardless. No need to anger her further by leaving her on the doorstep.

"Finally, what the hell's wrong with you? It's bollocks going to this funeral anyway, but turning up late?"

"I was out cold, Eva. Work." He shrugged his shoulders as if it was enough of an explanation. When he caught the look on her face, he continued. "Big case, kidnapping. Not slept for a few days."

Eva plonked her black leather handbag on the settee and slipped her coat from her shoulders.

"I'm surprised they've let you have time out, you know it's not as if you and Liv were family." Without waiting for an answer, she walked towards the bathroom. "You'd better get ready. Unless you're going casual?" Albie looked at his joggers and t-shirt then back at Eva. "I'll give you ten minutes, then we're off."

The journey could have been worse. Traffic in the tunnel at any time of day was horrendous. North London was an area he rarely frequented. Sometimes with work and on the odd occasion he visited his grandmother.

The rain accompanied them on the journey but the clouds to the north of the tunnel carried a heavier load and as if on cue, the heavens opened as they walked through the wrought-iron gates of the crematorium.

Albie pulled up the collar of his coat and inched under the large black umbrella Eva had the sense to bring from the boot of her car.

They hurried the crowd of mourners who hovered by the doorway and under the eaves of the church inside, out of the downpour. As Albie reached the doorway, he noted the lobby was full of people he'd rather not be in proximity with today or ever. He placed his hand in the small of Eva's back and guided her back down the steps.

"It's rather crowded in there. Don't think we'll get much of a welcome."

Eva studied his face. "Why are we here if you knew it would be this difficult? You know you could have visited her grave tomorrow."

"I owe it to her."

Eva laughed. "You keep telling yourself that, go on, beat yourself up. Olivia was a big girl, Albie. It was her job and poor skills in self defence that killed her, not you."

He stared at her. Her eyes twinkled. One thing he'd always admired about Eva was her loyalty. Not a noble trait in him, but in his eyes, admirable.

"She's dead, Eva. Have some compassion, just this once believe me when I say I made her life hell. Not recently, but when we first met."

"How so?"

"You know what I did in court? I blamed her for the muck up with the case." Eva shrugged her shoulders. "Eva, she nearly lost her job, a career she loved because of me."

"But she didn't. Now that's enough wallowing in self pity. They're going in. She strode forward, closed her umbrella as she reached the lobby, and placed it into a stand. Albie took the steps two at a time to catch her up, lowered his gaze, and slipped into a pew at the back of the church.

The service aired on the side of sorrow, rather than the celebration he knew Olivia would have preferred. In fact, the only person whose speech lightened the occasion came from a muted Maureen McNally, Olivia's foster parent from her teen years. But Maureen, a cuddly woman whose homemade food brought a smile to any face by nature, had a bubbly personality. A contrast to Robert, Olivia's adoptive parent, a man born into a family descended from nobility. He was a barrister who had once dabbled in politics. If only he could decide which political parties policies he agreed with and then commit.

The congregation were a real mix. Their singing voices echoed around the church, bounced off the walls, and disappeared into the high ceiling. Albie bowed his head when prayers were read, mouthed to hymns led by a choir, listened to the speeches from loved ones and the local vicar. He cringed at the thought the Olivia he knew would have hated the hypocrisy of it all.

Eva clung to his hand through the whole service and at one point, during The Lord is my Shepherd, he swore she dabbed tears from her eyes.

The Olivia he knew would have loved a few anecdotes of her life shared. Smiles on people's faces at her memory, 'In my Life' by the Beatles playing as the pallbearers carried her coffin from the church, and bright colours worn rather than the sombre blacks and greys worn today.

The sadness of the day to Albie was that Olivia's life, as far as the people here were concerned, began when she went into care at thirteen. It's as if before that she did not exist. What was sadder, her loss of life at twenty seven or her loss of life before she hit her teens?

Albie kept his head down until the congregation had left the church. The vicar's instructions were to either make their way back to the Devine's residence or join the family at the burial site. A plot bought by the Devine's for the last few generations.

Did she even want a burial? She wasn't a fan of insects and

screamed at the sight of worms when she dug through the soil to bed flowers in the spring. Fire petrified her though, it especially angered her if fires were started on purpose, and even more so if its victims were children. Albie nodded to Eva when she encouraged him to leave the church and follow the procession at a distance. Burial or cremation? Did it really matter now whether she had a preference?

Eve opened her umbrella and gave it to him to hold. At least he no longer had to hunch to ensure he didn't get wet.

"So what do you think, Eddie? Will this give you closure?"

Albie smiled at Eva, she was one of a few people that called him Eddie, she'd always been a cheeky cow.

"How do I know? Perhaps I'll feel better when it's just us here. When I can say what I'm feeling. Say goodbye," He shrugged and stopped walking. They were close enough, any closer would be an intrusion.

A noise behind caught his attention. A short woman dressed in a dark raincoat with shoulder length black hair, dappled with grey, and large dark sun-glasses out of place under the conspicuous rain clouds, hung back and watched the gathering.

"Another unwelcome visitor to the ceremony." Albie nodded in her direction. "Someone from her past, perhaps?" He made a mental note of trying to discover the identity of the woman before they left the cemetery. She may have known Olivia, perhaps a younger version.

Although they were too far from the scene to hear what they said, individuals throwing petals on the coffin shared words, heads bowed, tears shed and emotions high.

It was half an hour before they all filtered back towards the church. Ozzie and Maureen caught Albie's eye and nodded an acknowledgement, but apart from that the only person who approached them was Delilah Grange.

"What the bloody hell are you doing here?"

Albie watched the distraught figure stride between the grave stones in his direction.

Eva pulled on his arm. "Albie let's go, it's not worth causing a scene."

A small group gathered on the gravelled pathway and watched Delilah's determined stride.

"You've got a nerve. You're the reason she's in the ground." Her slap reverberated through his bones, precise, accurate, and heartfelt. She didn't draw a breath before pummelling his chest with small balled fists that knocked him backwards into Eva who stood her ground. It was just moments before grief replaced anger Delilah fell into his chest and sobbed.

Eva watched on as Albie lifted his arms to comfort his attacker but lowered them again as common sense took over. She stood on tiptoes, her mouth as close to his ears as she could reach. "Let's take our leave. We can visit another time. It will be less intrusive."

Albie didn't reply or even acknowledge his friend. Instead, he waited until Delilah's sobbing subsided. "I know this isn't what you want to hear but Liv and I, we were friends. I have to make my peace. Say goodbye."

Delilah raised her swollen bloodshot eyes to his, leant her head back and spat. Thick mucus ran over his closed left eyelid and down his cheek. Splattered spots of spit ran warm on his indifferent face. He fought the urge to wipe his face clean, instead he held her stare. It was only what he deserved. She'd let him off for the pain he'd caused her friend over the years.

"Okay that's enough," Eva squeezed between the pair, pushed her back into Albie to ensure some distance. "You've made your feelings clear. We'll respect your wishes."

This time when she manoeuvred Albie, he followed willingly. Without a word, she steered him from the graveyard, around the back of the church, and into the grounds of the crematorium. The benches were damp, and the rain was still falling, but Eva encouraged Albie to perch next to her on a bench while she busied herself wiping the remains of Delilah's attack from his face.

"You told me she disliked you. I wasn't expecting that much hostility." She smiled as she dispatched the used tissues into a nearby bin. "Well, at least you can cross her off your Christmas card list."

"Could have been worse." Albie leant forward, rubbed his hands over his face and sighed, a languid inaudible sigh.

"Hell Albie, either that woman's a complete nutter or you really did a number on her friend. I mean, other than what's in the public domain."

He rose from the bench, lifted his arms above his head, stretched on one side then the other and cricked his neck on either side before lighting a cigarette.

Eva scowled and coughed as he exhaled a cloud of smoke in her direction. She bit her lip, knowing better than to comment on his smoking habits, and instead led the way through a maze of identical plaque covered walls. Each inscribed with personal messages from loved ones, some with cones of flowers hung all gifts to the dead.

The only trace of rain left when Albie stood at Olivia's graveside were muddy puddles and drops blown from the leaves of the trees on the breeze. Eva stood behind him at a distance, she'd refused to wait in the car but still gave him the privacy he needed. For Albie, privacy was important for what he had to say.

His head hung but not in prayer. He wasn't one to ask for help from anyone. No, he was resigned to her death. In fact, death had courted her all of her life. She'd often joked she'd join the twenty seven club, if only she'd had any creative talent. Well, death had caught up with her in the shape of Nick Lansbury, it wasn't an easy, quick death either. He shook his head to clear his thoughts. This wasn't the reason for his visit and he refused to shoulder the blame for her death.

Albie cleared his throat and with no prepared speech, spoke to the petal covered casket.

"Hi Liv, I know what your thinking, I've got some nerve showing my face after only one visit to your bedside at the hospital. And you'd be right. I'll not apologise for my absence. I'd been absent from your life for years before we met up again. Instead, I came to tell you the truth about the Wilkins investigation."

Albie shuddered as a chilly breeze played with the branches of a nearby tree and inky clouds formed overhead, threatening another outbreak of rain.

"I'll not dwell on our relationship. I think we both know it was some kind of infatuation. You were so different. So many secrets danced in your eyes. You were intriguing. It was never love. If it had been, I would have put you before my career. Instead, you took the blame for my failings in the press and in your career. In court, it was me who told lies to save my skin. That's why I'm sorry. You were already so vulnerable and I took advantage of your growing feelings and trampled all over them for my gain. That's why I'm here. That's why I'm sorry."

He stopped, looked skyward, and blew out a lengthy breath refreshed by the cool raindrops as another shower took hold.

"You'll never see me again, Liv. You deserved better in life and I will not haunt you in death." He kissed the tips of two fingers, bent, and touched the freshly turned soil. He picked up a handful of the moist earth and scattered it over the casket.

"Rest in peace." He whispered and turned to leave.

3

Isabel looked at the gold-rimmed glass clock on the mantelpiece, nestled amongst the family photos. Each a memory of a happier time. She couldn't believe that just six months ago they were a perfect family. A thirtieth anniversary to remember. A party then off on a holiday to Wales, close to the place Iain had proposed all those years before. They were so in love and on the start of a wonderful journey together.

She fiddled with the sleeve of the cardigan, found a damp tissue and dabbed at the tears from under her red rimmed eyes. Isabel inspected each photo and tried to imitate the smiles on each face. She picked up a large photograph of her and Iain on their wedding day next to their anniversary photo. How could she still love him after such betrayal? This had to be why. Years of life lived together.

A soft cry from the baby monitor brought her back to the present. She looked at the clock again. Esther was late. It was unlike her to be away from Dillon longer than necessary. However, it was her last day. Perhaps her colleagues had laid on a farewell coffee. Isabel smiled, the crying from the monitor had faded and instead contagious chuckles rang from the gadget. Dillon was so contented, just like Esther as a baby.

Isabel made her way to the stairs. It was always better to get him while he was happy. The shrill ring of her phone stopped her in the hallway. She hesitated, they'd ring back if it was important. Ignoring the phone, she climbed the stairs to the spare room. Esther always called her mobile. In fact, very few people made contact on the house phone now. She swung open the bedroom door and her grandson greeted her with an enormous smile.

"Nana na na." Dillon cooed as she wrapped her arms around him and breathed in his sweet milky smell.

The ring of the phone interrupted their cuddle.

"I suppose we'd better get that. What do you say Dillon, shall we get that?" She bounced him on her hip as she manoeuvred them downstairs at a slow gallop. Then snatched the phone from the cradle.

"The MacDonald residence. How may I help you?" She sang in a voice she saved for the telephone.

"Mrs MacDonald? Isabel MacDonald?"

"Speaking."

"Mrs MacDonald, this is Mrs Lewis, Esther's supervisor. Sorry to bother you at home..."

"Has something happened? Is Esther all right?" Her grip tightened, and she pulled Dillon closer into the crook of her waist. He whined as she bounced him on her protruded hip, bounced him and pecked him on the head.

"That's just it, Mrs MacDonald. I don't wish to alarm you, but Esther didn't turn up to work today." Isabel tried to control the light shaking of her body. Her chest tightened, and the patterns in the wallpaper moved and merge. "Mrs MacDonald, are you still there?"

"Yes, yes... She left as normal this morning." The words left her mouth in a whisper.

"Sorry Mrs MacDonald. I'm sure there's an explanation. Perhaps her car's broken down. I just thought it was out of character for her not to be in touch, especially on her last day."

Isabel tried to answer, the polite words of agreement caught in the back of her throat.

"Let her know when she turns up. We wish her the best of luck in her new job. And ask her to call. Goodbye, Mrs MacDonald."

Isabel collapsed to her knees, and the phone slipped from her hand. Dillon struggled from her grip and crawled towards the toy box in the living room, giggling with each movement.

Isabel sat, numb from confusion, a recent mechanism put in place to deal with life's traumas. She could not cope with much more heartache. Slumped forward in defeat, it was easier to retreat into herself than face problems. She'd learned that over the last few years and gained a certain amount of perverse enjoyment from wallowing in self pity.

"Nana na na," Dillon squealed as he threw a toy over his shoulder. Isabel watched her beautiful grandson at play, oblivious of her deep rooted fear for Esther's whereabouts. Negative Nora, that's what Iain called her before their marriage fell apart. I always look at the worst-case scenario and double the horror.

Esther had not arrived at work, but even more unsettling and out of character she had not returned home to Dillon. Isabel glanced once more at the clock, three hours later than usual. Something was wrong. Isabel retrieved the phone from the floor. She didn't need Iain. She would sort this out alone.

4

Albie sat at his desk, thankful that he'd slipped back into his shared office without too much fuss and kept busy for the rest of the morning. He took pride because the pile of paperwork to action looked healthier than it had in a long time. A small achievement that he was aware would be short lived. Although he despised the paperwork side of his job more than any other part, in this case it had served a purpose. It had given him more to think about than brooding on the funeral he'd left just a few hours earlier.

Now, while waiting for Tanya to bring back his coffee and lunch from the local deli, he had time to think. He tapped the table with the fingertips of one hand and banged his flat palm on the desk with his other. The beat intensified until he pushed back his chair, jumped to his feet, and paced. The tick of the wall clock pulsed in his ear, a throb at his temple sharpened, a common occurrence since the attack on Olivia. It amplified his guilt into a horrendous, excreting puss that his subconscious fed off as it festered and grew inside his head. Time to think caused the throb to deepen. Images flashed in his head like a disjointed recognition while bile threatened to explode from the depths of his stomach. It's taste, bitter in his mouth.

He stopped pacing, leaned against his desk and faced the doorway, excited about lunch and Tanya's return. He gripped the rim of the desk with each hand, the rhythm of impatient finger taps deepened with his use of two hands. Laughter from outside the office spilled into the room as the door flew open, his thoughts, so real, eradicated as he moved to greet the man who'd entered behind an animated Tanya.

"Look who I found on my way to the deli." She gestured to the tall, slim man balanced on crutches in the doorway.

"You're looking good back on your feet. How's it going Frankie?" Albie helped him to the plush leather burgundy chair by his bookshelf, took Frank's hand in his, and gave it a firm shake. "You've had the plaster removed. Bet that's a lot easier."

"Yeah. I can scratch itches now without using mum's knitting needles. It's so good to be back. Just catching up. It's boring at home now." Tanya handed out the sandwiches and perched on the arm of his chair. Albie leaned back against the table and took a large mouthful of a chicken and mustard sandwich. Ploughman's Pickle? He coughed, erratic coughs from the back of his throat, reached for a glass of water and took a gulp. One day Tanya would come back with the actual lunch he'd ordered. He watched his colleagues chat. This was the first time they had all been together for a few months. He could live with tangy pickle for today.

"So Frankie, when are you coming back?" Albie asked, interrupting their banter.

"I'm ready as soon as you'll have me. I can work in the office until I'm fit to work a case again. Get up to date with some of your paperwork, Sarge." He smiled and nodded at the pile Albie had made inroads on that morning.

"Still as cocky as ever, then?" He smiled and sipped his coffee. "It's okay with me if you go through the proper processes. It'll be great to have you back. Someone to back me up again. Won't it Watts?" Tanya screwed her nose up at her boss, with her mouth full of chicken and mustard sandwich.

Albie settled back into his chair to finish his lunch and watched their interaction, adding an occasional comment, but on the whole he felt great at the opportunity to observe the camaraderie of his team.

A hesitant tap on the office door interrupted their hugs and goodbyes.

Albie shouted, "come." A young officer poked her head around the door. She scanned the room before entering, and scurried forward, her head angled so her thick black hair curtained her face. Without acknowledging the others, she stopped two feet in front of Albie and outstretched her arm to hand him a manila file.

"Frankie, this is the newest member of our team. Jana Kolska." Albie took the file and watched the polite nod from the youthful woman.

"There's another abandoned car, Sarge."

"Is it the same M.O. as the others?" Tanya asked, breaking away from Frankie's hug.

Albie opened the file and scanned the singular piece of paper.

"Found on a slip road off the A2. Both front doors open, passengers door damaged. Inside clean. A mud trailed from the woods led to an area in front of the abandoned car. Skid marks." He tapped the bottom of the page and grabbed his jacket. "Possible witnesses. Let's go." He turned to Frank. "Have a chat with Jana, she can find you a desk for tomorrow." Tanya hugged Frank one last time, grabbed her bag, followed her boss, and slipped her jacket on as she jogged to the lift.

5

Isla sat upright on a dusty-pink, velveteen, high-backed chair in front of a cluttered walnut dressing table with large brass flower handles, and a three-way mirror. She flicked a platinum blonde curl from her face and pouted her full lips. She twisted the bottom of the blood red lipstick case and painted her fleshy bottom lip with slow precise movements. One eye remained on a well-worn photo of Marilyn Monroe, in a similar pose, blowing a kiss to her adoring fans. It was dog-eared and stuck between the mirror and a metal clasp which held the creased image in place.

From the corner of her eye, she spied her own fan. He was awkward and insignificant when she first met him, but now he was loyal like a puppy, and infatuated by her. She'd picked her partner with precision. He hadn't been her first choice. To begin with, before he showed his darker side, Isla had been unsure of the traits she desired in a business partner. List making helped. She had made note of pros and cons of men who were loyal, would work for a cause, and were keen on justice—her type of justice. However, it took her a few months to recognise the personality type she could trust. Trust was of the utmost importance if she was to share her darkest secrets and desires with a partner. He had to be someone who would have no qualms of making them a reality.

Isla smiled. The smile she saved especially for Devon. She found a gratuitous enjoyment at his expense when he flushed with embarrassment and adjusted his trousers to hide his arousal. She brushed her top lip with the lipstick, left a deep red imprint on the tissue she used to blot her lips, then blew Devon a kiss. She had his full attention.

Isla slipped her feet into fluffy, kitten-heeled, slippers. At five feet five inches they added an extra inch to her height, and in her mind, to her appeal. She turned and walked towards Devon, easing his legs apart she shimmied between them and placed one hand on his chest. Isla had always loved the feel of silk on her skin, and the pale-blue baby doll nightie felt sleek under the silk negligee that slipped from her shoulders. Lamp light settled over the subtle silhouette of her hourglass figure, and a hint of her erect nipple strained against the material as she leant forward. Isla placed her hand over his and with gentle coaxing slid it from her hip where it rested and took it on a tour of her body. She closed her eyes and listened to his erratic breathing. His caresses became more urgent, exploratory.

Isla felt empty.

She learned in her first fumbled attempts at sex that she wasn't textbook aroused. She needed control, men, women, herself. If she was in control that was enough.

Awareness of the control she held over Devon in all areas of his life was why, with him, she could perform. Or at least show some aptitude of normality. She rubbed her leg against his bulge, and he whimpered. His eyes glazed over and she felt need squirm in her lower stomach. Her hand slipped from his shoulder to his chest. She knew that her release was in her own hands.

Esther was floating, she was astride an angel-winged white cloud surrounded by a faultless turquoise backdrop. Breeze buffered the cloud back and forth like the rhythm of a rocking chair. She tried to open her mouth to scream, but they sewed her lips together. Her throat rasped, and she struggled to swallow. She picked up an oar from the shelf above her head and paddled away from a fast-moving cloud on a collision course with her own. Instinct told her to paddle harder while trying to avoid the cloud in front. Too late, she was hooked to a multi-coloured cloud with a changing palette. De-energised, she slumped back into the softness that enfolded her and resigned herself to go on a dream journey. It was not until she passed a large Mexican death mask worn by someone on an opposite cloud did she take notice. When the figure opposite removed the mask from her face, she found what brief fight she had and resurfaced, terrified, but ecstatic to be alive.

Esther struggled to focus on her surroundings as the outlines of familiar objects blurred in and out of her vision. Blood red and black dominated the colour scheme of the room, reminding her of a Pulp Fiction poster. A throb in her temple kept in time with a drum beat that played in her head. She rubbed her fingertips across her forehead, massaging as she went to ease the throbbing. Each movement was heavy and restricted by the clank of metal. Esther looked down at the snake-like chains that constricted her movement. Esther's tongue stuck to the roof of her mouth. Adrenaline pumped at high-speed into the blood tracks of her body, pumped by an over zealous heart. Senses heightened, she leaned on her hand and pushed her body up and back until she hit a solid, wooden headboard which like a giant splint kept her upright.

Snippets of memory flashed in her head. Her eyes widened, and her voice threatened to escape in a deafening scream. Primal instinct or fear smothered the sound before it escaped her lips. She realised in a moment of clarity that she had choices, and the choices she made define the length of her life. By remaining inconspicuous, Esther might hang on to some control, and that was her chief aim. To remain in control of her life for as long as possible.

She glanced at her manacled wrists, lifted one arm and watched the solid manacles slip an inch, followed by thick links of chain. The metal edge left imprints in her delicate skin but was loose enough for blood to circulate. Large links of inch-thick metal made up an endless coil of chain on either side of her body. She followed the chain to a metal ring the size of a basketball hoop that hung flush against the blood red wall. The amount of chain coiled on each side of the bed eased Esther's fears. The length of chain gave her a certain amount of freedom, she rationalised.

A voice in her head whispered, you're a survivor. She closed her eyes and visualised her mother. She held a smiling Dillon in a tight grip on her thigh and swayed to a silent soundtrack. Esther walked towards the figure, arms outstretched to take her son. Just as he was within touching distance, Isabel turned and walked away. Esther curled into a ball. Her tears fell on her prayer posed hands. Please, she mouthed to the retreating figure. Isabel stopped and looked over her shoulder at the collapsed heap on the floor. She held up her free hand and beckoned her daughter to follow. Esther tried to scramble to her feet, but the chains restrained her. The more she fought to free herself, the tighter her encasement. With each movement the chains squeezed, a boa constrictor preparing its prey for death. Still she struggled until breath was squeezed from her wilting body.

6

Time had never dragged before. Isobel had never associated pain with the movement of the clock's hands before today. In fact, in her personal experience, a shortage of time had been more of an issue than too much. The click of a latch and squeak of the gate hinge drew Isabel back from the hypnotic action of the clock. She ran to the front door in time to catch the daily handful of junk mail scattered between an odd bill as they dived through the letterbox courtesy of Pat, their loyal postman. Obviously, his name wasn't really Pat (well, she didn't think so, anyway). It was Esther and Liam's nickname for him, not very original, but it stuck. He had delivered this round since she had moved in with her young family twenty-two years earlier. One constant in her ever-changing life. The only change she'd noticed with Pat was he'd gone from two-to-one round a day.

Isabel flicked through the handful of envelopes and threw all but an electricity bill into the bin behind the living room door. She sat on the settee in the bay window and slipped into the dip she'd worn in over the years. She inched back the crisp white net curtain. This was her chair, one she snuggled in to feed the baby, read, watch TV, and even knit when she went through her creative phase. More than anything else, this seat kept her in touch with the outside world. Gave her an insight, advanced warning of who was about to enter her life. Gave her control of who she let in and who to ignore.

The tick of the clock echoed in her head, a slow methodical pace. Isabel covered her mouth and sobbed dry tears for her loss. Her loss of control. With bitterness and a pinch of trepidation, Isabel dialled Iain's new number.

He picked up after the second ring,

"Hello." His deep velvet tones washed over her. It was too soon to chat with the man she still loved. "Hello, who's there?" His voice, a little clipped and impatient now, reminded her of the reason behind her call.

"Iain. It's me. Sorry to call. I know I'm the last person you..."

"Isabel? I've told you to give me space. What are you thinking calling this number? Sally could have answered." The velvet tone that enticed her when he first answered had morphed into a stranger's voice. A stranger teetering on rage.

"Don't flatter yourself, Iain. I rang because I'm at my wits end. Esther is missing. And you know what, fuck Sally." She slammed down the phone and took the receiver from the cradle, buried her face in the hands, and sobbed. She sobbed for her wasted life, for years of selflessness, for her inability to take control of the life. But overall she sobbed for her lost daughter. Poor Esther. Who looked out for her beautiful daughter? She wiped away empty tears with a crumpled, damp tissue and picked up the phone.

"Hello. Police please. I'd like to report my daughter missing."

7

Albie stood on the curb-side, distracted by a consistent stream of traffic that passed the cordoned off area at a slow pace. It seemed as if curiosity was a human trait possessed by the majority. As normal, there were rubberneckers slowing down to glimpse the turmoil and on the verge of causing another accident. A member of the public called the original sighting of the car in at five o'clock that morning by a man in his fifties, after travelling home early from a night shift. He had been reluctant to talk to the police, although what he'd witnessed weighed heavy on his mind. It was guilt that made him contact them. After sharing his worries, he retired to bed with a clear conscience.

Turning his back on the traffic, Albie focused on the wooded area which laid back from the footpath. It was dense with heavily leaved trees, brambles and well fed stinging nettles thriving along either side of a dry manmade trail. An ideal area for early morning and late night dog walks, it was quiet enough further into the woods for a person to feel isolated and vulnerable, especially in the early hours of the morning. Hidden in a busy place. Perfect for people just passing through to cause havoc. But it was also a spot known to locals as somewhere they could go if they were up to no good.

Tanya's work was quick yet precise as she searched inside and outside the car in silence. In fact, as an onlooker he could have been watching a silent movie. Each police officer an actor engrossed in their individual role while traffic sounds in the background were an added affect. Albie caught Tanya's eye and indicated his intention with a nod before he followed the pathway under the tree's canopies. Sheltered by the leafy branches, Albie scanned the greenery the further he walked the more he noticed an unpredictable depth on the brambles on either side. After a few steps, Albie had to tiptoe around muddy patches on the pathway where the heat from the sun was blocked. He slipped a few times, holding his arms out like an unbalanced aeroplane, and fell to the side into a tree trunk before he stopped.

"Shit." He slipped his soft leather shoe off and smelt the suspicious murky brown mud trodden into the instep. He flung it to the ground and gagged on the inhale.

"Dog owner's, bloody dickheads. Never pick up their dog's crap." He continued to rub the sole back and forth on the grass until the worst rubbed off or was caked in mud. Thankful to taste the freshness left by the early morning dew, still visible, balanced on blades of grass and dripping from leaves as he brushed the branches with his shoulders. Albie had not strayed too far from the scene, but the isolation he felt and the silence broken up by the intermittent buzz of distant engines sparked a dormant animal fear. He in a small thicket, closed his eyes, tuned out the buzz of the traffic in the distance, and listened. Birdsong, crickets, the chatter of squirrels, and rustle of foliage were distinct. It amazed him how such a small area ignored by so many people could be such a thriving habitat.

The chatter of his wildlife hosts became more purposeful the deeper he explored. Unsure of what he'd hoped to find, Albie took one last full turn of the surrounding trees. A glimpse of light flew out from behind the trees and danced and weaved towards him, then disappeared. He focused on the tree for a few seconds before he walked over. Behind the aged, thick, tree trunk were dense bushes covered in lethal spiky thorns, a threat to anyone who tried to enter. Albie knelt and untangled a piece of bright lemon material.

"Fuck." Blood blobbed on the surface of his thumb and on the point of a large thorn. Albie sucked the tip of his thumb then shook it in the air as if the action would stop the pulsating throb. He rubbed the piece of material between the fingers and thumb of his other hand, pushed it into his jacket pocket, and retraced his steps. They were coming to the area and looking for evidence but didn't even know whether a crime had been committed.

Tanya sat in the passenger's seat of the car. She has her notepad open and appeared engrossed in her jottings. Albie stamped as much mud from his shoes as he could then scrapped them on the curb to remove any other traces before strolling over to join Tanya in the car.

"Well? What's the verdict?"

Tanya slipped her notepad and pen into the small canvas shoulder bag pooled on her lap.

"It's hard to say, sir. All I know is, this is bigger than abandoned cars. It's the fourth in as many weeks. All stolen just days before being abandoned. Deep cleaned both inside and out. It makes little sense. Unless..."

"Unless it's connected to something bigger?" Albie turned the key in the ignition and tried to ignore the smell of dog's shit mingled with a burst of cool air. He waited for a gap, then pulled out into the traffic. "Let's see if we can make some connections."

Tanya nodded and fiddled with the radio. *News and travel on every channel. They could do without that* she smiled and turned the radio off. The journey back to the station was uneventful, roadwork and accident free, a novelty for the end of August.

As expected, Detective Inspector Sarah Masters had ordered an early afternoon briefing to discuss further developments in this mish-mash case. Albie had known Sarah for twelve years. He wouldn't have classed her as a friend. He was not one to invest enough time in people to make friends. In fact, in all honesty he had just one friend to his name, and it was her who invested time and energy into their relationship.

Sarah's change of time for briefings this week was unexpected and unpopular, because people are creatures of habit. Albie scanned the officers, most stood in the same areas as in each morning briefing. Somewhere deep in discussion with colleagues while others joked around. Some gulped bland drinks from the station's machines, others from the nearest newsagents or coffee shop. Many ate, some for the first time that day, others as a habit or for comfort. They were all so different, that's why they gelled as a team. Change was one area they could all agree on. Change to routine was difficult to accept.

Sarah's entry to the room appeared to go unnoticed by most. Albie was aware of every movement, from the effort she put into shouldering the door open to the measured steps she walked a scant distance to the central space in front of the boards. He studied the scribbles she made and images added. A draft caught the back of Albie's neck and he shuddered as he spotted the shake of her hand, the occasional tick in her right eye, and the quiver of her bottom lip as she spoke.

Inspector Masters made her initial apologies for her recent absences. Her voice thick and gruff from the result of a thirty a day habit that she'd spent most of her life trying to quit. Albie examined her features. Her complexion lacked its English rose blush which adorned her face all year round. A greyish tint darkened the skin around her eyes and she'd scraped her hair up into a tight, dishcloth blond bun. The suit she wore hung from her frame when a month before it had emphasised her hourglass figure. When had this happened? And he thought he was an observant person. Sarah Masters picked up a chopstick, her favourite pointing tool, and pointed at Albie.

"DS Edwards. Perhaps you could assist me?"

He slipped between groups of officers and retrieved the stick from her shaky grip. With one subtle movement he pushed a chair nearer to his inspector and gestured for her to sit. Instead, she stood tall and placed one hand over the back of the chair to support her slender frame.

"Right. We'll begin with the cars." Sarah nodded to Albie, and he pointed to each in turn. "First, what is the connection between these stolen cars? Including the one abandoned today?"

Tanya raised her hand, and Albie nodded. "PC Watts. How about you update us with the connections between the stolen vehicles?"

"Sir, although these cars have no common connections of make, age or owners they were all abandoned on different slip roads off the A2/M2 route."

"Many cars are stolen and abandoned PC Watts. Apart from the stretch of road, how else are they connected." DS Fawn's interruption was personal. Albie huffed, undid the top button of his shirt and stepped forward, but before he could speak Tanya answered.

"True, DS Fawn. However, each car abandoned had the front passenger and driver's door open wide. They'd parked so close to the exit of the slip road they were difficult to miss, even travelling at a reasonable speed. They were left in the early hours of the morning and both the inside and outside had undergone an extensive clean."

Masters appeared deep in thought. Seconds ticked away until Albie cleared his throat to fill the uncomfortable silence. All eyes were on Masters as if her insight were a message from a messiah.

"Sarah." Albie whispered, his eyes drawn to her restless hands and uncontrollable shaking.

"Good." She tightened her grip on the chair back. "As you can see. Each car has a photograph of a missing woman." Sarah took slow, deliberate steps and sat on the high-backed chair. "DS Edwards will explain his theory."

Albie held out the chopstick to Tanya, and she took the baton. She moved to the opposite board and pointed to the first image. "Before we discuss each individual girl, DS Edwards will explain the connections made by our team." Tanya lowered her arm and tapped a beat on her thigh to distract from her nervousness. She nodded to Albie.

"As explained, the four cars abandoned over the previous four weeks plus a fifth car this week have tentative links." He scanned the faces and gave the crowd a few seconds to digest the information and dispute if there was disagreement. "Good, we're all on board with the first connection. For the next part, you'll need an open mind. Just hook onto the facts. The first car was abandoned the last Friday in July. By the Monday, we've had all missing person reported." Tanya pointed her stick at the image of Claire Lance, a beautiful redhead with porcelain skin and bright blue almond-shaped eyes looked out at them from over her shoulder. One finger pressed against her pouting lips, tattooed with 'shh,' down its length. "Claire Lance, 26, an air hostess on her way to Stansted Airport to board a plane to the Caribbean, loved her job. She'd been at home in Greenwich. Her father contacted us when he hadn't heard from her. Claire always sent a message to let him know she'd arrived. She did not arrive at work. Her colleagues state that this is out of character. She was a reliable and efficient member of staff. From when she left her home at 2.45am on Thursday morning, both Claire and her red Nissan disappeared off the face of the planet."

Tanya moved the chopstick to the next image.

"So you're saying that Claire is connected to the abandoned car?" DI Fawn moved forward as she spoke. "And the others?" She asked while scanning the three other faces. Each as young, full of life, and beautiful as the next.

"Each woman reported missing after people found the cars abandoned in similar situations. All the women are in their late twenties or early thirties are independent. They come from unique backgrounds but have family networks from which they gain emotional support. Each woman is financially independence. We could label all of them as ambitious in their particular field."

DS Fawn raised her hand in the air. Albie held his breath, nodded, and waited for the onslaught.

"So. In a nutshell, your theory is that someone is stealing and abandoning cars but not before scrubbing them inside and out. Your thought process then somehow links this with an elaborate ruze to kidnap victims are of a similar age, ambition, and live within the vicinity of two motorways." Rachel Fawn laughed aloud. A long purposeful exaggerated laugh. "You really want us to suspend reality.

No disrespect, Marm." She turned her attention to Sarah, "but if that's everything, can we get back to work now?"

DI Masters pushed herself to her feet and steadied herself.

"Yes. DS Fawn. Your team can follow up on the abandoned cars. Find any links you can with the missing girls." Before Fawn could dispute her orders, she turned her attention to Albie.

"DS Edwards. Most theories are far fetched until proven. Your team are to investigate the women's disappearance." Her eyes wandered over the images one last time. "Remember, if your theory is correct we'll expect a fifth missing person reported by Monday. It may be an idea to inform local stations to take notice of all reports and not to enforce the forty-eight hours rule."

DI Masters dismissed them with a wave of the hand and last words.

"You both have to work together on this case. A united front. Understand?" They both acknowledged her comments with a blasé nod of their heads. She sighed and left the room, doubtful that either DS could have a successful working relationship together or with others. Both were as ambitious as the youthful women they just discussed. Sarah was sure that neither of them would hesitate to stab the other in the back if it meant they'd succeed.

8

After some thought, Albie had decided, he would walk the back roads to the Lance's home when he left the building, Claire Lance's father was at home. He'd been unable to work since her disappearance over a month before. A swift walk to their house would take fifteen minutes, twenty at the most. He'd noticed he had gained a few extra pounds recently, they'd taken up residence around his midriff. He'd even had to loosen his belt two notches. After weighing up the pros and cons of time versus health, health won out and vanity came a close second.

As he opened the door into the busy reception area, he drew his shoulders back, stood tall and pulled in his stomach muscles. He'd seen it so often in this job, men of no age at all thrown on the scrap heap, old before their time. Albie Edwards loved himself too much to even consider the possibility of ageing and knew that when it was inevitable, he wanted to be in control of his distinguished demise.

"DS Edwards, sir." A young officer behind the desk waved him over. "I can see you're on your way out but we've had another reported missing person."

Albie blocked the officer from view of members of the public seated in the waiting room.

"Okay, keep it down!" He leaned towards him across the desk. "Remember where we are. What information do you have?" The young PC folded the paper and slipped it across the desk. His head bent to hide the blush that crept up his neck.

Albie glanced at the address. "Call PC Watts and ask her to meet me at the address in twenty minutes."

A light warm breeze brushed his cheek as he hurried from the building. He reached for the handrail and took the steps to the pavement two at a time. At the bottom, he turned to his left. His measured jog lasted only fifty metres before he bent forwards, his hands on his knees, and sweat beaded on his forehead. After what felt like several minutes of gasping for breath, he'd decided he'd look into renewing his gym membership as soon as possible.

Thirty-five minutes later, Albie entered Auden Road, one in a maze of identical roads, each claimed the names of classic poets. Each pair of semi-detached houses a clone of the next. Auden Road portrayed an air of affluence, but not without a hint of home comforts. There was no announcement of poverty on display. Colourful annual bedding plants edged garden lawns. They showed individuality through the choice of hedge or bush, however even with these choices there seemed to be an unwritten code on height, colour and placement.

Albie had reached number nine before he'd questioned the length of the street. He shook his head, shoved his hands in his pockets and willed his aching feet forward. Only another one hundred and fifty-five houses to go. He sped up when he spotted a police car parked opposite the house. Albie headed across the empty road, surprised because only about three cars had passed him since he'd passed number nine.

"Fuck," Albie muttered under his breath as Jana emerged from the driver's seat of the car and walked in his direction. "Great, an amateur." He pulled in his gut, smiled, and nodded. "I didn't expect to see you here, PC Kolska. No PC Watts?" He scanned the area, hoping she'd pop out from behind one of the well trimmed bushes.

"No, sir. Just me." She slipped out her notebook and pen. Not unlike Tanya in the note taking department, Albie noted.

"Tanya was still questioning families and suggested that I accompany you and take notes." Jana waved her notebook in front of her face. A security blanket for a newbie, he thought as he walked through the gate. The garden was a replica of the others in so many ways. But with closer inspection the neglect was clear. Uncut grass, drooping petals tinged with brown edges mingled with weeds, and uneven branches on rebellious trees. Albie stepped back and examined the outside. It was unkempt, verging on shabby compared to the neighbours. The neglect was recent, the legacy of busy people or perhaps a broken home.

A petite woman carrying a baby on her hip answered the front door. She wore jeans and a blouse that hugged her curves and flattered her physique, as it would a woman half her age. Her coppery auburn hair was streaked with grey and twirled on the top of her head in a domestic top knot she made look seductive. She'd been crying. The woman concealed watery red eyes with a haphazard application of make-up and she squeezed a crushed tissue in her hand.

Albie showed his ID card. The baby dropped his rattle and tried to grab it between his chubby fingers.

"Dillon." The woman said as she bent to retrieve the toy from the step. Her voice was soft and melodic. "I'm so sorry, please come inside." She turned from the door and led them into a cozy living room. The faint smell of paint hung in the air. A clean shaved bespectacled man eased himself from the settee. His height was deceptive when seated and he stood at well over six foot. He held out a long sinewy arm and shook Albie's hand with a firm grip.

"Thank you for coming so soon, we were told that you don't consider missing adults at risk for forty-eight hours."

Albie cleared his throat.

"That is often the case. I'm DS Edwards, PC Kolska." He gestured to his colleague who was already busying herself taking notes. "And you are Mr and Mrs MacDonald?" They nodded in reply. "I understand you have both contacted the police about your daughter, Esther. You're worried because you expected your daughter home earlier today. Is that correct?"

Isobel MacDonald sat Dillon in a baby walker. He chuckled and picked up one of many toys scattered on the tray.

"It's not like Esther, she wouldn't leave Dillon." Isobel said as she sank to her knees in front of the baby and stroked his head. "She just wouldn't. He means the world to her." Tears trickled down her cheeks, and her entire body jerked. Mr MacDonald's awkward pats on his wife's back did little to console her. Mr McDonald picked up where his wife left off.

"Isobel's right, Dillon is the most important person in her life. She'd never willingly leave him. It's out of character."

"Does your daughter live with you?"

Isobel MacDonald dabbed her swollen eyes. "Yes, she moved into the main bedroom with Dillon when Iain left us. It made sense. She needed the space. Dillon has enough stuff to fill a house."

"So you're estranged, Mr MacDonald?" Jana asked, pen poised over the notebook.

"This isn't about me. It's about my missing daughter." His top lip tightened over his teeth and he fisted his hands.

Albie studied his expression and noted his deep frown lines. He had a slight flare to his nostrils, and his intense stare distorted his suave features.

"I'm afraid Mr MacDonald, if we are to have any chance of discovering your daughter's whereabouts this investigation will focus on anyone connected with her, including you. We will need your change of address and phone number. You can give it to my colleague."

"Look is there any way you can keep this low key? Sally won't like this."

Isobel jumped to her feet and lunged at the man in front of her, fists pounding on an unresponsive chest. "Fuck Sally!" she screamed while Albie pulled her back. "You spineless bastard. Our daughter is missing and all you're worried about is what slutty Sally'll say." She slumped forward in Albie's grasp, her energy dissipated enough for him to release his grip on Isobel's waist.

Albie swivelled a hundred and eighty degrees and positioned himself between the couple. "Are you okay, Mrs MacDonald?" He said as her breathing slowed. "I know this is a tough time for you but I'd like to check Esther's room."

Without saying a word, Isobel led the way upstairs. Portraits adorned the wall to their right, a family at different stages of their lives, smiles beamed from their faces. These were snapshots of memories from happier times. In the first two framed photographs, a family of four smiled down on them. They were Mr and Mrs MacDonald standing behind two children sitting upright and tall on red velvet cushion chairs. One was a freckled-faced blonde boy about five-years-old. He sat across from a round faced toddler whose red hair stuck up in short clumps on her scalp. As they continued to ascend the boy disappeared from the family photos. He must have been in his mid teens when he vanished, and the family became a trio. Albie stopped in front of the last photograph of the adolescent man. There was something familiar about the lad's face, but Albie's eye for face recognition seemed to lack of late.

Isobel hovered outside a door to their left as they reached the landing.

"It's in there." She nodded in the general direction. "If you need anything I'll be with Dillon." She backed away and held the top of the bannister.

"Mrs MacDonald? The boy in the photograph is your son, I presume. Is there any chance he'd know where to find Esther? Her haunts? Sometimes siblings share secrets they often know more than their parents."

"I doubt it." Her grip tightened around the bannister, and she turned to face him. "Liam's been in prison for the last eight years and he's not due for release soon." Albie went to speak, but Isobel MacDonald did not wait for a response. She was used to walking away before the questions became too difficult to answer. Everyone needed a coping mechanism. He watched the tiny figure and her rapid descent, the bannister a crutch for her frame and her pride. Isobel's disclosure would need to be followed up. He made a mental note, then continued into the spacious room which spanned the front of the house. Exotic pastel flowers dominated the walls, entwined in an intricate pattern. It boasted double of everything, windows, radiators, and sets of wall lights and reading lamps placed on identical bedside cabinets. The floral theme was continuous throughout the room, a claustrophobic combination of quilt covers, curtains and lampshades. A multitude of flowers. It reminded him of ivy covered cottages, a natural beauty on the outside smothering its host until it is damp and rotten to the core.

The room itself was bare. Stripped of identity. At first glance there was very little that belonged to Esther. He bent down and picked up a crime thriller from the floor next to a discarded pair of slippers and an oversized t-shirt, used as a makeshift nightdress. Albie crouched to open the draw in the cabinet on the side she slept. A jewellery box with a collection of cheap earrings, a cross on a chain, a charm bracelet complete with an assortment of charms, and a dress watch with a gold link strap. In the bottom draw she hid a collection of perfumes, make-up, an assortment of toiletries, a hair dryer, and brush.

He shook his head. In his mind this was temporary accommodation as far as Esther was concerned. No belongings were on show. It was as if Esther MacDonald was just passing through. A rose pink ribbon peeked from under the pastel flower frilled pillowcase. He rubbed the velvet ribbon between his thumb, and forefinger, then yanked. A small book followed the attached ribbon onto the quilt and for the first time that day Albie smiled and mouthed a thank you to no-one in particular. Esther kept a diary. He flicked through the pages, each covered with neat flowing ink. Not just dates and appointments, it was a journal. He hoped she'd shared her thoughts and secrets with this silent friend. He took one last look round the room Esther shared with Dillon, turned and headed for the stairs.

Jana stood by the front door, her notebook and pen out of sight.

"If you hear from Esther or think of anything that could help us find her, no matter how insignificant, contact us at the station." Albie said as he handed Mr MacDonald a card. "We'll be in touch soon." He turned to Mrs MacDonald and held up the dusty pink diary. "I found this in Esther's room. A journal, I believe. It could help us put together her last movements."

Mrs MacDonald stared through him and without a response walked passed him into the living room.

"Whatever helps you find Esther." Mr MacDonald said as he followed his wife.

Jana was halfway up the path before Albie shut the front door. "Hold up." He called after her. "I could do with a lift back."

"Thought you were on a fitness fad." He grinned, so she had a sense of humour.

"Who told you that?" He tensed his muscles and patted his stomach. "Whoever it was, they're liars. There's nothing wrong with my fitness." He opened the passenger door and eased his aching body into the seat just as the first spots of rain hit the windscreen.

9

Unfamiliar sounds weaved into Esther's dream. The soft tones of a saxophone accompanied by the tinkle of piano keys were soothing yet somehow disjointed. The music interweaved with a generous sprinkle of deep feminine vocals. Both were responsible for her gradual recognition of her new reality.

Esther inched her eyes open. She prayed she'd find the security of pink patterned wallpaper and her gorgeous Dillon giggling in his adjacent cot. It was a dream she clung to in desperation. Instead, she was overwhelmed by the rich reds and blacks of her nightmare. Her head was clearer than her previous conscious spell as she scanned her prison.

The room had a high ceiling with a chandelier that hung from decorative moulding. The furniture was sparse. A wardrobe, a chest of drawers, a dressing table, and a nightstand with lamps. The centre piece was an elaborate four poster double bed. Each item of furniture was from a time when items lasted a lifetime. A phrase her mother was fond of quoting when complaining about another excuse for a piece of furniture.

Esther wiped her eyes and tried to bury any thoughts of her mum. She dare not indulge in a single thought of her family if she was to stay focused and alert. In contrast to the old fashioned furniture. The sizeable room boasted speakers played muted jazz numbers from the two corners of the room she faced.

A large monitor hung in place of wall mirror that felt alien to the rest of the room. A green dot luminous against the black frame flicked like the blink of a cyclops and Esther's sudden awareness of the intrusion sent a shudder down her spine which she attempted to suppress.

She was being watched.

Through her fear and addled thoughts, Esther knew she needed a strategy and fear could not play any part in her plans. Esther had little doubt she was in unthinkable trouble, but if she kept calm and clear headed, she would overcome this blip in her life, and she would soon be in the arms of her loved ones. Aware that her first step to escape involved having a calculated mind, Esther reassured herself that if it was down to a battle of wills, she was ready for the challenge.

Raising her head, she faced the monitor. The flicker of light flashed like a coded message. She stared at the light for as long as her concentration allowed. A stare of intent. A stare of defiance. She didn't care. She was sending her own message. Esther MacDonald, the survivor.

Devon smiled at the screen. He had captured her defiant stare and enlarged the image on his central screen, which emphasised her glare of intent. There was no doubt in his mind that she was a fighter and as he studied her face, his excitement grew. Esther was one of the last components they needed to begin the game, which only enhanced his appetite for this fantasy world Isla had created.

Thrills were non existent until Isla had noticed his potential. Until he met her he'd felt as if he barely had a pulse. When she first told him he was special he'd tried to walk away. He'd glimpsed madness in her eyes for the first time that evening and it had spoken to him. It had recognised his needs.

The screens drew Devon back to the defiant stare from their latest victim before glancing at the individual screens, each showed identical rooms. Only one remained empty. They were almost ready to play. And the beat of Devon's pulse reminded him he was special.

"An interest in each individual game piece is unnecessary Devon." Isla traced a fingernail across his bare shoulder as she whispered, "It communicates vulnerability. A weakness we never tolerate in others, so we must hide it within ourselves."

His companion gave his hair a playful ruffle, then ran her fingers across his stubbled jaw. She slid both hands to his shoulders, kneading and manipulating him with massage strokes. Slipping her hands over the top of his chair, she twirled Devon to face her and straddled his lap. Her hands slipped to his chest as she eyed the large features of Esther on the screen. A smile crept across her face as Devon gripped her waist with his and mirrored the rotation of her hips. A moan escaped his mouth, an indicator she'd regained his full attention. Isla leant forward, switched off the central monitor, and shuffled from Devon's lap. Isla placed two fingers on his chest to capture the gallop of his heart.

"It's time to introduce the fresh game piece to the rules of play, don't you think?"

Devon grabbed her wrist and re-situated her palm over his pulsing erection. Knowing better than to speak, he pleaded for release with his half-hooded eyes.

"We'll finish this later." She wriggled her hand from his clasp and walked from the room. "You've got ten minutes. Get ready for some fun."

Devon sat stock still. His thoughts ran to memories of life before Isla when he'd been John Crane. Plain old John. The middle child of an ordinary middle-class family. A nobody, unnoticed, unloved, and unimportant. That's the life from which Isla saved him. She reinvented him and gave him a reason to live. She'd noticed death court him and his desire to end his miserable life.

He stood and headed to the closet and reached for one of three crimson shirts with piped black edges, and a black tailored-suit— a gruesome replica of the bedroom decor. He glanced in the long mirror. His attire was immaculate. He headed for the dressing table and removed a padlocked box from the top draw. He fiddled with the key until the pin of the lock released. The hinged top open upwards, and he ran his hands over a ribbed mask that stared up at him. The thin balaclava boasted a soft satin inlay that felt luxurious next to his skin. Crimson piping edged the eyes holes, nostrils, and zipped mouth piece. Devon studied his alter ego in the three paned mirror. The sewn on jokers smile had been his idea and how he wore the zip added to his menace. His formidable presence had earned him the name of The Enforcer. Since Isla gave him the name, he was no longer ignored. His role in life had changed, and his love of life had grown.

Devon kissed the tip of a small dagger, his choice of weapon today, and slipped it into a small leather sheaf strapped to his waist beneath his well-cut jacket. He paused before taking one last look in the mirror and mimicked the smile of his mask.

He would enjoy the next hour.

10

Albie stood stock-still in front of two transparent boards, unsure whether he'd unleashed his hypothetical theory on his colleagues too soon. From the response he had received perhaps he should have waited, but gut instinct and his years on the force told him there was a connection. The longer he sat on the connection, the greater the chance the case will escalate out of control. He was sure of that at least. Albie took a step back and studied each face for the umpteenth time. He heard Tanya's voice before he was aware of her presence. "Where shall we begin, sir?"

Albie moved to his left to make space for his colleagues. Tanya joined him while Jana kept a respectful distance. Still new to the role and unsure of Albie's expectations, Jana was annoyingly distant. He took a deep breath and shrugged off his unfair summary of the newest addition to his team. What he knew was time would tell whether she would make the cut. At the moment, he gave her a month, and that was being generous.

"Talk us through the missing women again, Tanya."

She moved to the table once more, Jana fumbled in her pocket for a notebook and pen while Albie leaned against a desk facing the board and cleared his mind of everything but Tanya's voice.

"We've gone over Claire Lance's story, I'll move on to the others. Adele, Molly, and Nina all vary in age. They are from unique backgrounds, and their family lives differ and workplaces. The similarities between them are at a push meagre. They all disappeared, at some point, on their drive to work. The obvious question we should ask is how a person and their car just disappears into thin air."

Tanya raised her eyebrows and lowered the chop stick she'd been using as a pointer. a distinct frown etched her forehead. "I keep asking myself if these girls will live to tell us of their ordeal. But now, with an abandoned black Ford Fiesta on the same route, what worries me the most is we're no nearer to any conclusions than when these women were first reported missing."

Albie took in the black circles around Tanya's eyes. "Let's called it a day, you go home and get some sleep. I think it'll be awhile before you get to rest again. On my way home, I'll take a trip back to the crime scene. See if we missed anything."

Tanya nodded and left without an argument.

Albie stepped from the curb and leant against his black Audi, his pride and joy. He'd saved relentlessly after his promotion before he could afford to buy the car and refused to acknowledge it as a status symbol.

The lateness of night didn't bother him. He'd enjoyed the detours he'd taken to reach his destination. In fact, the solitude gave him the opportunity to mull over the evidence and the video from a fresh perspective.

A crisp breeze grazed the back of his neck, and Albie pulled up his jacket collar. He rubbed his hands together then spun three hundred and sixty degrees, just as he had at the potential crime scenes of the other girls.

Each road was situated next to, or nearby, a busy A-road or motorway with a continuous stream of traffic passing through during the day, but more of a trickle at night. An area of greys and greens dismal in the faint flicker of artificial lighting. A place to pass through. Not a stopping point or even an area for meetings—illicit or otherwise.

He closed his eyes and listened. There was nothing but the distant drone of occasional traffic on the road below. Every so often, the call of a bird or screech of an animal caught on the air. The wooded area to his right sounded far more restless and alive than the neighbouring manmade environment which added to pollution in the area. In the first instant, from car fumes and now with crime.

Albie's thoughts clouded. He knew they needed to make a ground breaking discovery to move the case forward. He shuddered and leant over to fiddle with the heater. The air in the car was cooler than outside. He groped in his pocket for the keys. The smooth cotton he'd retrieved from the woods that morning was tucked in a plastic evidence bag where he'd shoved it, and in his hurry forgotten to bag it with the other evidence. With a slow shake of his head, Albie turned the key.

Bon Jovi sang through the speakers as he indicated to head into the nonexistent traffic. One thing Albie knew after watching the video, whatever game the abductor was playing, risk takers planned and executed it. He needed to take another look at the message they'd sent once again before calling it a night. Tapping the fingers of one hand on the steering wheel, he turned up the volume and joined in with the band.

11

As Albie expected, the department was full of people each with their individual roles to play in the investigation. To the untrained eye the entire scene looked like a chaotic mess, but Albie saw it as an unfinished symphony. In his mind, once each instrument in the orchestra had completed their own part, the individual sources would weave together to create a classical masterpiece.

He ignored the nods of recognition from a few of his colleagues, those who raised their heads enough to notice his appearance. The photo board beckoned as it did each morning for the last week. He winced at the thought the connection between the missing girls were recent. He scoured the boards to see if anyone had added any information since he last looked the day before—a much needed daily reminder of the missing girls and the urgency of getting them home. Every morning without fail he scanned their smiling faces, searching for the missing link. Just a hint of a connection between these young individuals that could give the team the vital lead they needed to bring them home.

"Leads?"

Tanya continued to stare, unable to break away from the carefree smiles of the youthful woman full of life. Vanished. She shook her head, picked up her jacket, and threw it over her shoulder before heading towards the exit.

"Let's find the common link." She replied and not waiting for an answer she strode to the elevator and pressed down.

Forty-five minutes sitting in traffic did little to help the pessimistic atmosphere that loomed in the car. Albie glanced in his side mirror and jerked the wheel at the last minute to force his way onto a slip road. Drivers rewarded him with a cacophony or hoots and hand salutes from a van driver. Tanya grabbed the rim of the dashboard to secure her balance.

"Watch it!" She tutted and glared.

"I'm not wasting anymore time. Look at the tailback to the tunnel. Do you want to find these girls or not?" Albie glared at his colleague through defiant eyes, daring her to disagree.

"Yes. But preferably alive."

Dickhead, he mouthed to the animated man behind as they took a left on the roundabout and headed towards Blackheath.

King George Street was nestled to the side of Greenwich Park, situated in an exclusive sought after part of the borough. Geoff, Claire's father, came to an abrupt halt in the doorway just as Tanya leaned forward to press the intercom to the right of the enormous metal gates obstructing their way. Albie pushed against the gate and squeezed through the smallest gap and followed the hunched figure back into the house without a word. Albie noticed the man's stoop seemed more exaggerated since he first met Geoff Lance. When they'd first approached him, a strong-shouldered muscular man had appeared, tall and proud. But over the weeks, he had whittled away to an unresponsive wreck.

"I hope you've come with news."

Albie hesitated. "Mr Lance, I'm aware this is a tough time for you."

"Why are you here? You won't find her in this house, you know."

Albie took another step, then paused. Mr Lance's hands hung by his side, clenched in tight balls, his skin stretched over bloodless knuckles.

Tanya opened a creased manila file and placed individual photographs of the girls. Each a duplicate of those on the board that had memorised her each day since Claire's disappearance. Abbie nodded towards the images, "Do you recognise any of these women, Mr Lance?"

He shook his head as he glanced at the smiling faces, pausing at the photo of the added redhead.

"Please take your time, do you recognise, Esther?" Tanya eased the one photo closer. "She is the most recent girl reported missing." She caught the corner between her thumb and forefinger and dangled the image in front of him.

Claire's father took one last lazy look, "We've been through this so many times." Geoff thumped his balled fists on the table, and the photos jumped in response. He turned to Albie, spittle flew from his mouth as he spoke. "I don't know the others. They've no links with Claire. And to be honest with you, Claire is my only concern. So get off your arses, use your brains, and find my daughter." He swept his hand across the table surface. The images of a smiling face scattered like hope floating on the breeze. He gasped for air and sobbed as he grasped the back of a chair to support his broken body. Tanya busied herself collecting the images and promising to contact him with any news of Claire. She took one more look at the hunched body, then hurried after her retreating boss.

"Bloody waste of time." Albie thumped the roof of his Audi, followed by a swift kick at the tyre.

"I'm not so sure." Tanya settled into the passenger's seat and watched while Albie indicated and pulled out into the trickle of traffic. "Did you notice his reaction to Esther's photo? He hesitated. There was definitely some recognition there. Whether it was her or something in the background I'm not sure, but he recognised something."

She inched down the window and took a breath of clean air. "I wonder if we'll get the same reaction from Mr Soul?" Her question hung in the air. She waited for a response, leant forwards and turned on the radio just to fill the silence. They turned off the roundabout and headed past the shopping centre before Albie spoke. "Stop at the pub by the river. We can eat, mull things over, then walk to Libby's flat. What have we missed?"

"Not sure." She said as he pulled into a parking space that had just been vacated.

Albie opened his car door then turned back to her, "Bring the pictures with you." He stepped from the car and took long strides towards the river. He scanned the wooden tables and benches, although the sun was high, a cool breeze caressed his skin and ruffled his hair.

"Grab that table." He pointed to one overlooking the river and just vacated by a young couple wrapped up in each other's arms. They nibbled each other's ears and ran their hands over each other, oblivious to the looks from the other customers. Tanya threw her oversized handbag down with a thud, beating a group of underage teenagers to the spot and giving them a piercing glare.

"Food?" Albie asked, already halfway to the pub door.

"Just some chips and a lemonade."

Tanya straddled a wooden bench and gazed across the river. The surface sparkled in the sunlight, the sway of the waves soothed her, and she inhaled a slow long deep breath. Damp, like dew on blades of grass, clung to the fine hairs on her exposed body. As a faint smell of rotten fish wafted in from the river, she turned her attention back towards the file which poked out from the top of her bag. She removed one photograph from the file. Took a quick glance at the people on the surrounding tables. They were all engrossed in conversation, so she laid it the image on the table top, then took her time to make a detailed study the image.

Albie savoured a mouthful of homemade chicken pie and glanced at Tanya's focused face. She'd been nibbling a golden chip for the last couple of minutes. He nudged her arm. "Whatever it is you think you'll find can wait until you've eaten." He licked his lips, sliced another chunk of pie, lay the fork on his plate, and leaned over and removed the photo from her reach. Tanya tried to take it back from his grasp. "Leave it. Eat your food. She'll still be here when you finish." She opened her mouth to argue, but Albie's raised hand told her it would be a waste of time. Instead, she tucked into a wicker basket of chunky chips. She pushed the basket away and Albie finished her unwanted chips and examined the photo again.

"What's the black mark poking above her collar?"

Tanya leaned towards him and followed the trail of his finger. Streaks of auburn hair that trailed over the girl's pale-blue shirt collar hid a partial feathered-pattern. She studied the detail, "It's a tattoo, at least I guess that's what it is, I can just make out wispy, wing feathers. It's not obvious and it may be an abstract inking similar to a bird's feather."

"It's a possibility, that's what Geoff Lance spotted."

Tanya picked up the image and inspected the background. It was a hazy back garden of greens, browns, and blacks. All held in place by a dreary overcast sky.

"I can't see anything of significance, but I'm not Geoff Lance."

"If the other girls have tattoos, we could be onto something. Grab your jacket. Let's have a chat with Libby Mann, you never know, Nina may be partial to ink art too." Tanya grinned at him and slung her jacket over her shoulder

"What's so funny?"

"It's good to see your enthusiastic again, sir. You must have needed the food."

12

The faces of smiling innocence taunted Albie from the file balanced precariously on his lap. The women's abductions were feeling like some kind of organised sick joke with the culprit in too deep to come out and admit that it's gone too far. Try as he might his theories faltered when he grasped for reasons. Why these women? How could so many disappear in such a brief time without a trace? What was their connection? He ran his fingers through his hair, closed the file, and slipped it back into Tanya's shoulder bag before following her into a spacious reception. A security guard leant over the desk engrossed in the sports pages of a broadsheet. He raised his head at the clip of Tanya's heels on the marble floors.

"Good afternoon. Can I help you?"

They both raised their credentials. "We are here to speak to Miss Mann."

"Is she expecting you?" He asked, scanning a list that looked sparse.

Tanya stared at him for a second, noticed his reticence, and added with a smile, "It is important and time sensitive. If you could?" She pointed to the phone and gave him the sweetest smile she could muster.

Flustered by her response, he reached for the phone with a shaking hand.

"I'll just call through." He mumbled into the receiver, then nodded toward the lifts. "112."

With a smile and secretive wave over her shoulder, Tanya led Albie to the lifts.

"No problem, sir." She said as the doors opened, and they stepped inside.

Albie balked at his reflection on the mirrored back wall as he entered the lift. He ran his fingers through his greasy hair and smoothed the front of his shirt with grubby hands. Twenty-four hours without a shower, he needed to go home, rest and indulge in some personal hygiene rituals. He glanced at Tanya; she was always well turned out and even though she'd benefit from a similar routine to him, with Tanya it never showed.

"Okay?"

Albie smiled at Tanya's reflection when she caught him stare. Her cheeks flushed, and she forced a cough to clear her throat.

"Sir, it just occurred to me, this lift is twice as large as my living room. How can they afford to live in this area, never mind these apartments?"

"We'll find out, shall we?" Albie led the way towards a door at the far end of a well-lit corridor. He rapped his knuckles against solid wood, which inched open at his touch. With his palm flat, he edged his way into a small entrance hall. "Miss Mann, it's DS Edwards and PC Watts. We hoped to ask you a few questions."

"Come in, I'm putting the kettle on, do either of you fancy a cuppa?" Her voice, melodic and soothing, had a trace of an accent that Albie could not quite place. The hall led into a spacious open plan living area with rooms leading off to the left and the kitchen on his right. The floors were stained wooden interwoven slats, complemented with neutral painted walls of cream or a similar off white, adorned with contemporary prints and large framed photographs.

Tanya poked her head around the kitchen door. "Thanks, tea would be great. Need a hand?"

Libby lifted the tray from the work surface. "No need, I've filled the teapot, it's brewing." She squeezed past the officer into the living room. "Have you any news?" She placed the tray on a solid pine coffee table and gestured to the settee. "Please, sit."

The officers both lounged into the plush cushions. Albie perused a photograph of the view of Greenwich Park from the Observatory. It was a black and white print, but mesmerising.

"A magnificent print. Which of you is the photographer?" He asked as he joined them and perched on the edge of the settee.

"Nina, it's her work. She was, I mean is waiting to be discovered. She was prolific before we married. Lately, her creativity in photography has taken a back seat."

Abbie smiled and leaned forward. He steepled his fingers and focused on their hostess.

"Miss Mann?"

"Libby, please."

"I'm afraid we have little to add to the information we shared with you about Nina's whereabouts. But we do have more questions."

Libby raised her hand and interjected. "Look, without appearing uncaring or uninterested, Nina isn't one of your snatched women." She picked up the teapot and poured the light brown liquid into the mugs on the tray. Her grip tightened around the handle, and she steadied the teapot with her other hand. Tears trickled over her cheeks, Tanya eased the teapot from her grasp and continued to pour.

"I'm sorry," Libby said. She rubbed a tissue over her cheeks, dabbed under her eyes, and screwed it into her clenched fist. "I know you're only doing your job. But Nina, she's streetwise. She deals with difficult customers daily. She wouldn't put herself in a vulnerable position."

Albie continued to watch Libby Mann, drinking in her response.

"We know your feelings about the abduction case, Miss Mann, but Nina's disappearance fits a pattern and is central to our investigation. Are you ready to answer some questions now?"

Libby lifted her head to face him. Unable to hold eye contact, she nodded and bent to inspect the beige rug beneath her bare feet.

“Nina was driving your car that day. Hers was in the garage. Is that correct?” Another nod. “How long had she been without a car?”

“It was the first day.”

“She worked the night shift, but you weren’t working. Why was that?”

“We were working the same shift. I’d been throwing up all day so couldn’t work.”

“So when did you last see her?”

Libby dipped her head further and her shoulders shook, tiny uncontrollable movements. Tanya nudged a clean tissue into her hand and whispered. “It’s okay Libby, take your time.”

Albie sipped his tea. A bitter after taste caused him to cough, which he attempted to stifle while trying not to contort his mouth.

“I was asleep when she left so I last spoke to her two days before she went missing.”

Tanya finished her drink, licked her lips and asked, “Has Nina got any tattoos?”

Libby glared at Tanya, unsure whether she’d misheard. “What sort of question is that..? Oh no, you haven’t found some..?”

“No. No, nothing like that. It’s just a question. It could be something or nothing.”

“We all have tats, us exotic dancers. Mostly they’re subtle, rather than explicit.”

“Did she have a raven tattoo?”

Her face drained, she looked colourless, porcelain pale. “No she hasn’t, but I have a raven.” She lowered her vest top and revealed a small tasteful raven flying over the mound of her bosom towards her cleavage.

Albie attempted to examine the decorative bird with nonchalance, but even with a swiping glance he could tell it was a fine design. He had two on his own body. They were private. Only seen by a chosen few.

"Uh, um." Tanya broke the silence. "Delicate art work, Libby. What's the story behind the raven?"

Albie stifled a grin. PC Watts was his true protege. Asking the right questions. Extracting necessary information and unlike him, she made the witness feel at ease. He felt a pang of pride as he sat back and watched her piece together the facts.

"So you were thirteen when you got a tattoo?"

"Yeah, like I said, a night out that got out of hand."

Libby picked up mugs, an obvious indication that for her the conversation was over. Tanya took the mugs from her hands and replaced them on the tray.

"Libby." She waited until she had her full attention. "This is important. I know this is difficult for you to talk about. And you no doubt think it's insignificant because of the timescale. However, it could apply to the case and if it isn't we won't have to discuss it again. Now what happened?"

Libby took a deep breath, entwined her fingers, and looked from one officer to the other. "Okay, but you've got to understand, I was young and stupid. It's something I've tried to bury.'

Abbie nodded, Tanya patted her arm, "We understand."

"I lived with my parents at the time on the outskirts of Blackfen. I had a small group of friends and we spent most evenings at the park or at each other's houses. This particular night I'd met my friend Kayleigh, she was two years older than me. She was pretty, adventurous, and daring. She'd arranged for us to meet two older boys in Lee Green."

"How much older?"

Libby studied her bare feet. "Kayleigh had met one of them already and said they were eighteen. I was scared about going, but she said they were okay."

"What happened?" Albie leaned forward in his chair. "How did you end up with the tattoo?"

She lowered her voice. "I got separated from Kayleigh and ended up somewhere with this bloke called Lester and his mate. Tools, they called him. I only had lemonade, but I lost time and when memories came back to me in snippets. They did things to me that left splintered scars. Things I want to rid myself of, but with this reminder." She pointed to her breast. "How can I?"

"So this happened fifteen years ago?" Tanya removed her notebook from her inside jacket pocket and scribbled. Libby nodded. "You were in Lee Green and the eighteen-year-old men you were with were as Iain and Tools?" Tanya continued to write as she spoke. "Any other names? What about your friend Kayleigh?"

"No other names. Kayleigh disappeared that night and turned up in the river Ravensbourne two days later. She'd been assaulted and drown."

Tanya slipped an arm around Libby's shoulder and whispered to her as she sobbed. Libby wriggled from under Tanya's arm once the tears had stopped. She blew her nose and tidied the cups onto the tray. This time Tanya didn't stop her.

Abbie stood and headed in towards the front door. "Thank you Miss Mann, you have been most helpful."

Tanya stood as well. She reached out and took one of Libby's hands in both of hers. "I will keep you informed of any updates concerning the whereabouts of Miss Anderson." And with a gentle shake of her hand she followed Albie.

Libby shadowed them to the door and watched them step inside the elevator. She closed the door and slid to the floor, hugged her legs to her chest, rested her head on her knees, and sobbed. She sobbed for her dead friend and she sobbed for the lost thirteen year old still begging for answers to unanswered questions.

They strolled down the stairs and across the half-filled car park in silence. Both officers still processing the latest information. Tanya closed the passenger door and waited until Albie had edged out into a gap in the traffic and indicated to follow the signs back towards Greenwich. Like a small excited child Tanya Watts broke the silence.

"So what do you think, sir? This could be a fresh lead. Or at least knowing that it's Libby with the raven tattoo and it was her car driven by Nina that night. The night she disappeared. That must mean something, right?" She petered off and focused on his unreadable expression.

"You did great Tanya." He reassured her. "You're right. It could be useful information but let's not get carried away. Not yet, at least."

Albie reached over and turned on the radio. Tanya concentrated on the buildings and scenery as it stretched out in the distance and they streaked past. During the journey, her mind replayed and processed the recent information shared with them a short time before and the more she digested the information the more she knew they'd caught a break.

13

Esther stilled. Footfalls outside her door put a stop to her exploration of the room. The chains that bound her wrists, ankles, and waist, though secure and inescapable, did not limit her movement within the large room. After her initial failed attempt to open the door, Esther was just thankful for the freedom of movement they had given her. The clink of the chains and the burden of their weight had become background noise in her silent need to keep busy. Keep thinking. Keep alert.

The thud of bolts drawn open mingled with the scrape of the chains startled Esther. Her body shook as she retreated into a dismal alcove in the far corner of the room. She hid as far from the solid oak door as possible. The key turned in the lock and clanked as it released. Her heartbeat pulsed in her ears and replaced the silence. Esther rolled into a tight ball like a vulnerable embryo. She backed further into the corner, ignoring the pain from the indent of the wooden framework pressed into her lower spine. She inhaled and scrunched her eyes. As a child, she remembered playing hide 'n' seek with her brother. She'd always lost the game because she'd thought all she'd needed to do was close her eyes to hide from others. It took her a while to realise she was wrong. Now more than ever she wished the game was that simple.

The squeak of uncoiled hinges and drag of wood on carpet unsettled Esther enough for a whimper to escape her lips. She parted her eyelids and laid flat, aware that she was no longer alone. From her hiding place she glimpsed white stiletto shoes and narrow ankles dressed in fishnet tights. Behind were a pair of black leather men's shoes. The fit was narrow and tapered to the toe. A tassel adorned each shoe and were polished to a mirrored shine.

So she hadn't been mistaken. The man and woman in the car were together. Esther closed her eyes once more, this time to help her rationalise her situation. There were two of them and he'd had a knife when they confronted her, so fighting would be out of the question—they'd overpower her in an instant.

But what if it was her only way out?

The woman sauntered over to the table where she placed a tray, "We have food for you. Sit at the table." The woman's melodic voice rang out in the silence. Esther froze.

"Listen." The voice continued in the darkness. "By nature, I'm an impatient person. I'll give an instruction twice and no more. So for the last time. Sit at the table and eat."

Esther cringed and attempted to swallow. The woman's voice cut through the air with menace. Silence buried into Esther, and goosebumps rose with the tiny hairs on her arms.

The man stepped into her eye-line and lunged at her head. His fingers dug into her scalp and entangled her hair. Her scream echoed around the room as she grasped at the roots of her hair to lessen the tension. Reflected in the shine of her assailants black leather shoes, her distorted face stared back, her wide ruby-red lips the only colour in her alabaster mask of pain.

She shuffled on her hands and knees to keep up with the man's movements. Contact with the rough tufts of carpet burned the skin on her knees, and tears stained her cheeks. Hands yanked her onto a hardback dining chair. Tension left her body, and she opened her eyes as the man untangled his fingers from her hair.

For the first time, Esther lifted her head and looked into the dark-green eyes of her attacker. She bulked at the pleasure that danced in his eyes from her obvious pain. His balaclava covered head reminded Esther of a sinister silhouette puppet she'd played with as a child. He was so close that his aniseed breath warmed her face. His zipped mouth turned into an unnatural smile and a gasp left her lips when he next tug of her hair. A quick snatch near her scalp left her skin taut and throbbing in the aftermath.

Esther watched her capture's eyes as they awaited a reaction to pain, and with each squirm his aniseed breath increased and his excitement grew. His fingers entwined in her hair and played with her scalp until tears dripped uncontrolled from her eyes.

"That's enough." The woman's voice sliced through her pain, and her assailant released her hair. Esther withheld her desire to run her hands over her sensitised scalp to regain control. "As I explained, I will give you an instruction only twice. If you are not obedient, then The Enforcer will receive great pleasure ensuring your compliance." He leaned closer until his fingertips grazed her hair, and she flinched from the action. His eyes smiled in unison with the silver zip. He shaped his mouth in unadulterated enjoyment. His mask was surrealism at its most unsettling.

Esther averted her gaze from the intense violation of her captures' stare and ignored the persistent throb that pounded inside her head. A haze of candlelight illuminated the crackers and cheese on the serving tray. Esther's stomach grumbled.

"Eat. You need to keep strong and healthy to be off to the best start possible." Esther examined the face of the attractive blond seated at the opposite end of the rectangular table. She lifted a glass and saluted Esther. "If you're difficult, The Enforcer can persuade you to eat. I thought I made it clear, you need to eat."

Esther took a bite of cheese on a crisp cracker which crumbled and stuck in the roof of her mouth. A mouthful of wine moistened her mouth and rinsed the food from her palete. Each gulp warmed her body. She knew her face would have a healthy blush, Caleb used to tease her about her inability to hold her drink. Lightweight, that's what he'd call her. The blush always gave her away.

After the initial mouthful, Esther couldn't hide her hunger, and unsure of when she'd next eat, her survival tactics took over. With each mouthful she studied her dinner companion on the opposite end of the table. Her features were unclear in the candlelight, but although disjointed her outward beauty was unquestionable. Carved cheekbones were prominent beneath a covering of soft shapely skin, pale in tone. And black mascara-covered lashes enhanced her deep-blue oval eyes. Drawn on fleshy ruby lips pouted out from a flawless face.

Esther swallowed the final mouthful of food from her plate, licked her index finger, and run it across the surface collecting crumbs which she sucked from her finger. Another sip of wine sated her its warmth quelled her unease. For an instant, she felt as if she was on a night out with old friends.

The woman leaned towards her and tapped her middle finger on the table. She painted the manicured nails the same colour as her lips.

"Finish your wine then we'll talk."

"Thank you," Esther pushed her glass away, "but I've had enough." Her skin prickled. The forgotten figure stepped from the shadows, picked up the wineglass, and replaced it to its former position.

"Drink. Second instruction given." The woman clenched her mouth into a false grin. Her eyes narrowed and retreated under her creased brow. The woman wasn't interested in her cooperation. This was a challenge.

Esther reached for the glass and sipped the rich liquid. Without the cheese and crackers the fruity oak tastes no longer warmed her, instead they left a bitter residue in her mouth. With each sip her head felt heavy, like a concertina pushed together with a throb of a repetitive drum beat constantly in the back of her scalp. Her eyelids ached, and she struggled to keep her eyes open. Her vision swayed, and she tried to focus on the large candlestick in the centre of the table which looked like a Dali exhibit. Her tongue was sour and stuck to the roof of her mouth.

"Listen." A distant voice echoed out of sync with the ruby lips that delivered the message. "We have a few minutes before you sleep. I'm delighted to welcome you to this worthy cause. The first of its kind, I believe. We will explain your part in this cause soon enough. We will share the rules with you tomorrow."

The woman placed her hands on the table's edge and pushed herself to standing.

"Tuck her in, will you? Oh, and no touching. Not yet." She said as she headed for the door.

Esther felt hands invading her body. Fingers brushed her breast and fixed under her arm, and the other hand scooped her up under her knees. Her head lulled back and her eyes shut before he'd even lifted her from the chair.

14

The prison building loomed over him like the mock welcome of a reluctant host. It had been some time since he'd entered this place and it was with some reluctance he did now.

The procedures undertaken to gain entry took time and were intrusive regardless of his position. Although a civilian would expect further unpleasant steps of an invasion of their privacy than he faced. He sat at a table in the middle of a room filled with replica tables, each drab and in need of a rubdown, and a new lick of paint. A stale smell, difficult to place, settled in his nostrils and lined his throat after each breath. It lingered for days on clothes, skin, and visitor's nostril hairs. That same smell bore a shade of defiance. It was a deep urge to be an individual in a world of conformity. The thought of ever losing even a small portion of his liberty would be enough to reinvent the scent he despised now.

Guards led the way and separated as they approached the table. Albie studied the t-shirt and tracksuit bottomed man who followed at a distance. Liam MacDonald was unrecognisable to the young lad in the family photograph hanging on the walls of his childhood home. He was muscular, he'd obviously grown, and the gym had been his friend in prison, judging from the stretch of his t-shirt over his chest. His biceps bulged under his sleeves. His hair had darkened, as had his stare. Probably a necessary trait picked up as a survival tactic in his current home. He threw himself onto the chair and angled his body at a forty-five degree turn away from his visitor without acknowledging Albie's presence.

"I am DS Edwards. Thank you for agreeing to see me, Mr MacDonald.."

"Let's get one thing straight," He said as he leant across the table. He was close enough that Albie could smell stale tobacco on his breath. "I'm not doing this for you. It's me sister. She's the reason I'm here. Why haven't you found her yet?"

A guard took a step forward and hovered on the periphery. Albie gave a slight shake of his head and raised his hand. The guard hesitated before he took a step back and relaxed his hands at his side.

"We are doing all we can to find Esther. In fact, that's why I'm here. Fifteen years ago there were a series of murders, young girls found assaulted and drowned in the Ravensbourne river." Albie laid the photographs of the dead girls in a neat line. Below, he added the kidnapped girls.

Liam prodded the nearest pictures with two long-nailed fingers.

"What's this all got to do with Esther? You should be out there now while you still 'ave a trail to follow."

"That's just it. I'm following a trail now." Albie eased the girls faces closer to the prisoner. "Take a good look Liam. Robson Shaw, he's our link, the man you murdered. I can't talk to him, you made sure of that. If you want to help us find your sister you need to talk. Tell us everything you know."

Liam brushed his sweat dotted forehead with the back of his hand. "Robson? What's his connection?"

"Each of these girls," Albie jabbed at the images once more. "They all had the privilege of having some kind of relationship with him. Do you recognise any of them?"

"I didn't know him that well. Our paths only crossed from time to time." He shrugged, stared at the photos for a while longer, then picked the one in the middle. "I vaguely remember her. She laughed all the time, loved to dance." Lines wrinkled at the corner of his eyes, and his cheeks dimpled at the memory. "Leigh. Yeah, she loved to dance."

"Did you ever see her with this girl?" Albie asked. He handed over a head and shoulders photo of Libby from his file.

Liam studied Libby's picture for a few seconds before handing it back. "Never seen her before. I don't remember her from the papers either. What's her connection?"

"None really. Just a friend." He slid one last photo across the table. The feathers were so black, mingled with a blue tinge, and the unmistakable outline of a raven. "Familiar?"

Liam tore the image from his grip.

"Where did you get this? Have you found her? Is she alive?" The chair squeezed across the floor from under Liam as he flung himself across the table at Albie. "Stop playing games with me. Where is she?"

Albie lunged out of Liam's reach, his back flat against the far wall, and watched as the guards fought to restrain him. They struggled to grab an arm each, flanked him on either side, and coaxed him back into his chair.

"What is it about the raven, Liam?" Albie asked from the safety of the wall.

"He'd brand 'em the girls. Tattooed them with a raven. The bastard." He made circular movements with two fingers on each temple as if to offset a migraine.

"Go on." Albie dragged his chair back from the desk that separated the pair and lowered himself onto the seat without taking his eyes from the man opposite.

"He'd get friendly with 'em. He'd make 'em feel a million dollars. Give 'em treats and all that. After a bit of time, he'd give 'em a personal present. He called it 'branding'."

"Where did they get the tatts? They look professional."

"A mate of his, Joey someone... Kohl. Joe Kohl, that's it. He went to art college. He loved the body art, good at it an' all. This is one of his."

Liam pointed to a cobra on his bicep that gave the illusion of striking from a different angle each time he tensed his muscles.

"One more question." Albie lowered his voice and waited until their eyes met. "Why did you kill Robson Shaw?"

Liam raised his bulk from the chair and leaned into Albie's retreating body, as if to share a secret. "It was self defence."

Albie struggled to control the tension in his voice and the slight shake in his body. He wasn't relishing the answer but knew he had to ask the question. "Why did you go looking for him that night? What set you off?"

"He'd branded my sister." Liam's scrunched forehead stuck out and covered his large piercing and unapologetic eyes. "She was fourteen."

Albie remained seated long after Liam left the room. His mind swarmed with questions. The links were there; he knew it. But Liam was scant on the information he would share with the police.

Albie tapped a rhythm on the steering wheel of his BMW and worked on ignoring the thoughts that had niggled away at him since he pulled up outside the prison. Until now, he'd refused to contemplate a rendezvous with Freddie Hurst, his biological father. However, time was ticking and with each minute that passed his insight and connections may override Albie's need to avoid his least favourite businessman.

15

The incident room changed within seconds. The exchanges between officers subsided to whispers, and then a silence of disbelief hung in the air as they focused one by one on the screen.

The faces of two clowns bounced on the paused screen in front of a black backdrop, the falsehood of their expressions unnerving and unnatural.

Albie broke the silence. "This video was hand delivered to the front desk by a courier bright and early this morning." He flicked through a few papers in his hand, then continued. "Now, I know the horror movie jokes will have already done the rounds, but I want you to remember that for the young women taken, the horror story they're living is no joke. Lights, Frank."

Frank reached for the switch, and a few officers shuffled in their seats as if settling down for the main picture at the cinema.

"Good," the smaller clown said, it distorted the voice, but the words were clear. "I hope by now I've grabbed your attention and I intend to be precise and to the point. After years of appealing to the police to reopen the Raven Murders case, in the hope of a pardon for

Robson Shaw, I am dissatisfied with your response. Rather than try to negotiate with a disinterested police force, we have taken the initiative. As it says in the Bible, '... an eye for an eye...' We say 'a girl for a girl,' until you imprison the real killer for the murders and pardon Robson Shaw." The clown frowned, and their fist hit the table. The second clown stared straight at the camera and grinned, then disappeared off screen as the camera panned to include three women slouched in chairs.

The names rolled off the clown's tongue like they were reciting a register. "Claire Lance... Adele Soul... Nina Anderson. We haven't finished yet, but you could finish it before the pain begins. Find the Raven Murderer."

Albie stopped the video and scanned the faces of his silent colleagues as they sat staring at a black screen.

Fawn's voice focused on them once more. "We've spoken to a teenager, he said, a blonde woman approached him outside the police station and offered him money to deliver the package to the front desk. He is coming in to meet with a police artist. We've sent the package away for testing, like we will with the video."

Fawn nodded to Albie, who cleared his throat, picked up the remote, and fixed the video on the girls slumped awkwardly and tied to chairs.

"They used force to kidnap these women. Their captors have warned us they have not finished. There was no mention of Esther MacDonald, but that does not mean that they do not have her. Investigating each of the women further must be top priority." He rewound the video again and paused on an image of the two clowns. "We have two suspects who refer to the Raven Murders and Robson Shaw. Shaw was found guilty posthumously of five counts of murder. These people believe they have a cause. Having a cause always makes people dangerous. So we must find them and stop them before they hurt these women." Albie turned from the painted-on smiles of the clowns to the solemn faces of his officers.

"But why would they take these women to acquit a dead man?

Especially if it was a watertight case," Frank asked as he pushed the switch and the lights flickered overhead.

Fawn stood and ran her hands down the front of her trousers, brushing out invisible creases. "I guess that's what we need to pursue, Frank. Find out how these girls are linked to a cold case and take another look at the evidence that convicted Shaw."

16

Esther covered her eyes against the streams of sunlight hitting her face. It was a rude awakening from a drug-induced sleep. Her hair stuck to her cheek in a strip. Her sweat had turned into makeshift glue and kept it in place. The heavy chains that ached her wrists clanged together as she picked the dried grunge from her eyelashes. At least she hadn't dreamt this time, she thought, as she tried to push last night's hours from her mind.

Esther eased herself onto her elbows and shuffled into a sitting position. Her muscles ached with the strain of each movement. She slumped her head back on the plush pillows and studied the room in the light of day. The walls and woodwork were painted in a variety of reds and black, however, the colours were not as dull as she remembered. And the carpet reminded her of a field of plush poppies, just like the field where Dorothy slept in Oz. In the sunlight, it was easier to make out ornate gold that covered the edge of the ceiling, a hint of luxury that also adorned the mirrors and picture frames. Esther's eyes rested on the black monitor centred directly ahead. The only item that did not fit the character of the room. Modern technology that covered the chimney.

A distant sound broke her train of thought. Her breath quickened, accompanied by a shiver. She sat upright, her neck elongated as she strained to hear. The clank of metal, the turn of a key. She followed the sounds, one lock... two... three. It reminded her of a warden unlocking prison cells. Was she in an institute of some type? She knew one thing for sure this was all a mistake. Scuffed footsteps stopped outside the door, and the key turned in the lock. Reason overtook fear and Esther patted the quilt around her legs. She flicked her hair from her face and straightened her back in a regal pose.

The woman entered with a tray of clothes. She did not even glance at Esther as she spoke. "Get dressed. You've got ten minutes before they come for you."

Esther lunged towards the woman who shoved her back towards the bed. "But I don't understand. Why am I here?"

"You'll know soon enough." She walked towards the door and when Esther didn't move, she said, "The quicker you dress the more answers you'll get."

Esther wriggled into the dark denim jeans. They were a snug fit, but comfortable. She examined the thick metal bracelets which encased her wrists, picked up the t-shirt, and shook her head in disbelief. The seams held together with silver press studs, they'd thought of everything. She grabbed the hem and pulled. She smiled at the memory of Dillon's angelic face. His body rolling from her at changing time and his shrieks of delight as she grabbed a chubby arm and leg to roll him back and undo his babygrow.

A loud sob escaped her mouth, and she smothered the sound with her palm. Esther concentrated on taking deep breaths. Dillon would have to be a no-go area for her thoughts if she was to remain sane and level-headed. She splashed some cold water on her face from a bowl in the corner and untangled her hair with her fingers.

Heavy footfalls approached from a distance. She turned to the bedside clock. The loud tick of anticipation counted the minutes until they opened her door. She perched on the edge of the bed, her feet dangled like a little girl awaiting a call from the dentist.

17

The air tasted sour on her tongue from the aftertaste of citrus juice he had asked her to drink. Her face scrunched with each bitter mouthful. A blindfold tightened in a secure knot at the back of her head was thick and coarse. It was so tight that light spots danced in front of her eyes. Esther drew in a deep breath and filled her lungs with cold air. She shuddered as her skin cooled crept. Unsure whether the temperature had plummeted or fear of the unknown had sent the shivers, she shuffled the way a hand in her back directed. Esther inched forward, step after cautious step. She wanted to use her hands as a guide, but ties that dug deep into her wrists restricted them.

"Stop." Esther stilled and her high-pitched plea echoed. Every muscle in her body tensed to remain balanced. His body barged her sideways smack into a damp wall. His rough hand grasped her underarm and his fingers dug into her flesh. Breath tinged with aniseed heated her neck as he whispered.

"Stay snug against the wall. I'll tell you when to take a step." Fingertips traced an escaped tear down her cheek. Her lips tingled as they traced her mouth. "Listen, you are alive, but there are no guarantees how long you will live." He shoved her once more into the wall. "And that would be a disappointment. We haven't even played."

Her legs buckled, and acrid vomit hit the back of her throat. She clung on to her consciousness. In her mind, that was the difference between survival and defeat.

Each step was a painful act of faith. Each step could be a step off the edge of a precipice. Esther cursed the fact that with every movement the trust between capture and captive grew. She cursed her own worsted thoughts, and that she had to put her life into his hands. The hands of the enemy.

"Final step."

The ball of one foot contacted the ground, but a shove in the back unbalanced her and she tumbled. Her knees hit the hard surface first, and pain jolted through her entire body. The thud of contact between her shoulders, chest, and the ground ricocheted the pain, and she inhaled filth, grit, and dirty water. She spluttered and heaved. A hand spanned the back of her head and forced her face back into the putrid puddle. Esther held her breath and counted. She got to six, and she was wriggling and squirming against his hold. At eight, her frantic movements jerked her into spasms. Her desperation faltered by then. The final number she remembered reciting was twelve.

"Esther... Esther, open your eyes." Aniseed breath. She inhaled and stared into the darkness. Shapes emerged. A haze of objects. Movement. "Esther, meet your competitors."

A flicker of light haloed human shapes as it danced back and forth. Her own gaze met with many pairs of eyes. Some pleading, others half shut, but all similar animals faced with attack.

At the centre stood the elegant woman. Fine hairs stood on the back of Esther's neck as she remembered what happened if you didn't follow her instructions. A painful throb pulsated at the crown of her head as the woman circled the group. Her frown mingled with a callous curiosity. The tilt of her mouth revealed too much pleasure in her captures torment. They were a desperate audience.

"We have a complete set of opponents, and you know what that means?" The woman pivoted in Esther's direction.

She smelt aniseed. He was close. Too close. "Can we begin? Are the games ready to begin" Excitement tinged his voice.

Stilted silence, a breath held in unison, and a shared terror of anticipation hung in the air.

"In due course. First you have all asked the questions many times individually. Who are you? Why am I here? What do you want from me? You have even suggested that I... we have made a mistake or we've chosen the wrong person." She paused and turned a full circle and challenged each pair of eyes.

"We will attempt to answer your questions now and explain your part in the game." She gestured to the man behind Esther to join her before she addressed the girls. An inhalation of breath felt like it drained the room of oxygen. Fear prickled their faces and their bodies collapse inwards.

"I am Isla and I love to play games." A childish smile enhanced a sparkle in her eye which gave her a certain innocence. She turned to her companion. "Why don't you introduce yourself properly?"

He fiddled with the zip on his balaclava. The fabric grin manipulated into a manic sneer with the action.

"Hi." He turned and waved to the girls. "Some of us have had the pleasure of meeting unofficially." A few of the girls lowered their heads, and a whimper escaped from one.

"I am Devon and I'm devoted to Isla. I enjoy games, but I prefer to take part." He strolled towards the girl opposite Esther. Her eyes bulged and body danced in erratic jolts. A tender brush of his fingers caressed her cheek like a lover's gesture. She squirmed and gagged. "Yes participation, my favourite pastime." He hovered inches from the victim and absorbed her fear.

"Back to your questions. The second: Why are you here? We choose each of you for very different reasons. Each reason leads back to a particular time and event that will be meaningless to you. Despite this, we choose you."

Devon sidled up to her and lowered his voice. His words incomprehensible to the group. "Devon will address the next question and as The Enforcer of events it is essential he shares with you the importance of your contribution."

Devon drew back his shoulders and puffed out his chest. He then raised one jewelled finger on his left hand. "First, you are each a participant in the games. A contender. Second, you will take part in various missions. Each will have either a positive or negative outcome. Next, do not trust anyone. Your life will depend on your reaction to others. Finally, there is a goal for you—freedom."

He swivelled with slow, deliberate ease and faced each girl in turn. "Only one of you will survive." He breathed in the fear in the room and absorbed the loaded silence.

"You are probably wondering who you can thank for your fate. Look no further than your nearest and dearest." He ignored the looks of disbelief and continued. "We all have secrets. Some families have more to hide than most."

"Don't look at your imminent demise as unfair. I call it Robson's Revenge."

Isla took one last look into each of the girls. She exaggerated a yawn and brushed past Esther towards the stone steps.

18

"Any information yet about Kayleigh? The body found in the river?"

Frank cleared his throat and tried to ignore all eyes drawn to him, each expectant on his words of wisdom. "It checks out. Kayleigh Lambert was a sixteen-year-old from Bexley Village when her body was disposed of in the Ravensbourne river. The killer subjected the victim to a sexual assault before strangling her and dumping her body."

Albie added notes to the space below a picture of the young girl's bloated corpse, then drew lines between the images to update connections between victims.

"Did anyone take the rap for the murder?" DS Fawn's attempt to hide her curiosity forgotten, opened her notepad and waited.

"A dead end I'm afraid, Shaw. Robson Shaw was found guilty of the murder, after his own death, as were three similar murders during a four-year period which began with Kayleigh."

"Any witnesses? Further information?"

"Well, Libby Mann was a witness. Not to the murder, but as the last person police could find that had seen Kayleigh alive. She was thirteen at the time with strict parents. Her memory was sketchy at the time and the description she gave of the young men they'd met outside The Tiger's Head pub led nowhere." Albie paused and made eye contact with Dawn in an unspoken apology.

Tania broke the silence. "There must have been other witnesses, if not to Kayleigh's murder then surely to the others?"

"Um... yeah. There were for each. In fact, there is one name that pops up in three out of five of the cases. A local man. A Martin Piper, he was twenty-nine at the time of Kayleigh's death. He was a youth worker at the church youth club and worked on a family stall in Lewisham Market to earn some extra cash."

"Obviously, whatever he had to say I guess, wasn't that useful then?" Fawn said as she continued to scribble.

Frank scanned the files. "At the time they classed him as another unreliable witness. They dismissed much of what he had to say as hearsay or speculation."

Albie waited for silence to elapse, then summarised. Once he concluded that they didn't have much to go on, he shared the tasks out while updating the boards. "Just before you go." Albie waited until it was almost silent. "Although we only have a few avenues to pursue, remember we have a couple more than yesterday."

Albie caught Rachel's eye and nodded towards their office. "Do you have a minute?" The DS followed her colleague into the cluttered room and closed the door on the chatter outside.

"What's on your mind?" She strode to the chair facing his own across a paper-laden desk and stood behind it, tapping her fingernail on the wooden frame.

"DS Fawn, I need your teams full support in this case." He raised his hand before she could interrupt. "An active case. Suspected abduction. One video communication from the perpetrators and as yet nobody. Yet worst still, no real clues... just vague connections and a hunch."

"Go on.." A grin spread across her face at his obvious discomfort.

"I will be upfront and honest with you. We need results. We need something before one of these kidnappings becomes a murder investigation."

She watched as he paced back and forth. She couldn't help but relished the anguish he attempted to hide behind a nonchalant frown.

"How can we assist?"

Albie smiled, pulled his chair from the desk, gestured for her to join him and opened the familiar manilla file he'd removed from Tanya's bag earlier. "I need your team to keep up with the abductions case. Question as many people as possible, visit the sites, and insist on interaction with relatives, friends, neighbours and anyone else who could have even the slightest tenuous link. This is with the victims, if they were in, or live in, the surrounding area of the snatch sites."

She flicked through the pile of paperwork already collected. "We're on it. Really, you want us to retrace your steps. Worried you've made mistakes? You want to cover your back?"

He snatched the file from her grasp and scowled. Flustered by the silence, Rachel stood and turned to leave.

"Rachel, wait." He raised his fist to his mouth and cleared his throat. "We've got to put this to one side. All this bullshit and competitiveness. You know it's difficult for me, asking for help, especially from you. These girls are still alive. Are you willing to have any of their deaths on your hands because of your pride?"

He walked towards her, placed the file in her outstretched hand and whispered a thank you as she left the room and shouted for her team.

"Coffee?" Tanya asked as she sidled past DS Fawn.

He looked at his watch. "A quick one while we update."

"What did she want?"

Albie tapped his pen on the table. "Coffee. Then we'll talk. Oh, and get the others in here."

Jana adjusted the back of the passenger seat in his car like a cuckoo settling into another bird's nest. Albie loosened his tie, unbuttoned his top button, and eased two fingers inside the edge of his shirt collar. Sweat gathered on his forehead and neck, a claustrophobic reaction because of the close proximity of a virtual stranger. The electric window screeched as a three inch gap let refreshing air into the car and Albie breathed it deep into his lungs. He turned the engine over without a word and pulled out into a stream of traffic, regretting sending Frank out already. As a result, Tanya had to accompany him rather than be a familiar passenger in Albie's car. Jana sat with the car seat upright and her back rigid. She stared ahead silently. So silent that Albie's eyes were drawn to her chest. Reassured at the slight ascension, relieved that he'd witnessed proof that she was still alive.

"So, how are you enjoying your first few weeks with us?" His voice felt stiff and forced. But he waited for a reply and kept his eyes on the road ahead.

"Yes, it's good. I mean I'm learning so much, especially working with Frank. I mean PC Gibbs."

Albie nodded. "Frank's a good copper. We'll be in Lee Green soon, d'you know what we're doing?"

"We're gathering as much information about the local area from as many people as possible who lived here fifteen years ago when the body of Kayleigh Lambert was found."

"Good. Now, where would you go first to dig into the past and expect to get some answers?"

"Public houses, Sir. Oh, and we should also ask about any tattoo parlours around, or someone in the local area renowned for their ink work."

Albie checked the road, screeched through an amber light, and tapped out an unrecognisable beat with his signet ring on the steering as they fell back into silence. He pressed his foot down on the accelerator, uncomfortable with having to make anymore attempts at forced conversation.

19

As midday approached, heat settled like a claustrophobic blanket. It seeped through the tightest gaps and enveloped them like a lover's caress. Tanya peeled her jacket from her body. Unprepared for the mini heatwave weathermen had been hinting at for days and slick with sweat, she wished she'd put a plastic fan in her bag and some body spray. Her damp thighs rubbed together as she walked, and she thought about Marilyn Monroe. She'd had the right idea, Tanya closed her eyes and imagined a cool breeze lifting her skirt.

"You okay?"

"Course, the heat is intense. It just caught me by surprise." The houses all looked the same. Pre-war houses. A typical council estate where Eastender's were rehoused to escape the carnage left from the bombings after the Second World War.

"Which one is it?" Tanya asked.

"Over there," He leaned across the roof of the car and pointed to the house at the end of the street at the bisection of a crossroads. "Wait up. I'll come with you."

"The boss said you're not to get involved. It's an interview, and he's expecting me."

Frank shook his head and opened the car door.

"I don't like this Tan, I'm here and like you say it is just an interview so there're no worries." He adjusted the crutches and manipulated his body to standing. "Anyway, why should you get a cup of tea and biscuits while I wait in the car like your pet dog?" Tanya smiled and led the way. It was good to have Frank back, but she knew to share that would feed his ego, and he was cocky enough.

The house was half hidden, surrounded by overgrown trees and bushes, each one bigger than the last. Even the pathway competed with splatters of moss, entertaining a variety of weeds that planned to overgrow and devour the garden path.

"Watch your step, Frank." She warned as the sole of her sandal slid beneath her and she grabbed a bush to gain balance. A cross of black industrial tape covered the doorbell, so she looked for a knocker. After a few moments of looking, she rapped on the front door with her fist.

A scuffle ensued behind the door. A dog sprung at the glass panel, and an intense continuous bark dared her to enter.

"Shut up and get out. I said, shut up." The voice from the other side of the door was authoritative, and Tanya took a step back. There was a yelp and a scramble, then all went quiet and the door opened.

"Come in. PC Watts, is it? I was expecting you." She walked passed a trim man with no hair and a dark grey beard sporting a pair of grey-framed glasses. He noticed Tanya glanced towards the door on the left behind which the barking and scraping continued. "He's all right. Don't worry about him, he is harmless... d'you like dogs?"

Tanya ignored his question and introduced her colleague instead.

"Take a seat. I'll get some drinks and biscuits. How do you want your drinks, hot or cold?"

"Cold please." Tanya scanned the room with pleasant disbelief. It was spotless. Wooden cabinets shone, glass glimmered, and the soft furnishings were show house standard. Tanya felt she should slip her shoes off her feet out of respect for the light beige carpet that moulded to their shape. She allowed herself to relax into the floral suite and dwell on the contradiction between the garden and the interior of the house. Frank hobbled behind her and supported his weight on the crutches as he inched onto a dining room chair rather than struggle down onto the settee.

"Well, this is an unexpected surprise after the overgrown mess of a garden. I won't mind drinking from the cups here now."

"Nice place." Frank agreed, wiping two fingers across the wooden dresser on his right and inspecting them. "Not a speck of dust."

Tanya had reached for her second chocolate biscuit by the time Frank had been through the niceties with Martin Piper. He thought he'd led a relatively sheltered life. He'd grown up an only child and was born at home. He'd lived in the same house all of his life and kept himself busy.

"Has the area changed much in the last ten years?" Tanya took a sip of iced lemonade and used her fingertips to dab her mouth free of crumbs.

He sat for a moment and pondered the question as if the answer he gave was of great importance.

"Well, yes and no, I suppose. In the majority of the area, there have been few changes. The inevitable changes are the people, I suppose. You know, people move on. They grow up and have families of their own. Some move away."

"So let me get this straight." Frank waved a biscuit in his hand as he spoke. "You have lived here all your life."

Martin nodded.

"We need to ask you some questions relating to ten years ago when a murdered girl's body found in the river Ravenbourne."

Martin Piper placed his mug on a coaster, linked his fingers, and leant forward. "Ten years, that's quite a while ago. I don't know if I'll be of much help."

"Mr Piper, you made a statement about your whereabouts on the Friday evening in July. A dog walker discovered the day before the body of Kayleigh Lambert in the river."

"They said at the time I was unreliable. What makes you think anything has changed? If I was unreliable then, I would be diabolical now. Do you realise how many girls they found dead over those few years? Are you aware of how many statements I had to make to the police?" He wrung his hands, rose to his feet, and paced back and forth across the small living room.

Tanya and Frank exchanged glances. She made notes while he pursued the original question.

"We are interested in the Summer of 1995. July the twenty-first. What were you doing at the time? How were you making a living and why were you dragged into the investigation?" Frank watched him pace once more than asked him to take a seat.

"I was helping out on my old man's stall at Lewisham market mainly. The family had a pitch there for years. Early mornings were a killer, especially during the winter months."

"Were you working that weekend?"

"Well yeah, but I didn't help set the stall up on a Saturday. I had a lie in because I helped at the local youth club on a Friday night and afterwards some of us went for a few at the local."

"Local?"

"Rose of Lee, up the road, its name changed to Dirty South a while ago. It's shut down now. Was a right nice pub as well."

Tanya flicked to the next page of her pad. "Tell us about the youth club."

"It was just a place the teenagers met, played table tennis, darts, hung out with their mates. I volunteered there with two others, you know, doing our bit for the community."

"So you were in your late twenties and spent your Friday nights with a bunch of sixteen-year-olds. Why?"

"It's hard to explain. It was just like that then none of us earned big money. We volunteered, but one bloke paid for a few rounds in the pub afterwards. We'd go out on a Saturday, couldn't afford two nights in a row."

"What can you remember about that night, the Friday?" Tanya was poised, pencil in hand.

"We'd had some trouble over the few weeks leading up to that day. Some older lads hanging about outside, intimidating the younger boys, and bothering the young girls. You know, no big deal really. That night two girls I didn't recognise were following them about. They were mucking about to begin with. I noticed, as we were locking up, they'd upset one girl. One of the lads had a grip on her arm and she was raising her voice. Asked him to stop." He stared ahead as if replaying the event in his mind.

"Did you intervene?"

"Course, the bloke wrapped her in his arms, told me to piss off. I asked her if she was okay. She didn't answer, just stared at me. Then her friend shouted abuse. I jogged after the others and caught up with 'em just outside the pub"

"What happened then?"

"That's it. The next day they found the girl dead in the river. That's it. I never found out what happened to the other girl, the one wrapped in the bloke's arms. She's not dead, is she?"

"No, Mr Piper. She's not dead. So it was the abusive girl that died?"

"Yeah, you know what, it sounds bad but I don't remember her at all. No matter how I try, even when the police showed me a picture of her. She could've been anyone. The memory that stays with me are the haunted eyes of the little girl I left behind with them." He covered his face with his hands, his body moved in a slow rocking motion.

"Thank you, Mr Piper. We've got enough information for now. Please contact us if you remember anything else about that night."

They left him in the same position and let themselves out into the stifling heat.

20

A buzz droned in Esther's head. She fumbled blindly for the alarm, but there was no clock and no bedside cabinet. She opened her eyes, sat up and stared at the unfamiliar surroundings. Her limbs ached with each movement and she slammed her palms against her ears as the buzz drilled into her skull.

The monitor on the wall opposite the bed sprang to life, interference played with the images until the picture settled to show a large dim room with other women chained to the walls. Esther scrunched the sheets between her clenched fists as snippets of her memory flickered into the forefront of her mind.

The melodic voice she recognised infiltrated the room.

"Good to see you girls."

She sank beneath the covers to block the intrusive camera from her sight.

Esther's breath caught in the back of her throat and she choked in her desperation to inhale clean air. She sprang from the bed and covered her partially clothed body. Spasms shot through her limbs. As she concentrated on controlling her breathing, beads of sweat settled on her cool forehead and dripped into her tangled hair. She cowered on the floor behind the bed to hide, but it did nothing to protect her from the voice.

"I'm pleased to see you all." The voice blared through the speakers once again. "The contest will begin soon, but to begin with you must all be part of the formal introductions. It is important you remain seated in front of the monitors and follow my instructions."

Esther's hurried step reflected her heartbeat. She sat erect on the chair and leaned forward only when the voice continued.

"Each of your faces will be shown on the screen. You are to say your name, age, and one other piece of information about yourself. Be precise. You have only a short amount of time to appeal to the other contenders and get them onside."

A tear-stained face filled the screen and Esther felt a pang of hope. She tried to focus on what the woman said, but could not help being drawn to her gaunt face and blank eyes.

"Name and age?" The voice echoed around the room, and the woman on the screen choked out her words.

"I'm Claire, 26." She wiped a tear from her cheek. "I live in Greenwich and I'm an air hostess,"

One face merged into the next. "Adele. 30. married and just want to go home." She shrugged and stared ahead.

"Nina, 26. I'm a nobody. I'm just trying to live in my ordinary life."

Esther tensed as her face illuminated the screen. She cleared her throat and spoke with clarity. "I'm Esther, age 23. I'm confused, baffled at what's going on. Why was I taken? I have a life with my family." As her voice faded, her head flopped forward and her whole body collapsed inward. Crying was not an option. She caught her lip between her teeth to stifle a sob as it deteriorated into a muffled whine. The interference and buzz resumed for a few moments before the voice brought back her attention to the screen. Esther's limbs shook at the balaclava covered face that filled the monitor and the smell of aniseed assaulted her memories.

"Observation was an important part of those initial introductions. Now from what you know about each other, I will ask you to make a decision. Who do you feel should take part in the first task? You're in control. It's imperative to choose carefully as your choice could decide your fate."

Esther edged back in her chair as his masked face grinned and the tip of his tongue traced his zip edged lips. His eyes sparkled, and his unseen expression embedded dread which rattled through her shaking body.

"Use the screen to select a number. Each number represents a contender in the order of introduction. Once you choose your number, we will share your choice of person, and their task, and then we'll begin."

Esther locked eyes with her masked attacker hypnotised by his artificial presence and devastated by the cool shudder he inflicted at the base of her neck. Her first instinct was to hide, to become invisible. Instead, her movement restricted her own desire to find out the outcome of this bizarre game they'd been dragged into, so she continued to stare at the screen and when asked she touched a number.

A central light flashed. Anticipation built in her gut, and Esther held her breath. The number two illuminated the screen and seconds later an intrusive camera followed sobs of devastation from the bent form of Adele.

"Ladies, you have chosen your sacrifice." The masked figure addressed the woman on the next screen. "Adele. That's enough, the more you fuss the worse the task and the worst the task the less likely you are to survive."

The sobs subsided into muffled moans. He held a large red edged manilla envelope in his gloved hand. He scanned the content of the paper inside and hesitated before he delivered the message.

"Adele, you have fifteen minutes to prepare for the challenge. We will take you to a lake and you will dive for a bundle. When you retrieve it, you will bring it to the bank. You will be responsible for the life or death of a living creature." He turned his attention to his silent viewers. "You are all responsible. Each of you voted, and Adele was your choice."

Esther coughed and hitched cool air into her lungs. The screen buffered, and it broke the hypnotic spell. What had they meant by being responsible for the life or death of a living thing? Her stomach contracted and the acrid taste of bile painted the back of her throat. A shadow of panic clouded her mind as the clocks tick vibrated in the corner and filled the room with a countdown to a woman's fate.

The monitor screen buzzed to life, and a covering of frantic flies teased the lens. The gradual appearance of a grainy image came in and out of focus, then settled on a stretch of water. In front of the water stood was a figure in a wetsuit. She was shoved towards the edge by the demonic masked monster Esther had grown to hate.

Esther leaned forward in her chair. Her hands were numb from clinging to the chair frame. A morbid fascination kept her caught up in the masked man's movements. He crouched and picked a bag from the bank, then he heaved it in front of the camera. The bag wriggled.

21

DS Rachel Fawn wondered how she'd been talked into interviewing family members of the victims, which was surely just a routine activity. She flicked through the file as young PC Conrad pulled into the side road where Adele Soul lived with her husband Paul. What a waste of time. She tutted at her own stupidity. Since she had competed with Albie Edwards, she'd grown to admire his insight and dedication to the job. He had many traits she tried to live up to herself. Yes, he was annoying, argumentative, and sometimes just darn right arrogant, but he got results and demanded respect.

"Come on then. Let's do some detecting." PC Conrad glanced back at his boss as he manipulated his thin, lanky body through the open car door. He noticed a trace of a smile on her face and grinned like an excited puppy expecting a run in the park.

The man who answered her loud knock surprised her. He had a rugged chin, olive skin, and hypnotic lavender eyes. She took a step back and braced every muscle in her body. "Mr Soul?"

"That's me." He said as those lavender eyes scanned her body and locked with her own before he entranced her with his smile.

DS Fawn saw a charmer who could well be untrustworthy, even

though she found him attractive since he was the husband of a kidnap victim. She toyed, for a split second, with the idea of playing his game, but rejected the idea just as quickly.

"May we come in, Mr Soul? We just have some follow up routine questions about your wife."

Paul Soul studied her ID and grinned. He opened the door and walked inside. They followed him into a spacious hall, neutral colours had been used to decorate the area, even the furniture added little in the way of colour. Sunlight filled the room, which added to the sterile feel of the place. It felt more like a showroom than a home. "Mr Soul. I have a statement made by you after you reported your wife missing. Two days after you last saw or heard from her. Is that correct?"

He bowed his head as if contemplating the question and when he raised his head Fawn could not help but notice the lavender in his eyes had darkened, as had his complexion. He pulled a cigarette from a pack balanced on the edge of the windowsill behind him. He then lit a match and puffed on a cigarette until the end ignited. Smoke looped from his mouth as he exhaled and sat balanced on the arm of the settee.

"Exactly, you've got a statement so why are you here bugging me and not out there searching for her?"

"Like I said Mr Soul, this is a follow up. We can find new evidence at any point in an investigation and we need to pursue all areas of the case. This will include interviewing anyone who can shed light on your wife whereabouts."

"I don't know where she is for god' sake. I was the person who reported her missing." A low growl left his lips. Once again he took a long drag on his cigarette and exhaled.

"Precisely, you were the last person to come forward who'd seen Adele alive. Two days after she'd gone missing. Why was there such a gap in time before you call us?"

Paul Soul stood and paced the room as he explained.

"I phoned because it worried me. I'd found out she hadn't arrived at her parent's house."

DS Fawn scanned the information written in his original statement.

"Had Adele planned to visit her parents then?"

Paul Souls lowered his head and spoke to the floor. "We'd had a disagreement."

"It must have been a bad disagreement between you two, to think she wasn't coming home."

"Look, this has nothing to do with Adele's disappearance. I'm not saying another thing. Our private life is just that, private. It's none of your business." Paul Soul inhaled and turned his back on the officers before blowing out a translucent cloud of smoke.

"I think you'll find any information that can help us solve your wife disappearance is very much our business Mr Soul. Would you rather do this in your own home or are we going to take you to the station for questioning?"

Paul sighed. He shook his head defeated, took a final drag on the cigarette, and stubbed it out in an ashtray on the windowsill. "Go on then. Do your worst."

Fawn straightened in her chair and cleared her throat.

"When did you argue and what cause the argument?"

"Adele had an anonymous tip off. Some nosy cow texted her with pictures of me kissing another woman. The first two came through on the Saturday morning before she went missing. She went mad, throwing stuff, hitting me, and screaming. I'd just managed to calm her down when three more came through. Those were more.. well, you know."

A thrill of excitement shot through Fawn's body at the sight of Paul Soul's discomfort and she had to force the smile from her face as she continued.

"No, I'm afraid we don't know Mr Soul, you'll need to explain."

He paused and stared into her eyes. "Look, it was a short fling right, nothing serious. It was a mistake, but the photos were explicit. It's always been Adele for me, no-one else."

"What happened then?" DS Fawn continued to keep her expression blank and watched as Paul Soul frowned and bent his head.

"She grabbed her bag, coat, and shoes then walked out. Not a word. She just walked out that door. I've heard nothing from her since. Not a word."

"Didn't you go after her? Try to contact her? Or perhaps contact her friends to make sure she was okay?"

He raised his head. His intense stare drilled into Fawn and it took all her strength not to break eye contact.

"Look, it's not the first time we've argued. I know Adele, she needs time and familiar surroundings to calm down. When it's happened before she's always turned up at her mum's eventually, and once she's got it out of her system, she always comes home and we sort it out."

"Not this time." DS Fawn shocked herself with the blunt tone of her statement and she was quick to continue. "So when did you first call Adele's parents?"

"Just before I contacted the police." He lit another cigarette and inhaled.

"So you say that you had a violent argument with your wife about your extra- curricular activities, she stormed from the house in a distressed state. Then she drives off in her car and you leave it seventy-two hours before trying to contact her or inform anyone of her disappearance? Now I understand your distress, Mr Soul, but you must see how this looks." Fawn paused for a moment, and when there was no reply continued.

"What were you doing from the moment your wife left to the time you contacted her parents?"

"I went for a drink with mates. Then stayed at a friend's."

"Names, Mr Soul? Is there anyone who can vouch for you during the missing hours?"

He reeled off a list of names, including the woman he'd spent the night with. DS Fawn stood and ushered PC Gibbs out of the room.

"Thank you, Mr Soul. We'll be in touch when we find any new information regarding your wife."

Paul Soul took one last look at the officer, then turned and stubbed the cigarette out in the ashtray.

22

The sticky heat of the afternoon evaporated into a cool, calm evening. The artificial darkness from inside Esther's prison-like room made it difficult to establish the time of day or the temperature outside. The chill that caressed her body resonated with the tension that pressed heavily on her shoulders and crushed her lungs, making it difficult for her to breathe. The reality of their situation was clear as she watched the task unfold on the monitor. The immediacy of the horror she felt at Adele being nominated took time for her to absorb. Esther felt relief at her escape from nomination with a poisonous mix of anguish for the poor woman chosen to complete a task. She focused intently on the slice of life being played out on the screen, partly out of solidarity and partly out of a morbid interest.

Adele stood solid. Her eyes fixed on the wriggling bag. She followed each motion as it swung backwards and forwards towards the water. Her agitation was clear. She wriggled her chained hands in front of the masked man once he'd flung the bag out of her reach. Seconds ticked as she jogged on the spot, anxious to follow. As soon as Devon released the chains Adele plunged into the water like the curved neck of a swan searching for food. The impact splashed high above the sides of the bank.

Esther fell to her knees and shimmied closer to the images flashing before her eyes. She etched on the elegant ripples that danced on the surface, which was the only evidence that Adele and the wriggling bundle had ever existed. Her fingernails dug into her bare legs and blood pumped in her ears and an ache built in the cavity of her chest. Like watching a film at a suspenseful moment. Relief exploded as Adele thundered from the water, holding the bag above the surface. With one hand she used an unorthodox stroke to fetch a path to land. She threw the large black bag to safety and pulled herself onto the damp muddy bank. In slow motion, she dragged her limp, exhausted body a few feet. He yanked open the zip of the bag, and a golden furry bundle released.

Esther's tension fed on hysteria on the horrified face of Adele as she struggled to awaken the water-worn animal. The boney body twitched beneath her urgent touch and relief broke in the form of a smile on Adele's face. The bundle jumped to unsteady feet and shook. It's saviour laughed as it soaked her with a splatter of lake water. It stopped. Frantic, the dog went down on its haunches a slow growl left its mouth. It watched a figure crawl from the water nearer to Adele.

Esther stood and ran to the monitor. She banged the screen and screamed at the unsuspecting nominee. The moment of realisation imprinted on Esther's mind forever, she watched helpless as hands gripped Adele's ankles and dragged her back towards the water. Adele's screams pierced her heart. Her desperate grab at tufts of grass and clumps of weeds were useless against the unexpected force of her assailant. Like a crocodile that dragged its next meal under the surface, this predator was fast and furious. The blonde curl protruding from the black swimming hat left Esther under no illusions of the perpetrator's identity. She watched as the woman's long, white fingers with ruby red tapered fingernails forced Adele under the surface. She struggled back to the top once... twice, her arms flailed. First there were sprays of water, then just bubbles, and finally stillness.

Devon stared into the camera, his mask unzipped.

"You chose well. She saved the dog, but unfortunately for Adele someone had to forfeit their life for the dogs survival. Let's call it the Jokers card. Sleep tight. Oh, and one of you may have a visitor tonight."

His grin reached his eyes, and his laugh rattled through her skull.

Esther rolled into a ball on the floor and sobbed. The pain from her the last few days intensified. She uttered a silent prayer, the first since she was a young girl when they imprisoned her brother. But tonight rather than pray for another's safety she begged for her own.

23

Albie pulled into a side street off of Lee High Road and looked across at Jana. "Right, are you ready?"

She nodded, and they both stepped onto the pavement and walked back towards the main road towards the Old Tiger's Head.

"Do you know the area, sir?"

Albie slowed his pace and scanned the shops.

"There was a time when a crowd of us would go to the local pubs. If we couldn't get into the pubs in Blackheath, we'd have a wonder down the hill and try our luck here."

"Has it changed much?"

"A bit I suppose, but I'm not that old y'know." He nudged her arm and grinned, not sure whether she had taken him seriously. She smiled back and waited for him to continue.

"The Rose of Lee. Now, I remember getting in there a few times when it was open. Live bands played there sometimes. One singer, before my time, sung about characters from a book. She was on Top of the Pops. Do you know who I mean?"

Jana shook her head and bent to enter the pub under Albie's outstretched arm. As pubs go, it was fairly quiet for an early evening.

Although they had an evening menu, it was basic and Albie was aware of several good quality local restaurants where he would have preferred to eat. He wasn't clear what he expected to get from this visit, after all it was The Rose of Lee where the group used to drink. But locals were locals, and they had more than one pub to choose from after they'd locked up the youth club fifteen years ago.

Out of courtesy, he walked to the bar and flashed his ID.

"I'll have a Coke." He turned to Jana, "Drink?"

"Same please." She perched on a bar stall and tried to ignore the looks from the men in the opposite bar.

"Quiet in here. Is this normal?"

A robust middle-aged platinum-blond gazed at him with a cheeky glint in her eye as she placed two tall glasses on the bar.

"Yeah, I suppose it is. It gets busy later, at the moment it's mainly locals and a few stopped off for a quick drink after work. Are you still on duty?"

"Yes. We hoped to ask you a few questions." Albie said as he picked up the glass and took a long, cool drink. The woman watched him, leaned closer, but kept quiet.

"Have you worked here long?"

"Long enough." The blond bit her lip and traced her finger across the back of his hand before she changed the subject. "That's a shame I thought you might fancy keeping me company. I finish my shift in half an hour. What do y'all say?"

Albie blushed and took another gulp of drink. He gritted his teeth and fixed his best smile on his face.

"Tempting as it is, I am here as part of an investigation. Perhaps you could help though? It's an old case, so it's locals who may help. Ones who've been around for over ten years. Could you point out any hopefuls?"

Her smile deepened, "Other bar," she gestured. "The older guys in the corner. They started calling this their local when The Rose of Lee changed management and name."

The blond leaned across Jana, who shuffled back on the stool, and placed her hand over his. "Are you sure you don't want to hook up, you know, when you've finished? I could help you relax. You feel tense." She winked, tightened her grip, and smiled.

Albie untangled his hand from her grip, ignored the woman's comments, and Jana's vivid blush, then walked through to the other area. It was busier than the front, yet quieter. The customers were all probably regular's and used to each other's company. He spotted three men in the corner, each one nursed a pint like a golden chalice they'd guard with their lives.

"Can I get you a pint?" He addressed all three as if they were mates, and it was his round.

All three eyed him with suspicion, but it was the stockier of the three who spoke first.

"It depends, don't it?" He looked at the others as if he was about to share the funniest joke in the world. "It depends what you want in return."

The two others backed up their spokesperson with nods and tightened the grip on their pint glasses.

"Just a chat. Let's call it a walk down memory lane. Nothing heavy. Old news, really. What can I get you?"

He took their order and asked Jana to do the honours.

"Do you mind?" He asked. He pulled up a chair and introduced himself to the group. They muttered clipped introductions then the group sat in silence until the barmaid bought a tray of drinks to the table leaned all over Albie in one last attempt to gain his attention.

"You're all locals then?"

They looked at each other and nodded.

"How long have you lived here?"

Joe, the stockier man, spoke first, again.

"Grew up here. I lived nowhere else. Not like these two. Both travelled at different times. They wanted me to, but it never interested me. I like my home too much."

Albie turned his attention to the other two. "Were either of you travelling ten years ago?"

"How should I know off the top of my head?" Anthony, the only one with hair, swept it from his face.

"Fair enough. Let's see if I can refresh your memory. How old would you have been in 2000?"

"I'd have been twenty-two. Yeah, I travelled at the end of 1999 into the beginning of 2000, backpacking. Why?"

"Did you go too?" The third man nodded.

"August of that year, were the two of you travelling during the month of August?"

"I wasn't. I was back home from April 2000." Albie turned his attention to the only man who had yet to speak.

"I went back to Malta in June. I was out there for two years before I came home."

Albie thanked him and turned his attention back to his two companions.

"Do either of you remember several murders that started in August 2000 and ended in March 2002? Young girl's bodies were found strangled and dumped in Ravensbourne."

They both appeared deep in thought before Joe answered.

"Yeah, you couldn't help but know about it, it was all over the news. If you were a local and a male, they questioned you. Didn't they?"

"Yeah, it was a scary time for families. It was August, light until late in the evening, but few women on the street on their own. Scared they was."

"August, the body of a young woman, Kayleigh Lambert, was found." Albie slid a photo of her across the table, the one used by all the newspapers at the time. He followed it up with one of Libby Mann, was an attractive fourteen-year-old, with a smile that lit up her whole face. "You may have seen her with this young girl, they both frequented the area the evening before Kayleigh's death."

Joe pointed to Kayleigh's picture, "I remember her being in all the papers for months. I told the police at the time the same I'm telling you now, I never saw her in the flesh. Not that night or before." He took another look at Libby. "Don't recognise her at all, it's the first time I've seen a picture of that little girl. Who is she?"

"Someone who we now have reason to believe was with Kayleigh that night."

Anthony swept his hair from his forehead, gulped his final swig of beer and wiped his mouth with the back of his hand. "So what, are you saying there was another girl involved that night, I mean apart from her?" He pushed Kayleigh's photograph back towards Albie.

"Do you recognise either of the girls?"

He licked his top lip and took one more look. "I dunno, it was a long time ago. Like Joe said, that girl was plastered all over the media for months."

"And the other..?"

He went to stand. A silent look flickered between the men, and he moved towards Albie. "Same again?"

Albie followed him to the bar, even though the question wasn't aimed at him.

"Well? Do you recognise her? Perhaps you remember something about that night, even the slightest thing? It may seem insignificant to you, however, it may be a vital piece of information to us."

Anthony gestured to the barmaid and spoke to Albie in a whisper. "Not here all right. I can't talk here."

Albie nodded and placed his card under his empty glass.

"Well, thank you for your time. Enjoy your evening." He walked to the nearest exit followed by a silent PC Kolska. "Did you get all that?"

Jana closed her notebook and assured him she had noted all the relevant information she could from the discussion.

"Excuse me... you..."

"I don't believe it." Albie said, as she turned in the voice's direction.

PC Kolska smiled and waited to see how this conversation would pan out.

Albie's practised false smile spread across his face, "I'm still on duty Miss. Sorry, but I can't spend time with you."

"I know that you told me already, there's no need to make a scene." She scanned the faces of the surrounding people each appeared immersed in their own conversations. "That bloke you were talking to asked me to give you this."

She took his card from between her finger and turned it over in the palm of his hand. On the back, in capital letters he'd written, I KNOW HER. I'LL COME TO YOU. Albie called after the blonde, "Thanks, perhaps next time, ay?"

She blushed and shouted back, "I just might hold you to that."

Jana stood next to him, notebook and pencil in her hand. "Shall I note that, sir?'

He strode towards the car shaking his head at her unexpected remark. "Funny, Jana, very funny."

24

Devon yanked his mask from his head, threw it on the winged back chair and lounged back into it, one leg hung over the arm and he swung back and forth while he waited for a reaction from Isla who inspected the skin around her eyes in the mirror.

"Day one of the games was full of twists and turns. I loved your cameo at the end," He said. "What a twist."

Isla paused and watched Devon's limbs twitch. She was used to his hyperactive energy and knew if she rode it out and remained calm he would eventually yield and his mood become less animated.

He jumped to his feet, grabbed her shoulders, and began an aggressive massage. She placed a hand over each of his and talked to his reflection.

"Devon, stop." He responded after a few erratic rubs. All motion stopped except for a telltale twitch that flickered in his eyelid.

"Today was a total success. You shone as The Enforcer and showed great strength of character throughout. The games ended on a note of tension which is an important memory for the contestants to be left to ponder. And on a personal note, the outcome should be enough for them to take us seriously."

The twitch in his eyelid quickened, and he stuttered his reply. "As a… a reward, can I… I visit Esther tonight?"

Her smile intensified, "You don't need to visit anyone tonight Devon, your reward is right here."

Isla loosened her robe, and followed Devon's stare as it wandered across her exposed breasts. She leaned back as his hands followed the trail his gaze had taken just seconds before and closed her eyes as he bit down on her nipple. No amount of pain would eradicate her need for revenge. Pain was her only route to excitement and had been since she could remember. She didn't care who inflicted the pain—she only hoped to feel.

She felt a slight hitch of excitement from the adrenaline rush of forcing Adele's head under the water? Devon was the only person in this moment with the ability to get her close to the pleasure of pain she had felt earlier.

25

Esther raised both hands to the knotted makeshift blindfold secured at the back of her head and entangled in her hair. She winced with each intricate movement she had to attempt to undo the knot without yanking her hair from the roots. The soft opaque material fell from her eyes and she grimaced against the intrusion of light. She flinched, closed her eyelids, then edged them open as her eyes adjusted to the light's intensity.

Opposite her on a large board was a hand-written script and a tripod with a portable camera that winked at her in a rhythmic beat that matched her pulse.

She turned to the figure beside her.

"You don't expect me to read from the board, do you?" She edged back and winced from his face only inches from her own. There was something creepy about the big red nose, white face, and painted on smile that sneered at her obvious abhorrence. His white-gloved fingers dug into her shoulder like the claws of a falcon. So deep she could hear the scrape of nail on bone. His teeth yellowed against the pallor of his face, grit together while his voice fought for release.

"You will read every word from the board, exactly what we've written, any deviation and one of your friends will give up a treasured part of their body. Have I made myself clear?"

Aniseed polluted her immediate air supply. Bile rose in the back of her throat, and she nodded in reply as another clown placed a hand on her forearm.

"When I say, look into the camera and read the words."

A wave of nausea made her speechless. All she could do in reply was nod. Hands dug into her shoulders once again. Thumbs indented the soft skin between her shoulder blades and her body responded by straightening. Now the clown could move closer and she whimpered as his crotch pressed against her torso.

"Ready. Now."

"My name is Esther. Esther MacDonald." She swallowed, her mouth was tacky. She closed her eyes, desperate to control the quiver in her voice as she spoke. "I was taken. I do not know why they took me. Others are with me, other women, women that were kidnapped. You must help us. I'm talking to the person responsible for the Raven Murders. You know who you are and you must confess to spare our lives." Her lip trembled. A pain shot down her spine as the clown punched her in her lower back. She laid her hands flat on the table, even still her hands shook, and she tried to calm her breaths. "The police closed the case without finding the real killer and unless they take this seriously other young girls will lose their lives." The words on the board ended and Esther stared straight at the camera. "Save us. Please save us..."

"Enough. You've said enough." The clown said as he leaned over her shoulder, his breath on her neck. "Hold my glove in your mouth, Esther." The cotton filled her mouth until she gagged in response. "That's what happens when you add to the script."

Esther's eyes filled with tears as she inhaled through her nostrils and dragged hungrily at the air like an addict inhales their first hit. The clown circled the blindfold around her neck and tightened his grip as he knelt to eye level and exhaled aniseed. His painted on smile demonic as he watched her widened eyes weep with fear. Esther struggled against the restraints and breathed erratically through her nose. Her efforts to stay alive exhaustive. A white pain shot behind her eyes as he tugged a little tighter.

"Devon, that's enough. You've had your fun. Replace the blindfold and get her back to her room."

The clown leaned into her at the same time he released his grip on the blindfold. "If you promise to keep quiet, I'll remove the glove." His whisper and the trace of his finger across her cheek were soft. Hairs raised on the back of her neck, and erratic heartbeat echoed in her ears.

"Better?"

Esther gasped as he removed the balled up glove from her mouth. She felt the tingle of life return to flush her cheeks and her head fuzzed with relief.

"Beautiful." The clown's fingers traced the blotches of blood as they rose to the surface of her pale skin. His lips hovered over her mouth and she held her breath once again. "Do you feel that? Sexual desire and fear are near cousins." He got to his feet, then bent down and hoisted her to standing.

"Thank you Devon. Let's take Esther back to her room." As they moved towards the doorway Esther's knees buckled and her body slumped towards the floor. Supported under her arm and around her waist, she kept moving forward. Carpet cradled her bare feet, and she knew she was back inside her room.

"Lay back, get comfortable, and rest. We may need you again in a while for another TV appearance."

Isla had removed her red nose and curly wig. White patches mingled with red smeared face paint awakened the horror of memories from her past. Memories she couldn't quite remember and had probably buried for a reason.

Esther clung to Isla's hand while she fiddled with the knots that bound her wrists.

"Are we going to survive? Me and the other girls? What have you got planned for us?" She rubbed her chafed wrists and stared at the distorted faces watching her, unable to blink in case her question remained unanswered.

"I have no idea. It depends on the outcome of the appeals. You are all responsible for your lives. Convince the police to reopen the case. Set the wheels in motion for the real killer to reveal themselves. It's up to you."

Esther gripped her ruff and pulled her grotesque face closer, "Please, explain." A sob caught in the back of her throat. "Explain why we're here. How can we overturn something that we know nothing about? I don't understand."

Isla yanked away from her grasp and left the ruff in Esther's tightened grip. "All you need to know is my brother was not a killer. Someone killed those girls, but it wasn't him."

Esther rose onto her elbows. Her eyes narrowed, and she spat the next words through gritted teeth.

"Well, if you think my brother killed those girls, you've got it all wrong. He would never hurt another person."

Isla stood and stared ahead. She swayed back and forth like a mother rocking a baby.

"No?" She said with a disjointed grin on her make-up strewn face. "Well answer me this, Esther. If he can kill Robson, then what makes you think it was his first time?"

Esther lowered her head and fiddled with the ruff. The nylon felt like sandpaper between her fingertips and the coloured dots swirled in a blur as tears threatened.

"Get some rest."

She heard the door nestle into its frame, then lay back on the bed and let the tears flow.

26

Albie stepped from the car, strolled to the entrance of the building. He took the steps two at a time and stood between the doors and Jana. The smile brightened her face and had since they left the pub.

"Look," he said with one hand on the door. "I know you think it's funny." The smile slipped from her face and looked at her hands. "The barmaid chatting me up, but how d'you feel about it being our little secret?"

He waited for a reply which was not forthcoming and tried to ignore the grin she fought to hide. Albie went to speak again, instead just shook his head, walked through the door and held it open for Kolska to follow.

"Anything for me?" Albie asked at reception.

An officer with glasses perched on the end of his nose flicked through a small pile of messages and handed Albie two slips of paper. "All there is, as far as I know, Albie. Oh, yeah. DSI Masters has asked for a meeting between you and DS Fawn as soon as you return."

"Thanks Tim. Is Fawn here yet?"

"Just went up about ten minutes ago." Albie watched as he tapped on the keyboard. Whatever she was doing before Albie interrupted had him engrossed.

As the lift ascended, Albie gave Jana several instructions, including comparing notes with Tanya and Frank. The lift came to a stop, and he bounced on the balls of his feet as if to prepare for a hundred metres sprint. He headed in the opposite direction to his colleague and they went their separate ways without another word.

As Albie approach the DIs office through a maze of corridors, the difference between the decor on the higher-ranked officers floor and the basic neutral colours and cork boards covered with paperwork on the walls where the foot soldiers worked angered him. Although he was always intrigued by the paintings, hung intermittently along the corridor, the fact that they were prints didn't alter the overall pretentiousness of the comparison.

Albie tapped his knuckles on the wooden door. He waited until she called for him. He entered and sat in the chair she directed him towards.

"Albie, thank you for joining us." DI Masters glanced at her watch as she spoke and managed a terse smile.

"DS Fawn and I were just discussing the connection between the two cases you've been following up. I must say, the link between the two is tenuous, and unless you can convince me otherwise, a waste of everybody's time."

Albie looked from one to the other and felt a stab of determination in the pit of his stomach as he prepared to argue his case. "Detective Inspector, I understand your misgivings but before you decide can we discuss any links between the cases? Could I ask PC Watts and Gibbs to join us? They have useful feedback too."

"I asked for their notes on the way to the office. Here." DS Fawn handed him Frank's notebook, and he scanned the pages.

"Right, let's catch up on your findings and decide how to proceed now." DSI Masters gave him a moment to process her comment, then continued.

"Who did you talk to in the public house? And what information did you get from the customers?"

Albie shook his head and explained that he was waiting for a response from Anthony Locke, who was reticent to talk to him.

"So essentially we have had two teams working on the same case and between you, on paper, we could not show inadequate progress. In fact, it would be fair to say, we are none the wiser."

DS Fawn cleared her throat, "It wasn't a complete waste of time. Mr Soul admitted to an argument with his wife. He's made a habit of cheating on her, and the weekend she went missing she'd found out he'd been with another woman." DI Masters waited for her to continue, but when she remained silent, the DI turned to Albie.

"I have got nothing concrete, but I have every reason to believe Anthony Locke will put some light on the circumstances of the murders ten years ago. And once we have established a link between what happened outside the youth club and the men involved, it may give us insight into why women are disappearing now."

"All ifs and buts." The DI shook her head. "It's just not good enough. We need solid evidence, or at least a reliable lead to connect the two cases. Our focus should be on the live case, our priority to find those girls before they turn up as corpses."

Albie got to his feet, "I am listening but I believe the two cases are linked and working two teams, one on each case, is exactly how we will find the women."

DS Fawn stepped forward, "I was unsure when I was first asked to check old witness statements, but I have to agree with DS Edwards, it is too much of a coincidence for the cases not to be linked. Given more time, I believe we can come up with the information you require to justify using both teams on the case."

DI Masters looked from Albie's steely, determined frown to the gentler questioning gaze of his colleague and addressed them both.

"You understand that I have to account for every penny spent on this case at the expense of others? Especially with both teams engaged in what could ultimately be the same investigation." She faced the window which overlooked a parking area.

"You've got twenty-four hours to find a link that establishes a connection between the two cases. A substantial lead. God help us if you're wrong about this."

"Thank you." DS Fawn took it as the perfect time to leave while they were ahead and nudged Albie to follow.

"Not so quickly, DS Edwards," the DI gestured to the chair he'd just vacated. "Before you go, I want to clarify that I am livid with the way you have dealt with this case with and once it is over I am seriously considering whether I want you as part of this unit. I am the person who gives the authorisation to collaborate on an investigation. If you needed the support, it should have come directly through me. How do you think I looked when I was challenged by above and had to blab my way out of a tight corner as far as funding the operation goes?"

"If this is a bollocking about lack of funding, your rant will land on deaf ears while there are still women missing. Sorry. Next time it all goes through you. I should have asked permission, but even DS Fawn, who detests me, sees the importance of us working as a team on this one."

DI Masters narrowed her eyes and spoke through gritted teeth. "Next time, you keep me in the loop or face the consequences." She brushed past him and walked into the corridor. "Do you understand what I'm saying?"

He nodded and walked in the opposite direction towards the buzz of the investigation room.

27

Esther opened her eyes. At least she thought she had. With difficulty, she searched for a familiar object and settled on the bedside lamp. It became her focus because it was familiar, and the lamp gave her a desired connection with home.

Intermittent throbs at the back of her skull were reminders of the violence of the previous day. There was no question in her mind that her captures had drugged her again. Esther clung to the sheets that covered her naked body and dragged them with her as she sidled up the bed. She sat upright against propped up pillows and stared at the monitor on the opposite wall. A black screen stared back at her. At a glance, she could see no evidence of activity, interference, or images on the screen. This morning there was just silence. The silence was menacing, and she felt that it waited in anticipation to unbalance its victims. As she dressed under the cover of the sheet and coordinated the movement of her arms and legs to the best of her ability, the terror of the unknown kept her on guard. It was then when she decided that she would take care, at all times, not to expose herself to the masked man's pleasure.

Breakfast stuck in her throat, even though porridge should slide down Esther couldn't help but choke. The only way she kept down the contents of her stomach was the knowledge that she had to stay alert and strong for whatever lay ahead.

The monitor buzzed to life and Esther shrank back into the pillows, rounded her shoulders, and wrapped her knees against her torso in a tight hug. Seconds stretched into minutes before the woman's image jumped onto the screen. The initial relief Esther felt was short lived as she recalled the woman's calculated drowning of Adele.

"Good morning, ladies. I trust you all slept well." She paused for just an instant before continuing. "Day two of the game. How exciting. A new game, and a new vote for a new contestant. Don't let yesterday's experience torment you. The voting system is the same as yesterday, however you have less choice today. Images and numbers will flash on the screen and you will have ten seconds to make your choice."

The woman's melodic voice seeped into Esther's brain as if injected through a syringe. A soothing tone with the promise of hope disguised the pain and devastation the women would face. Esther's hand padded blindly on the screen ready to choose the next victim and as she pressed a random number, she slid to the ground. She forced herself to lift her head in time to see a number flash on the monitor, her heart thudded, breath caught in her throat she leaned forward and put her head between her knees. The room spun, and she gasped for breath.

"Esther," the man's velvet voice trickled over her so close she jumped and spun full circle convinced he was in the room.

"We have chosen you. This as a special moment for me because we will work together on this task."

Ester shuddered but kept listening to his deceptive tones.

"The previous outcome means there are not enough contestants left for the games to be effective. You have a very important role to play tonight. You are my accomplice in the next abduction."

She shook her head, unable to process the enormity of his statement.

No. She mouthed as the horror of the task hit her smack in the gut. Esther felt the other girls relief, unrealistic sighs floating on the air. The knowledge that they were safe, for now at least, made her dig deep for the courage she was determined to show. She lifted her head back towards the screen, but the familiar fuzz of white specks whirled across the dark background like the fear that danced in her heightened sense of danger.

Time, so often a two-faced friend, had no sympathy for Esther. Before she made sense of her task, plan an escape or even a way to communicate her desperation with anyone, the door opened and both figures from her nightmares entered the room.

The balaclava clad man rushed towards her in one swift movement, wrapped her in a tight grip with one arm and twisted his other hand in her long curls, and yanked her head back. His aniseed breath was hot on her cheek.

"I am so excited that we chose you for this task, see." He rubbed his hardness into her hip. "I have the pleasure of preparing you." He forced her onto the wooden chair and tied her hands behind her back.

"Wait, Devon. I need to explain our expectations and I need her coherent for the instructions. She has to understand the forfeit if she doesn't bring her back."

Devon backed away while Isla spoke to Esther and paced in the background. Thoughts shot around Esther's head like a shooting star bouncing off walls inside a closed building. The raised goosebumps on her arms reiterated what she already knew. They were unpredictable.

Isla struck her cheek so hard, Esther yelped.

"Look at me, not him. Listen carefully. I will explain your part in the task. If you don't follow the plan precisely, the next time you see your son will be in a coffin." Isla fixed her stare on Esther's, "Good, I have your full attention."

Esther listened to every diabolical instruction and evil idea with the knowledge of Adele's murder playing over and over in her mind. She couldn't call their bluff. "Why?" She sobbed in response, "What have any of us done to you?"

"I'll make it clear soon. I'm sure if you put your mind to it you could think of a reason you are here, but for now you have to play the game." Isla strolled towards the door, paused, and added, "Oh, I nearly forgot this has to be authentic. All yours, Devon. Do your worst."

Devon unzipped the mouth of his mask. His permanent grin distorted as he skulked forward. He pressed his face close to hers; he pulled his arm back and punched her stomach then pulled back and caught her jaw. She fought to stay conscious. Tried to work with the punches. One thing she held onto was that it wasn't just her life she fought to save now. Dillon would only remain safe if she went along with their warped plans.

The man's mask had slipped, and he gasped for breath, a grotesque monster. He pulled her head back and licked off dried blood from the corner of her eye and mouth.

"I'll be back for you," He said as he untied her wrists and left the room with the same speed with which he entered. The shudder that crept through her body merged with a quiver until her whole body convulsed and she hung like a puppet without its master. Blood and tears mingled with snot and ran over her lips until she wiped her hand across the pink marbled mess. Esther sniffed up and forced herself to stand and hobbled to the sink. The cool water trickled down her face as she dabbed her split skin with a blood red flannel.

In reality, all she wanted to do was curl up to sleep in bed. Instead, with a renewed effort, Esther changed her clothes. They'd be back, probably sooner than later, and she needed to be ready. Not a petrified wreck, but the strong woman she'd always been. She had to prepare to fight for the life of her son and the other victims in the house.

She sat and waited.

28

"And so it begins," Albie said under his breath as he hung up the phone. He scanned the room, unsure of his next move until he spotted Rachel Fawn in a far corner office curled on a chair flicking through a file while writing in a notebook. He crossed the room in what he hoped was a casual stroll, then put his head around the door. "Fawn, we're up. A woman's body has turned up, they think it could be one of our missing ladies."

"Sorry, Edwards, it's not your call." She slammed the closed file into his stomach hard enough to tense his muscles and lift his hands in defence.

"You can't be involved in our investigation. Focus on the cold case and I'll be in touch."

Albie followed her woven trail through a maze of desks, collecting her jacket, phone, and colleagues along the route. "But we're twiddling our thumbs here."

She turned and forced a smile. However, her telltale frown gave away her surprise. "DS Edwards, we will keep you up to date with our findings and inform you of any connection with the cold case. Promise." She wriggled her fingers at him and her grin spread as the lift doors closed.

The Tarn was a small park situated back from a main road and bordered with tall green metal railings. There were two ways in and out of the park. As Fawn entered the gate and stood at the top of a steeply curved concrete pathway memories of childhood flooded her mind. Some fond, others best forgotten. Like many public spaces and building in the area, The Tarn had an interesting history which she was aware of as a child, although now it was a blur in her memory.

She skimmed the information board and noted that the park closed at four o'clock at this time of the year. It boasted a large elongated lake and was a secluded place to go about your business undetected. Rachel walked down the slope towards the lake and tried to control the speed of her legs as they carried her to a wooden hut just at the bottom. A police officer stood with one eye trained on a few geese that waddled in his direction. He was engaged in conversation with a man dressed from head to toe in green. The park keeper could so easily disappear into the foliage and go unnoticed. His skin was translucent. A damp sheen glistened across his forehead and Fawn could sense he would feel clammy to her touch. The fresh-faced officer had a few wispy fair hairs of his chin and for a moment he reminded her of the Lion King in his adolescence.

Rachel stood between them and opened her badge as an introduction. She turned to her companion, "PC Johnson, take Mr..?"

"Knight." The young PC held a hand towards the park keeper in introduction.

"Mr Knight to the hut and see if we can rustle up a hot drink for him with plenty of sugar." She turned back, her questions now aimed at the PC. "Before you go, what have you uncovered so far?"

He cleared his throat, his cheeks flushed, and he spoke louder than necessary. "A body. DS Fawn, Mr Knight, discovered a body this morning." He nodded towards the stooped man who sat on a bench with his shoulders covered with a thick blanket. Even so, his whole body shook with small erratic movements, but noticeable to the onlookers who were gathering thick and fast.

"How many colleagues do you have with you? We need to put a stop to the gathering audience."

He spoke into his radio and within seconds two officers rounded up the visitors and guided them towards the only entry and exit now open in the park.

Fawn smiled as another officer escorted Mr Knight towards his hut. Then addressed PC Johnson, "Shall we walk and talk? You can start by going through what you saw when you arrived at the crime scene and any information you've drawn from the witness."

The walk was short, but with a steep incline that led back up towards the road. Shielded by a tall metal spiked fence covered in foliage was a stone well. Metal mesh had been removed from the well's opening and the drop exposed, but the area was hidden from the public. Rachel glanced at the plaque this was once an ice well where they stored ice for use at the local palace kitchen. She leaned against the well, stood on tiptoes and gripped the side and bent forward. The drop was minimal and curled up at the bottom was a dark-clothed body. Initially, the bare white feet, hands, and pale face covered in a tangled of black hair looked like separate body parts. A flash of an unwanted memory unsteadied her, and she pushed from her mind the image of a dismembered life-size doll mingled with the real body parts of a victim.

Fingers dug into her fleshy upper arm through her jacket and jumper and she was thankful to feel her feet on solid ground.

"Sorry," A PC loosened his grip, and a blush tinted his cheeks. He lowered his gaze and tapped his foot. "Your balance wavered a bit. I thought you would join the victim."

Rachel steadied herself, thanked him, and tried to remember the last time she'd eaten. "So, I suppose we're waiting for reinforcements before we remove the body, are we?"

"I have hit on good authority that they'll be here within the next five minutes." A familiar gruff voice reached her before Leo rounded the bend with a bag full of equipment. "It's been a while Fawn, this is normally Edwards and Watts remit. I am honoured."

"Leo, it's good to see you." She felt heat rise from her chest and creep up her neck. He smiled at her and waited for her to continue. Fawn cursed under her breath at her adolescent reaction. "I'm afraid you're stuck with me today. Edward's has been banished to work on a cold case."

Leo moved to the side so his colleagues could start, then turned back to Fawn, "I've no complaints. I'd rather look at you than his miserable mug. You've already put a smile on my face." He winked then squeezed between her and the well, he mirrored her movements from earlier. "It looks like a tight squeeze. We must set the equipment up before we can go much further. Still, I'm sure you've got witnesses to interrogate."

Rachel watched him intently, hypnotised by the movement of his lips, before she realised he'd stopped talking. She pulled on the hem of her jacket and rubbed her hands together.

"Okay, I'll leave you to it."

"I'll come and find you when we're done." He said as she retreated.

The young PC paced towards her as she made her way down the slope and around the lake, a focal point of the park, calm waters with light ripples made by ducks in their constant hunt for food. He held out a packaged sandwich and a bottle of water while trying to fend off some inquisitive geese that looked ready to jump him for his food.

"I thought you could do with something to eat and drink. Its only cheese and salad. I wasn't sure whether you were a vegetarian? I've got a BLT if you want to swap."

Rachel took the offering and gave him a genuine smile, ripped open the packaging, and took a bite.

"Thanks, this is fine." She said between mouthfuls. She washed the food down with a few gulps of water and wiped her mouth with the back of her hand. Her stomach gurgled in appreciation. Fawn sat on a wooden bench, near the park keeper's hut, to finish her food and attempted to chew. A host of professionals walked towards the well. Between them they carried equipment of all shapes and sizes to the top of the park. It wasn't long before the whir of an engine vibrated on the breeze. Rachel stood, put the final piece of sandwich in her mouth, and threw the wrapper in the bin.

"Shall we talk to Mr Knight now?" The PC tailed her as if he was her shadow until they reached the hut. The man sat, crouched over, his elbows rested just above his knees, and his palms covered his face. He had removed his khaki green hat and exposed a thinning scalp of grey-flecked chestnut hair. He had a bald patch which reminded her of a monks scalp. She sat next to him, a persons' width away, to keep a professional distance.

"Mr Knight. I am DS Fawn and I need to ask you a few questions."

He raised his face from his hands and turned in her direction as if she'd disturbed him from his thoughts.

"I don't know if I can tell you anything more. The others have already asked me plenty of questions."

"I know Mr Knight, and as soon as I've finished, I'm sure you can go about your business. Have you had a cup of tea? Something to eat?"

"No... I can't stomach food at the moment."

"This shouldn't take too long. What happened when you arrived at work. Take your time."

"I was late, I've started parking further away and walking, you know." He patted his stomach. "Wife says I'm heading for a heart attack. Anyway, the gate was ajar. I wasn't worried at first 'cause Fred another keeper sometimes stops for a chat and a cuppa first thing."

"So when were you first suspicious?"

"It was the damaged padlock, that and my gut told me. I knew something wasn't right."

"Think carefully, Mr Knight. What were your next movements?"

"Well, normally I stroll the whole site. You can never be too sure of damage some young vandals cause. I find all sorts, even dead animals." She nodded for him to continue. "I always take the same route, a creature of habit, it happens as you get older. But not today, for some reason I went to the ice well first. I don't know why... I just did."

"You're doing well, Mr Knight, please continue."

"They'd balanced the wire mesh that covered the well, on top of a bush near the external fence. A putrid stink hung on the air, clung to the hairs in my nose, scuffles scratches drew me nearer to the hole and I glanced over to see.." He turned away, wretched, and dry heaved.

"Did you touch anything, Mr Knight?"

He took a deep breath of fresh air, "No, I ran to the hut and rang the police. It was when I put the phone down that a chill ran through me. I knew they'd been here, in the hut. They've nailed a note to the back of the door. I didn't touch it, I ran." He hung his head and clasped his hands together in his lap as they shook.

"You handled the situation well, Mr Knight. Thank you for your help. I think you should go home now and try to rest. If we need you again, we'll be in touch."

Rachel strolled over to the PC, who seemed to have made friends with most of the geese. "The note, where is it?"

"He's got it, I think. The DS down by the bridge at the other end of the lake."

"DS? I'm the DS on this case." She raised her hand to shield her eyes from the sun and tried to make out the figures who stood on the bridge.

"I know, that's what I said, but he insisted that you are working two cases together."

One person on the bridge waved, but Rachel had not needed an invitation and had covered half the distance already. Her nostrils flared and sweat trickled into damp patches under her armpits as she swung her arms to the march of her feet. The distance between them was enough to quash her internal beast who had been ready to rip him to shreds. By the time she reached DS Edwards and his sidekick Watts, her grimace was under control and she'd reminded herself that her professionalism must remain intact.

"Edwards, Watts. You're full of surprises, aren't you? Haven't you got somewhere else to be?"

"Aww, I thought you'd be pleased to see me." Albie hunched his shoulders and frowned.

"Look, you've had your orders from Masters. One phone call, Edwards, and you'll be off both cases. Is that what you want?"

Albie took a step forward and blocked the conversation from

Tanya, who had turned her back on them to watch the ducks paddle through the water.

"Rachel, just think for one minute. Before you make a phone call, there's no reason we can't just work together, you know, under the radar." He moved in closer and ran his fingers with a tentative touch down her arm.

Rachel wriggled from his reach. Tucked her shirt further into the waist of her trousers and held her hand out, palm up. "I'll pretend I didn't hear that, Edwards. Now hand over the note and go do some detecting. I'll see you both back at the station in an hour."

29

Esther felt the warmth of the woman whose head rested on her shoulder and lolled back and forth with the motion of the car. Her body trapped her, and the woman was the only thing separating her from the masked man. Her thoughts were on escape. Her desire to take a chance and throw herself from the car was overwhelming. She knew, however, that the chance of survival from the fall was slim. Escape from the monster near her minute, and the consequence for an attempt to escape, unthinkable.

The woman beside her stirred, moaned, and then stilled. She could never leave another innocent woman to the horrors she'd endured since being taken.

Determined, Esther decided at that moment that they'd survive their ordeal. They'd find a way. The more of them there were, the greater was their opportunity of survival. How could she keep them on side? All the girls were scared and fighting for their lives. Their captors were clever. They turned one against the other. Thoughts swirled and entwined but kept her occupied. Even when the masked man removed his glove, leant across the limp body between them, and rubbed his hand between her thighs, she remained focused on the road ahead.

Isla stared at him in the rear-view mirror, "Devon, there's plenty of time for that later. For now, keep your hands to yourself. Is there any movement from Delilah yet?"

Devon kept his hand in place until Esther scrunched her eyes. His fingers played over her crotch, pinched soft flesh through her cotton panties. His eyes remained drilled into her profile, which she kept blank and unmoved. He leaned closer and bent over Delilah's torso, his breath heavy with aniseed.

"You're mine, Esther."

Esther sat rigid, a tremble ran through her and then she felt calm, like the stillness before a Tsunami. The cool skin of her companion and her unhurried heartbeat slowed her own and enabled her to think through the fog.

She placed a hand over his and ignored his intrusion.

Devon smiled and withdrew his hand.

"We won't rush this, Esther." He said as he gazed out of the side window.

"We have a plan. Don't we, Isla?" He exchanged a glance with the woman in the car mirror. She inclined her head in agreement, her eyes fixed on the scene as it played out on the back seat.

"See baby," He ruffled Esther's auburn hair that framed her pixie face. "I'm not in the habit of negotiating. I'll suit myself." He clasped her right breast in a vice-like grip and dug his knee into the side of her thigh.

Delilah stirred below him, so Devon adjusted his weight and watched her face. She turned her head away as if instinct warned her of his presence. Devon, impatient and frustrated, leaned forward and licked her face.

"Devon, sit back down we're only half a mile away. If she remains unconscious, she'll be easier to move from the car."

They drew up outside the house, and Delilah responded to the first flicker of light. Unfamiliar with her surroundings, she kept her eyes partially closed. Her thoughts sped through her mind like traffic on a motorway. She cast her mind back to the meal with her client.

She felt warm and clammy and quickly established she was sandwiched between two bodies. She clamped her eyes closed. Her decision made, she'd play dead. She'd always thought it best if you ever found yourself in a dangerous situation. Asleep was as good as dead.

30

DS Fawn stood as Albie negotiated his way around their shared office, which both of them rarely used at the same time. They'd never worked so closely together. In general, they were in competition.

"I've just heard there's another missing person. I'm told they're an acquaintance of yours."

Albie's lips tightened and he frowned. "An acquaintance, yes, I suppose that's probably the best way to describe our relationship. Delilah Grange was Olivia's best friend."

"Oh, right? Anyway." Rachel shuffled some papers on the desk between them. "How are we going to play this? Masters has hinted that you should be off the case.. 'Too close' she said. She'll want answers soon."

Albie leaned on the desk and moved towards her. "She's right, I'm too close. Could you look into her disappearance?"

She raised her palm in front of her and shook her head. "We can't solve the cases without the extra support of your team."

"I wouldn't put you in that situation, Rachel. But what if your team continued looking for the missing girls while we investigate the cold case? We could link up and find the connection without causing Masters any sleepless nights."

"And if there are no connections?"

"We've just have to find the women alive… I don't care how. We've just got to find them."

Rachel pulled a cigarette from a box in her draw and rolled a lighter backwards and forwards in her palm before answering, "I'll call my team and refocus them on the kidnapping cases."

"Here," Albie held out a thin file. "This is what they have given us, so far."

She took it from his hand, "I better get on with it, then." As she left the office, the words, 'Filthy habit,' followed her from the room.

Albie stared at the paperwork piled on his desk. Where to begin? He picked up the message Tim had slipped into his hand earlier. It made sense to get out of the station before he stepped into an altercation with DI Masters. A meeting with Anthony Locke. That was reason enough.

Tanya swung the strap of her bag onto her shoulder, picked up her jacket, and folded it over her bent forearm. She took the car keys from Albie's hand and pressed the button to call the lift. "There's no way you're driving," she said. "You need a rest from the wheel."

"What are you on about?"

"Come on, sir. We've all heard what happened to Delilah Grange. I know there's no love lost between you, but there is history."

"Back off, Watts. They call it 'private life' for a reason. We're not involved, anyway. I handed it all over to Fawn."

"Yeah, right?"

By the time they reached the car, he'd given up on the discussion of who would drive and had to smile as she handed the keys back.

"Okay, sorry. It's none of my business. Drive, if it helps."

Albie opened the passenger door threw the keys over the car roof into Tanya's unprepared hands.

"No, you go for it. Assertiveness suits you."

A grin remained on her face as she negotiated a path into the ever building A2 traffic.

Greenwich Park was always busy as soon as the sun made an appearance and today was no different. He scanned the surrounding area. It had been a while since his previous visit to the park. So much had happened since he'd had to meet and pacify Eve after neglecting her for weeks.

Tanya cut into his thoughts, "Where did he say he'd meet us?"

"Down the hill, outside the Maritime Museum."

Tania nudged him, "Need any help, sir? It's quite a steep hill."

"Cheeky cow. I can replace you, you know? Sometimes it's better than working with someone quiet, no questions asked, no small talk. You could learn a lot from Jana." Albie stumbled after his colleague his feet moved quicker than the rest of his body and he careered towards the bottom of the hill.

"Thank you, sir. I'll remember that when you need help on the way back up the hill." Tanya leant against the truck of an ancient tree and pretended to hide a yawn. "By the time you make it down, Mr Locke will have got fed up with waiting and left, or we won't recognise him because he would have aged so much."

Albie's guttural laugh knocked him off balance, and he held his arms like wings and hoped they'd glide him to safety. He wiped invisible grass from his clothes and composed himself.

"Mr Locke." He called to a man in the distance. He was as tall as Albie, and he plunged his hands in and out of his pockets, and bounced from one foot to the other. He raised a hand, a sign that he'd seen them, then kept his head down and stayed put.

"What do you reckon?" Albie asked his colleague.

Tanya smiled in Anthony's direction, "He's not exactly happy to see us, is he? Let's hope he can help. I'll get drinks in the cafe`, you can meet him and grab a table. He may relax more with just you, I could be anyone."

They walked towards him together, curt introductions were made and Tanya walked ahead.

"Thank you for agreeing to meet Mr Locke."

Anthony pulled his sunglasses from their resting place on the top of his head. "Like I said, I remember seeing the girl that night but it's complicated and I don't know whether the memories are real."

Albie led the way to a table just vacated by an elderly couple.

"Is this chair taken?" He asked a man on the table closest and placed it at their table for Tanya.

"What? You're worried about how accurate your memory is because of the time lapse?"

"Well, partly. Fifteen years is a long time, and I'd been drinking for much of the evening. But it's more than that, I've got early onset dementia." He tapped his fingers on the table in an annoying repetition and scanned the area as if he was on a secret mission.

Tanya placed a tray in the centre of the table, poured two cups of tea from the pot, and slid a mug of coffee towards Albie.

"Help yourselves to milk and sugar. Take any of the food you fancy." She reached across and picked out a mars bar, opened the wrapper, and took a large bite. Then she sat in silence.

"So do you have a patchy memory or do you doubt your ability to remember accurately?"

Anthony slurped from the teacup, grimaced, and added a heaped spoonful of sugar. He stirred the tea and looked Albie in the eyes.

"A bit of both I suppose."

"Why don't you tell us what you remember and leave it to us to decide whether it's useful?" Albie placed the photo of a young Libby Mann on the table followed by one of Kayleigh taken a week before her death.

Anthony put his cup down, picked up a photo in each hand and studied them closely. His face was an unemotional until a cloud of reminiscence settled in his watery eyes. He wiped away a wayward tear before he replaced his sunglasses. Albie was unsure of whether he wanted to protect them from the sun or to cover up his unexpected emotion.

"Both girls look so young." He choked on his words and coughed into a handkerchief. Once he had control over his breathing, he continued. "Well, I suppose they were just that." He turned his attention to Albie. "What is it you want to know about them?"

"Anything you can remember. How well did you know them? When did you last see them? During the time the girls turned up murdered, were you ever suspicious of anyone or did anything unusual happen? Sometimes in hindsight a hidden memory can obscure reality and time changes perspectives."

Tanya popped the final piece of chocolate into her mouth and followed it with a sip of tea. She opened her notebook and leaned back in her chair, poised to write.

"I knew both the girls. Libby I only met her once, but I knew Kayleigh more. She was seeing one of my mates."

"So how well did you know her?"

Anthony lowered his head and shook it. "Me and Kayleigh had a fling. I'm not proud of it, but we were both young and couldn't keep our hands off each other." He rubbed his hands over his face and through his hair, sighed, then continued. "About four months, that year, the year she died we met up at every opportunity we got."

Albie drank the last of his coffee, "Who was the mate she was seeing?"

"You should know that. Haven't done your homework then?"

"I know what it says in the case files, but it would be better to hear it from you. See, this is the first I've heard of anyone else that close to either of the girls. It shows how thorough they were when they investigated the murder, doesn't it?"

"You could say that, but the reason it's not in your case files is I was long gone once they found Kayleigh. No one knew about us, we were extra careful. Kayleigh's fella wasn't someone you wanted to cross. If he'd found out I'd have been dead..."

Tanya leaned forward, "So you're telling us not one of your friends or Kayleigh's, for that matter, knew about what you were up to on the side."

Anthony's stare didn't move from Albie as he replied, "You make it sound calculated and sordid. I think you have to put things in perspective and remember we were kids. Just kids unaware of the consequences of our actions. We were just living for the day, having fun."

"Well, either the killer just came across Kayleigh that night—the wrong place wrong time scenario—or they'd been watching you both and ended it at any cost."

Albie picked up a picnic bar from the mountain of choice on the table. Opened it and bit. A mixture of peanuts, raisins, and biscuit fixed with stringy toffee and melting chocolate kept him busy for a minute while Anthony gathered his thoughts.

"That's ridiculous," Anthony slapped a hand to his knee. "We were only messing about. Whoever killed her had already killed before. If your theory was true, surely you'd be searching for a practiced killer. Not some jealous boyfriend."

"Who was her boyfriend, Anthony?"

"Robson Shaw."

"Okay, he's the bloke named in the report. Tell us about him."

"Robson was all right. He could be cocky and liked the girls. He was a year or so older than me and used to hang about with wrong-uns. He'd be known as a gang leader by now."

"Any idea why he was murdered?"

"He was killed two years later, knifed by some kid angry about how he'd treated his sister."

Albie nodded to Tanya. She stood, put her phone to her ear, and walked away.

"So, Shaw? Do you think he killed these girls?"

"His family was loaded, they lived in one of those massive houses off Blackheath. I went there once for an after party. Weird people, his dad was there and seemed to have a thing for the young girls that went with us."

Albie waited for Tanya to rejoin the group, "So did you see Kayleigh and Libby the night of Kayleigh's death?"

Anthony eyed both officers and took time to reassemble his memories of that night. He stumbled over his words as he relaid his memories.

"We were messing around outside the youth club. Some blokes were locking up the hall. Shaw mouthed off at them. He thrived on arguments, loved fights. He would keep on 'til someone took a swing at him just to shut him up."

He paused, drained the rest of his drink, and wiped his mouth on the back of his sleeve. "I was only hanging around for Kayleigh, we'd planned to meet up after the pub. She'd make up some excuse, a headache or something, and leave. It had worked before." His voice cracked and he took a long breath.

"And did you meet?"

"That's the thing. She had Libby with her, so we left. She still left early, but Shaw and a couple of other followed them. He didn't trust her, he said he'd heard she was a slut and had been messing around."

Tanya put the end of the pencil in her mouth like a cigarette, "So, you thought it was okay to leave two young girls to make their own way home. You knew those idiots were following them, that one of them was angry, and the next day you disappear halfway across the world with work?"

He thrust out his finger and wagged it at Tanya; she retreated into her chair as he gritted his teeth and spat out his words.

"I knew this was a mistake. I didn't have to contact you, and I've changed my mind about talking to you now." He swallowed, went to continue, but knocked the chocolate bars off the table and rushed to the exit.

Tanya caught Albie's eye and mouthed sorry.

Albie picked the chocolate bars up from the floor and placed them in Tanya's open bag. "Don't be too hard on yourself. You reacted how any decent person would. We've got enough to go on for now, anyway. One challenge at a time..." She laughed as they began the trek back up to the statue of General Wolfe at the top of the hill.

31

Albie slammed the car door and zigzagged his way across the road, avoiding slow moving traffic. Agitated drivers beeped, but he didn't give them a sideways glance. The entrance of a sleazy building between the garage and sex shop fixated Albie. It was just fifty metres from a monstrosity of a church, Gothic in appearance. It was so near, its bell tower was a beady eye that watched the comings and goings and reported back to God.

Albie had stopped questioning long ago how debauchery and holiness could share a pew in the same street. It shouldn't have, but it just worked, one balanced out the other. As some would say, they were two ends of the same problem.

He extended his hand to the smart suited bodybuilder who straddled and filled the whole doorway. The doorman ignored his hand and stepped aside, "He's in the office. Knock twice, he's expecting you."

"Come on bro, there's no need to be uncivilised. What's wrong? Are you too worried about witnesses to pull a knife on me this time?"

Albie didn't wait for an answer. He knew his brother had always had a short fuse, but wasn't stupid enough to respond in front of an audience. However, he'd have to watch his back for a while.

Inside, people hid in dark corners and half-dressed girls manipulated their bodies around poles, gyrating in cages suspended from the ceiling. Waitresses bent over to serve customers, with intimate parts of their bodies barely covered by micro skirts and cherry-string bras over breasts.

This place was an anthill in his father's thriving empire, and he was the legitimate heir as Freddie continually reminded him each time they met.

Albie walked to the bar asked and for a large brandy. He turned to face his surroundings and hitched his elbows on the bar behind. Manipulation, abuse, and corruption. Albie remembered a time he admired and adored his father. In fact, he so nearly joined his venture as a teen. He was at his most vulnerable and craved his love and attention. That was then.

The golden liquid tasted smooth on his tongue, but hit the back of his throat with a warm burn and followed its path towards his stomach. He placed the glass on the bar, thanked the barman, weaved between the tables towards the back of the building, and into the desolate hall that led to the back office. Two knocks, the door opened, and a man ushered him into a well lit room decorated in rich golds and burgundy.

Two men, adonis replicas, who wore tailored suits identical to his brothers, stood like statues and guarded the door he'd walked through. Albie stood tall in a central position in the middle of the room and fixed his feet like roots into the hardwood floor.

"Son, it's so good to see you again." His father coughed, a low and gravelled hacked as he spoke which prolonged each word. "Come closer," he said as he stood with the support of his spacious, polished-oak desk.

Albie remained still, planted to the spot, secure, knowing that he could defend himself against an attack from any direction. He hardly recognised the hunched figure, that until recently, had stood sturdy and upright as a feared and unexpected force of nature. Surprise had always been his main weapon against his adversaries, whether subtle disarmament or explicit demolition, he'd conquer those who dared to challenge his empire, and he always won.

Freddie straightened, the hunch on his back was less exaggerated. He walked to the front of his desk and in three strides was close enough to throw his arms around Albie, who stiffened in response and remained frozen to the spot. Freddie leaned in. His voice was so soft that Albie scrunched his forehead in concentration.

"You know I want the best for you, son. Nothing but the best. Even if it means keeping my distance. I've stayed away. No more. Do you hear me? No more." His grasp loosened, and he took a step back. "Now sit down with your old man. Let's have a chat."

When Albie didn't respond he pulled the chair away from the table. "Come on, son, humour me."

Albie sat in a chair the shape of a waltzer, his back moulded into the foam-padded cushion as if it recognised his body. "Freddie, I haven't come for a visit or a trip down memory lane."

"The missing women, right? I've no idea how you think I can help or why you think I would."

"You're right. I'm not here to ask for help to find the missing women, unless you know something about the abductions. It's more about a cold case."

"What more photos to look at? Such fun," Freddie shook his head and placed his hand on the envelope Albie had thrown across the table. "What's with the cold case? Not enough to do with girls snatched from under your nose?" He opened the seal and shook the contents haphazardly over the table. They both turned the individual photos face up and Albie arranged them in some kind of order.

Freddie sat in silence while he scanned the images. He raised a few of them to the end of his nose, then backwards and forwards to focus. "The Rose of Lee. I remember when that pub was open, you're going back a bit, aren't you?" He snorted. "That was my turf at one point and I remember the fight I had to keep it. That pub especially. Doubled the profits over a few years."

"Do you remember what was going on there to up your income?

Did it have anything to do with these women?" He waved his palm over the images like a magician about to perform a trick.

"We had this lad in the area, a right geezer, thought he was the next... well, me. He had a handle on things around the Lee area. You know, stuff off the back of a lorry, a bit of dealing-nothing too heavy. In fact, no notable profit ever came my way while he was alive."

Albie tapped his foot to an imaginary beat, "Just cut the crap and get to the point. How did this involve the girls?"

Freddie grinned and wiped spittle from the corner of his mouth with the back of his liver-spotted hand. "There he is. That's me boy. I knew you were hiding in there somewhere. What's so important about these tarts?" He waved his hand at the photos on the desk, much as Albie had a few moments before.

"Those tarts, as you call them, were young vulnerable underage girls who were violated, killed, and dumped in the Ravensbourne river over ten years ago. About the time your so-called geezer was alive and making transactions in your name. Look. It could have so easily have been your precious daughter."

Albie saw the gesture too late. With a wink from his father, the thick arm of a bodyguard encircled his neck and tightened across his windpipe. Albie raised his hands, latched onto the arm, and at the last minute pushed them under his assailant's arm to release the pressure. He stared ahead, determined not to struggle. Freddie's expression remained unchanged by his son's response.

"You know better son. Never question my decisions, you know family are off limits, as is the comparison of my angel to these stupid little girls who went in search of trouble." Another wink and the bodyguard loosened his grip and retreated to his place by the door.

Albie rubbed his neck and loosened his tie, "All right, you have a right to your opinion, it's not important to dwell on the girls involvement with these men. It's more important to focus on the crime. Who killed them and why? I know that Shaw died a few weeks after the last murder and was found guilty posthumously of their murders, but who else was involved?"

"You've got your murderer, Shaw. Once he died the deaths stopped, as you've just explained."

Albie shook his head and rubbed his eyes and cleared his throat before answering, "Too easy though, isn't it? Surely even you can see the convenience of accusing a man who's dead. Especially as the man convicted of killing Shaw is the brother of a kidnap victim."

"So what do you want from me?" Freddie's cough crackled with phlegm and spat into a handkerchief retrieved from his trouser pocket.

"Names." He stared at his father's hollow cheeks, once chubby from the food that comes with wealth and flamboyance. He'd decomposed before the devil paid him a visit to plant the kiss of death on his skeletal frame. "Names of others involved with whatever criminal activities took place under your watch. I know you well enough Freddie, you won't want this to connect to you." Albie gestured to the photographs on the table. "Especially if it goes viral. Look, give me something to go on and I'll try to keep your name out of the investigation."

Freddie wiped his mouth with the handkerchief, walked around the table, and leaned to within kissing distance from his son.

"What's wrong with you, son? I'm not a grass and you know it." He leaned closer, his voice lowered, hindered by the rattle in his throat. "You don't need me, son. You've already found them in the Old Tiger's Head. My sources tell me Shaw's little gang usually gather there every evening for a few pints after work. You're on to them, Albie." He poked a boney finger at Albie's temple. "Use this, son, the puzzles ready to solve. Then you can find those girls and set them free, that's if you find them in time."

Albie stood and pushed his legs back against the chair. His father's odour of underlying rot disguised by an expensive aftershave was unmistakable as he inhaled. The chair budged an inch, no more, but enough to slide to his right and take a backward step.

"Well, it's obvious you're unwilling to help. So it's time for me to leave." The bodybuilder blocked his exit. Albie turned to his father,

"Freddie, call off your thug. I've got some serious work to do and you've wasted enough of my time."

"Remember, it's all up there." Freddie pointed to his own head, then waved his hand towards the door. "Move, let him through. Goodbye, son."

32

"Come on, baby. Open your eyes," A hand cupped her jaw and fingers dug into her cheeks. "Listen, I know you're awake, sweetheart,"

Delilah caught her breath as the fingers dug deeper. Aniseed clung to the hairs in her nostrils and caught at the back of her throat. She struggled to escape the grip. She rooted her feet to the floor, and she pushed her back against the resistance of the car seat. She inched her lids open and came face to face with steel-blue eyes. He'd covered the rest of the face in a fabric mask which smirked at her, unchanged and zipped.

The car door opened, and Delilah looked for the first time at the other person who flanked her. She stared at a face she recognised, a face framed with an abundance of auburn hair. A face that had stared out from newspapers and television screens for the last few days. Her immediate reaction was to make it known to Esther MacDonald that she recognised her and that people were working hard to find all the victims. That it would be all right. Instead, she looked past her into the glassy eyes of a blonde woman bent down in the doorway. She reminded her of a dog attempting to understand a human instruction. Her head moved from side to side, alert and intrusive.

The woman grabbed Esther's forearm and tugged her from the car. She then leaned forward and examined Delilah's face. Her stare so intense Delilah lowered her head to escape her stare. The woman's chest rubbed across her profile as she cupped the man's face in one hand.

"Bring her with you. Let her rest and eat before her initiation."

"What is an initiation? Why am I here? Listen, my family are rich. Contact them and ask for any amount of money. They will pay any demand for my safe return."

"Devon, remember initiation is later." She ignored Delilah's pleas and disappeared up the stone steps and into the main entrance.

A shudder began at the base of Delilah's spine and crept up to her neck a vertebra at a time. Her mouth went dry and the hairs on her arms stood up in goosebumps.

Delilah sunk back into her seat as the warmth from his hand burnt a trail up her thigh. Her voice was a whimper, "Aren't you supposed to take me somewhere now and prepare me for something?"

Devon's sewn on smile didn't change. The only visible warning sign she spotted was the angle of his head and the sparkle of those ice- cool eyes behind the balaclava. She slid away from him and out of the car, unsteady on her feet, and just able to hold herself upright. He followed her in silence.

"Which way should I go?"

He gripped her arm and dug his fingernails into her flesh. She took a hasty breath to conceal the pain and followed his lead. The building was Victorian. A detached and isolated house on its own grounds. There was something familiar about the surroundings. So distant in her memory it could be a place she'd visited as a child.

"Where is this place? It's familiar to me." The words had left her lips before she could catch her thoughts. The sharp slap across her cheekbone whipped her head to one side. A grunt left her mouth and her own hand covered the area he'd struck. He gripped the back of her head and dug his fingernails into her scalp, entangled in her sleek deep brown hair. Delilah tried to yank herself loose from his hold. Instead, she instinctively bent towards him, anything to ease the agony caused by the pressure of roots being torn from her scalp.

Devon paced towards the back door through an ivy-covered archway. A flower covered feature in a rustic stone wall. He paused, contemplated his next move, and completed a ninety-degree turn. He followed the meander of a moss ridden pathway to some outbuildings, followed by a reticent companion. Her hair gripped like a horses reign and she stumbled behind too afraid to make the slightest noise. Devon stopped the keys rattled in a lock and the door creaked open. His hand relaxed in her hair, and she raised her head. She heard the crack before she felt a heavy object. Disorientated, she held out her arms to lessen the impact of the fall. There was another crack, this time in her wrist as she hit the floor. Her arms outstretched, he flipped her onto her back and dragged her inside of a dilapidated wooden structure.

Chains hung from joists in the ceiling which Devon secured around her wrists. She cried out at the contact.

"Keep that shut." He clamped his sweaty palm over her open mouth. "Let's see if this place is still familiar to you after a few hours in here."

Delilah clenched her eyelids, wrinkled her nose, and held her breath. She opened her eyes a millimetre at a time, and to her relief the monster had vanished.

33

Anthony Locke strolled into the Old Tiger's Head like it was just another day. He'd been careful not to draw attention to himself, especially since his meeting in Greenwich. He slipped his phone from his trouser pocket and read the text for the fifth time that afternoon.

Meet in the local after work,
come alone as we need to talk,
just the old crowd together again
JK

He grasped the handle with a firm grip, paused, straightened, and took a deep breath. The door moved towards him and he stepped back, opening wider to let two tottering women, engrossed in conversation, out onto the pavement.

"Your welcome." He said to their retreating backs with a sarcastic smirk. They continued to meander along the pavement. One woman placed a hand over her mouth and giggled, the other shouted, "Silly old sod."

Old? He didn't think of himself as old, mature perhaps, but not old. He ran his fingers through his coarse dyed hair and walked into the dim quiet bar that housed a few people either enjoying their own company or in deep conversation. He peered around the barmaid to the other bar. There was already quite a crowd gathered, including some faces he didn't recognise.

"A pint of Guinness," he held out a tenner, "Oh, and a Jim Daniels." He leaned towards her and winked. "Get yourself one as well, love." The barmaid's frown turned to a grin as she snatched the note from his grasp and without a word went off to pour his drinks.

"Tony, In here. We've got you a Guinness."

Anthony swigged back the whiskey, picked up his pint, and followed the voice into the other bar.

"Where've you been, mate? We've been waiting." Joe wiped foam from his top lip as he spoke.

"Yeah, I know. I had to work late."

"Right, is that everyone?" Someone shouted over Joe's shoulder.

Joe stepped back to reveal another group of men sat squat on the chairs around the corner table. Anthony studied them from their expensive suits, polished shoes, and crisp white shirts sleeve decorated with large studied gold cufflinks. Not only did they wear Dolce watches, but they wore their waxed-hair sculpted. He recognised them. He'd never seen them before, but he recognised their type from whispered rumours. They were the heavies sent in as a last resort. The bloke you hoped would remain a rumour. The type you hoped you'd never have to share the same air they breathed. He lowered his gaze and took a step back, hoping he could mingle in with the crowd and that no one realised he was late. Faces he recognised gave him a nod, others raised their pint to him. Anthony acknowledged a few who he could call acquaintances, then averted his eyes and waited for Joey to speak.

"Right, I'll make a start then, first thanks for showing up. It's a good turnout. Better than expected. You're probably wondering why we've contacted you, especially as some of you haven't been on this stomping ground for a good ten years."

"Yeah Joe, why're we in this dump?" The shout came from the back of a small group assembled by the back doors.

"Your dump is another man's local cheeky bastard. Listen, if we have fewer smart arse remarks you'll be on your way before you know it."

He scanned the faces for a response, then continued. "You've probably seen on the news or in the papers about kidnapped girls. That's why you're here."

"What the fuck are you on about? Why would you get us all to meet because of something like that?"

"Good point, Dodger. And I'll ask these gentlemen to explain." He directed their attention to the suited men at the table opposite Anthony.

They all stood in unison. The stockiest stepped forward, flanked by the others. His stature and stare demanded respect.

"Freddie Hurst thanks you all for attending this meeting." Silence stunned the room. Like fear induced statues, grown men froze, unable to apprehend the importance of the next words.

"For those of you who are unfamiliar with the Hursts, Freddie controlled the local area for many years. I'm Dominic his son and he's asked me to speak to you on his behalf." Dominic drained his beer and placed the glass on the table behind. "These girls going missing aren't the problem. Ten years ago there were other girls, they didn't just go missing, they were killed and dumped in the river. Thing is, the filth have jumped into this cold case like it was an old sewer and are wading waist high in the shit."

"So are they connected? Is there any truth in it?"

Dominic spun on the balls of his feet in the voice's direction and puffed his cheeks like a cobra ready to strike.

"That my friend has no relevance to the conversation we are having here today. My father has sent me to clarify that regardless of what may or may not have happened ten years ago, it was unsanctioned by him and he wishes to disassociate his name from any lines of inquiry connected with Robson Shaw and what was going on behind the scenes at that time." He scanned the unemotional faces while they digested the information he'd given on them then turned to his tribe. "Well, we'll be on our way if there are no questions."

"Hold on a minute." Anthony stepped forward, unsure what had urged him to challenge this bloke. "Are we getting any explanation why the coppers have linked the cases? Some of us were around then and will need to know what you expect us to say if we're asked about the murders."

There were a few muffled grunts and half nods of agreement. Dominic paused, smiled at his tribe, and took up his position in front of Anthony.

"All you need to know is that you are to not implicate Freddie Hurst in any conversation you have. You should avoid his name at all costs. If your name gets back to us, you'll be watching your back for the rest of your life. And no, I don't have to explain anything to you or anyone else."

Anthony held his stare for what seemed like an eternity while heads around him bowed and people fidgeted from one foot to another, with rings, watches, chains, any distraction to escape the heavy air of power being battled out in their presence.

Dominic nodded to the exit and his tribe move to the door, the first holding it open. Dominic closed the distance between them and prodded Anthony in the chest. Without breaking eye contact and through gritted teeth said, "Don't slip up Anthony Locke, we know you better than you know yourself and I'd love to be the one to teach you a lesson."

Anthony followed the expensive suits to the door. They'd parked cars illegally for easy access. He couldn't see anyone's face once they were behind the tinted windows, but he could feel their stares. He re-entered the bar where conversations were stilted and held in small huddles.

Anthony sashayed his way between tables to the other bar.

"Oi, Tony mate over here." Joey's voice echoed in his head and he cursed himself for not leaving through the other doors while he had the chance. He needed time to digest the warning interwoven with the instructions given by their unwelcome visitors. Anthony wasn't ready for a discussion with the boys. If he ignored them he'd make them suspicious, and they'd end up asking too many questions he'd rather dodge. Instead, he raised his glass, "Any of you want another?"

The barmaid lined them up, and he made two journeys, each time he negotiated his way through groups of customers and an assault course of tables and chairs. Finally, he placed a Guinness on a spare beer mat and balance on a squat stool that he'd grabbed from the table behind.

"So what d'ya reckon, Ant?" Joey leaned forwards, and the others waited for his reply as if his next words would be those of a prophet.

"About what?"

"What that tosser said. Do you think the cases are linked?"

"How would I know? Anyway, you heard the man, as far as they're concerned that's not the point. The point is, we've got to keep our mouths shut."

A bald man in the corner slurped his beer and wiped the froth from his top lip with the back of his hand. "But it's not that straight-forward, is it..? You were there. Involved. You know what happened, I mean what really happened."

"Shut up Dodge, a lot of us were around then. No one's mentioned that knob-head that used to help out in the Youth Club and how much he enjoyed hanging around the young girls." The group went quiet, and he lowered his voice. "Look, I know as much as you do about what went on back then."

"Don't give me that, Ant. You had the hots for those girls Robson was seeing, you had second dibs if I remember rightly."

The knuckles of Anthony's fingers were white from the grip of his glass. Heat rose in his chest and he took two large swigs of beer, but sweat beaded his forehead and trickled from his sideburn into his ear.

Joey put one hand on his shoulder, "Dodger, Tony has said all he's gonna say on the subject. He's right, all we've gotta do is keep our mouths shut and forget the name Freddie Hurst. That's all we've gotta do. Anyone wants another?" He picked up his pint glass and made for the bar, but turned before he'd taken two steps, "Give us a hand Ant." He said to his somber friend. Tony caught up with him at the bar.

"Thanks Joey, but I think I'll call it a night. Me Mum's got dinner on the table and you know what it's like since the old man died, she watches me like a hawk."

Joey nodded, "See you around, mate." But Tony had already headed towards the exit.

34

Heat seeped into her skin and Delilah inhaled deeply, but instead of salt in the air, dirt and grit tickled the back of her throat and stuck to the fine hairs inside her nostrils. Delilah clenched her eyes shut until they wrinkled, as did the top of her nose. Even subconsciously she knew the reality of her predicament, but there was still a chance that it was all a terrible mistake, an illusion. She ran her tongue around the inside of her mouth, and it stuck to the roof. The crunch that rang in her ears when she bit down confirmed her fears. She was delusional if she thought she was lying on a beach by the sea. Someone had strung her up by her hands. Her shoulders throbbed and her limbs felt as though they were no longer attached to her body. Her feet stretched to touch the ground but the slightest movement sent a shock of pain through her whole body and she screamed in desperation.

A steady crunch intruded her thoughts, and she pursed her lips to silence the howls that wanted to escape her mouth.

Delilah looked down booted feet, which stopped in front of her. So close she inhaled the leather, a smell that reminded her of her father. As a child, she'd always shine his shoes just to get a whiff of the leather. She creased her eyes closed as he lowered onto his haunches. He leaned in and dug his fingers through the flesh and hooked her bottom jaw. She fought against his upthrust, desperate to avoid his gaze. His grip tightened, and streaks of burning light blurred her eyes. She moved with his thrust to avoid the shots of white hot fire that burned through her with each counter movement.

"Open your eyes Delilah," Aniseed overwhelmed her like before. "You need to open your eyes at some point and the longer you resist the greater the pain."

Air shifted like a light caress as he rose. He circled her as if stalking his prey. Sweat beaded her forehead, fear drenched her armpits, and choked her with each breath. His unseen smile penetrated her vision and danced before her lidded eyes, daring her to defy him. Her numb arms moved with the yanked rope and fire ripped through her shoulders and her neck then shot through her spine. Her cry belonged to someone else as she clambered to hold on to consciousness.

"Your choice, Delilah. It's a simple request, but I'd much rather you rebel, I love a fighter, they excite me in so many ways."

Delilah stiffened and drew away from his touch. She knew he traced his fingers across her skin, an invisible touch. Repulsed, her skin squirmed. He relaxed the rope and circled her weakened body again before he crouched and buried his fingertips deep into her jaw bone. He'd established his authority, and against every fibre in her body she raised her head in unison with his gentle force and unglued her lids. The gradual influx of light blinded her at first and she had to concentrate until the outlines sharpened and came into focus.

"Good choice, Delilah. For a moment there, I thought I'd have to give you your own way and sew your lids together." He caressed her cheek with the back of his fingers and then whispered, "But what good would that have done either of us? I know, I for one would rather you were ready to play the game like the others."

Delilah listened. She wanted him to explain, but instead she stared into deceptive eyes that in any other circumstances would gain her trust. For the first time in her life she felt vulnerable and lost.

"Enough." In one graceful movement he was on his feet and

releasing her from the restraints. "You'll think twice before giving your opinion without being asked, I'm sure."

Devon held her momentarily as the rope loosened. The momentum at his release winded her on impact.

"Up." he said "On your feet."

His words were a distant whisper compared to the pounding in her head. She gasped for breath as his boot contacted with her chest, but her body did not respond. Delilah lay still, parts of her dead, the living parts raw and exposed.

Devon's hands pulled at her limbs one last time before he hoisted her into his arms. With her eyes squeezed shut, Delilah could concentrate fully on survival as she inhaled aniseed marbled oxygen.

35

lbie looked again for the umpteenth time at the laminated message found secured to the back of the park keeper's door.

We like to play games,
we play fair most of the time, unless..
we have a point to make or a message to share.
It's up to you to decide why Adele had to die.

"This is a definite message from a calculated killer, or killers, if we are to believe the videos."

"Why kill Adele? They mention games. Are they seriously suggesting that kidnapping and murder are games?" Tanya leaned back against an abandoned desk. She tapped the underside of her chair while watching her boss pace back and forth across the stage with the incident boards as his backdrop. The death mask of Adele in the additional image out of place against the backdrop of carefree, smiling faces on the opposite board.

Fawn also followed Albie's movements. The soft rhythm of footfalls calmed rather than agitated her, as he so often had in the past.

"How did she die? We know they threw her into the well in a few inches of gathered rainwater,"

"We're still awaiting confirmation but drowning appears to be the unofficial cause of death." Tanya scoured the scant notes from information she'd deciphered from Leo, in between promises to call him for a date and pick up from where they had left off. She had to admit it tempted her. She tore out his number and folded it, creasing each length with her fingernails. She turned her back on her colleagues and slipped the note under her bra strap so as not to forget.

Albie stood still, one hand cupped his mouth, and his eyes fixed on the image of a pale, bloated Adele. He shook his head as if thoughts and ideas would all fix together like puzzle pieces if only he could shake hard enough.

"Well," he raised his head, looked from one to the other, and included Frank who had just entered the room. "Any ideas? Thoughts? Connections?"

"Water. I'd say that connects the cold case deaths with Adele's if drowning is the cause."

"If that was the cause.." Fawn interrupted. "Okay, facts. They all had the same tattoo. Someone must be able to tell us who was capable of artwork in that decade. What about the locals who knew the girls? We need to dig deeper."

Albie raised his hand, "Hold on. The cold case is my territory, you need to focus on the here and now remember."

"How can you stand here and discuss the note found on Adele's body and tell me to back off?"

His lips etched into a smile, which she ignored.

"Okay, you've got me. Working as a team on both cases has to be the way forward, but it will only work if we keep each other informed."

Frank took the truce as an opportunity to interrupt. He slipped a note into Albie's hand. "You need to call this number, sir. They apparently have important information about the case. They wouldn't disclose it to anyone but you."

The scrawled mobile number stretched across the paper wasn't a number Albie recognised, unlike the name written in capital letters and underlined twice.

He walked towards the exit. "Sorry, I've got to follow this up."

The air was crisp even though the sun shone. Albie stood at the top of a metal fire escape at the back of the building and scanned the area within close proximity. The stairs were rarely used since they had relocated the car park to the front of the building. The brick walls overlooked a sparse concrete area riddled with weeds and varieties of moss that thrived in a bleak, damp environment. The only sign of life was four-legged with more sightings of rodents in and around the rubbish dumpsters by the day.

Albie stared at the piece of paper in his hand and inhaled, the crisp air caught in the back of his throat. Not for the first time in the last few years he wished he still smoked, even just the odd cigar. Surely it didn't count unless you inhaled. Once again, he tried to focus on the piece of paper. He pulled out his phone and dialled the first three digits, then ended the call.

A thin damp sheen covered his skin despite the cool air that stroked his flesh. It prickled and he stalled. In all the years since he'd become a police officer, he'd only known his father to contact him once. A conversation that had saved his career but at the cost of his relationship. It was the fallout that concerned him most. This phone call would not be advice or support from a loving parent. It would inevitably cost him, and he would be delusional if he thought it would not compromise his position on the force. Freddie could destroy him whenever he wanted.

Albie rummaged through his memories to a time and place when he needed reassurance. The voice of logic rang unsullied in his ears, 'Freddie has several traits, many we'd rather not delve into. As a family man he is loyal, Albie. Blood will always run thicker than water in Freddie's world. No matter what you think, he will always love you in his own way and because of that truth you're protected.' Good old Uncle Morgan, the only constant in his life and still an advocate for his wayward brother-in-law. On reflection, Morgan was right about Freddie's old East End duties to family. That was probably the only reason he hadn't been outed before.

Albie had no choice. Resigned, he jabbed the number into his phone, took one last look around, held it to his ear, and waited.

"Albie, I knew you wouldn't keep your old dad waiting."

"What do you want Freddie?"

"Straight to the point. That's my boy. You get that from me, and your natural charm." His laugh evolved into a guttural coughing fit and Albie removed the phone from his ear until it subsided.

"Listen Freddie, I'm running on borrowed time. Have you got anything for me or not?" A door slammed below and shouts echoed as someone emptied rubbish bins and rats scurried. Albie took a step back and leaned into the apex of two walls.

"I got to thinking after you visited. I sent Dominic to check out the local area, do some digging. You've been talking to the locals, I know. My memories are resurfacing as we speak."

Albie squeezed the phone in the palm of his hand and concentrated on giving a nonchalant response, "Look, Freddie. I haven't got time for your games. You either want to share or you don't. I have murders to solve."

"I'm not gonna discuss this over the phone. Greenwich Pier in an hour. You'll see another side to me if you're a no show, son."

Albie leant against the rusted railings and tried to compartmentalise his thoughts; to clear his head. Freddie complicated each part of his life. Every time he had dealings with him, he doubted his accomplishments and ability to be the person he professed to be. Freddie had the ability to cause him to question his own ambition and which base desires he was willing to exploit to ensure his success. He'd once been asked what his definition of success was. His reply was: 'The same as everyone's, surely, be the best you can be in all you do. It doesn't matter how you achieve it, just make sure you reach your goals.'

He emerged back into the office, head lowered, hooked his finger through the tab on the inside of his jacket collar, threw it over his shoulder, and strolled towards the exit.

"Albie?" Tanya sidled up beside him with a file in her hand. "Are you off somewhere? Need company?" She offloaded the file on Frank's desk. He raised his hand in a gesture of thanks and continued to study the paperwork under his nose.

Albie remained tight-lipped, shook his head, and pressed the arrow down. "Not this time, Tanya. What I'd like is for you to cover for me, understand?"

She'd half raised her shoulders. Defiance brimmed in her eyes before she spotted his firm frown. She lowered her shoulders and gave a slow, subtle nod of the head.

"What should I say?" Fawn was already observing their interaction from a distance. "She'll want an answer."

The lift shuddered to a stop and the doors begrudgingly stuttered open. Albie walked inside and swirled to face her, "Just say someone has called me to a family emergency. I'll contact her as soon as I can." He winked, grinned, and mouthed a silent thank you as the old doors juddered shut.

36

The sun shone bright and cheerful like the pretence of a summer day, but the wind whipped off of the River Thames to destroy the illusion. Albie pulled his jacket collar and rubbed his hands together to fend off the unexpected chill in the late afternoon breeze. He loved the river, well any stretch of water really, as a child he'd watched boats ferry people backwards and forwards, and marvel at the rhythm of the vessels under the control of the tides and currents, both as predictable as they were unreliable.

He was deliberately early and had time to scan the area. Freddie preferred to be at a meeting point first. Probably from years of experience of having to watch his back. That was the reason Albie arrived early. Any way he could rattle the old man would give him more control of the situation. Arriving before Freddie and his concierge also gave him precious time to organise his thoughts, and this was the perfect location.

Albie looked at his wristwatch. He was forty-five minutes early. He probably had an advantage of about twenty minutes if his prediction was correct. Plenty of alone time to absorb and order his thoughts. The first real opportunity he'd had since the cold case had become part of the investigation.

He listened to the slosh of the waves against the boat docked at the side; it was rhythmic and soothing to his soul. He breathed slow, deep breaths. The cool gush of air cleansed his airways and expanded his lungs.

The cases had tentative links, but regardless, they were links he could not ignore. The murdered girl Kayleigh and her friendship with Libby Mann, who should have been of one kidnap victims. The raven tattoos, although common now, with tattoo parlours springing up in high streets, but less popular ten years ago and so easier to narrow down. Albie shook his head. He knew there was more, otherwise Freddie wouldn't have made contact. He dug deeper. People and their secrets, skeletons from their past. People were experts at rearranging their memories. They often omitted essential facts because they'd rewritten their pasts to exonerate their sins or heighten their pedestals.

Freddie's reasons to meet were to exonerate his own part in the murders and pass the suspicions in another direction or be to misdirect completely. The purpose remained to be seen, but he knew he'd have to be open to either.

Albie felt Freddie's presence before he spoke. A subtle shift in the wind's direction wafted a hint of some expensive scent that hid the distinct aroma of decay. His habitual cough kicked in as he attempted to speak and Albie's emotions were compromised for a split second. But memories of the monster his father had been when he was young were far too awful to ignore.

"Deep in thought again? You were always inward thinking as a lad. I had to drag conversation from you."

"Did you ever think I just didn't want to talk to you, like now? I've only agreed to meet because you have information. Not for small talk."

Freddie croaked, spluttered a growl, and his face lit up as he tried to control a coughing fit. He waited until he could squeeze his words out coherently. "Always one to get straight to the point. No messing about, 'ay, Albie?" His son stared, his features stoic as he refused to engage. "All right, have it your way. I've been taking a walk down memory lane the last few days. It's not all great, I can tell you."

"Oh, I see, you've come to me because you've had a gush of conscience. Not interested." Albie pushed himself off the wall with his foot and headed towards his brother and another henchman. Both blocked his path.

"Nice to see you again, Dom. Now piss off and let me pass." Albie bowed his head and charged like a bull attacking a matador, but they stood firm.

"You want information, you say? Well, listen." Freddie's faint voice reached him from its journey on the breeze. Albie straightened, gave the human barriers a final chest thump with clenched fists and teeth, then retraced his steps.

Freddie had settled on a bench. He'd cupped a handkerchief over his mouth and nose as if breathing through a layer of cotton would help him control his rasping cough.

"I'm listening." Albie said and perched on the bench close enough to hear the tales he knew his father was about to weave.

"You understand the time you're talking about is just a speck in my lifetime and I can make mistakes, just like the next person."

Albie studied the old man. He nearly made some throwaway comment about him being disillusioned to find out Freddie was only human. Instead, he ignored the remark and allowed him to continue.

"Life was different then, a slower pace. I was at the top of my game. I had my finger in all enterprises in South East London and was left to get on with it. I'd reached the pinnacle."

Albie interrupted, memory lane was fine, but he needed to move Freddie on and fast. "What do you know about the murders? Were you involved?"

Freddie filled his lungs again and struggled to hold back another coughing spree. He noticed Albie's stare. Salt tears settled in the creases of loose skin under Freddie's eyes and dribbled down his cheeks. They could have been tears, but Albie knew they were a reaction to the wind.

"Albie, I may be capable of many things but the cold-blooded killing of these young girls?" He shook his head. "There was a gang back then. They did some running and selling for me. You know that young bloke Shaw took a knife to the stomach, and the murders stopped, right?" Albie nodded. "Well, it went quiet for a while then people started talking. The word was out that he was a scapegoat. The murders were down to someone else. Some sick bastard who got his kicks from squeezing the life out of the poor kids."

"Word was? What does that mean? You've dragged me here to listen to rumour, gossip I could have got from the neighbours? The murders stopped."

"You're right. I just wonder whether there were other reasons the murders stopped after Shaw's death? Especially if someone set him up."

Freddie pushed his hand down on the arm of the bench and steadied himself with the other arm. He rose and inched his back to a near upright position. He fiddled about in the inside pocket of his jacket, pulled out a folded envelope, and handed it to Albie. "I've called in a few favours. Dug deeper. I think you should look into these names for the reasons I state in the documents. This is one for you, Albie, I know I owe you. All I ask is that you keep me out of it."

"I knew there'd be a catch." Albie looked at the frail man beside him and really wished he could feel something, anything. "Are you saying, someone could implicate you?"

"Read into it what you will. Just do your job, son. Oh, and here's a freebie, the kidnappings are connected. There's no doubt in my mind."

Albie followed the men's path as they disappeared into an ambling crowd of tourists. His brother looked back once with a sneer that told him all he needed to know about family loyalty and brotherly love.

37

The stout, squat, bald man would have looked like any other man going through a midlife crisis if it were not for the adornment of piercings and colourful inks that fought for a place on his weather-beaten skin. He stood back and watched his minions emblazon their talents on those willing to pay for the pain as long as the outcome reflected the imagery in their imagination.

On the whole, they gave customer satisfaction and received few complaints. More often than not, they complimented his guys and girls for their skills. Each one was a modern day artist in their own right. They used their artistic skills to gain a sufficient income to live and survive on a day-to-day basis.

Joey Kohl surveyed his shop with pride. He had realised his childhood dream. He was ambitious in his own little niche in an industry that had taken time to become mainstream. As a young boy, he was fascinated by an old uncle's faded ink of an exotic woman, with the name Rita strategically penned across her provocative body. When he found out the story behind the image, it inspired him towards his ambition.

His Uncle had been in the Navy and after a drunken night, anchored up in some unmemorable harbour, he had an epiphany.

Joey hadn't liked the sound of that. However, on the back of this epiphany his Uncle had realised that his one and only love, Rita, was at home in sunny England. He just knew that if he didn't return to her immediately, she would be snapped up by somebody less worthy than himself. Pitiful and wallowing in his own misery and a bottle of scotch, he braved the etchings of a permanent statement of his love and devotion for this woman. It was engraved on his skin by an irrefutable backstreet artist. He never finished his story, but one look at Auntie Rita was enough to know that they had completed the work from a drunken description rather than a photographic memory.

"No mate, you've done well. I need a break even if you don't..."

Charlie, one of the best tattooists in his employment, raised his eyebrows as he walked through the doors at the front of the shop and lit up. Joey watched him inhale as if his life depended on the nicotine hit to his bloodstream. He picked up his cigarettes from the side and wandered out the front to keep him company.

"Char, how's it going?" Charlie took another drag on his cigarette and looked at the pavement. He spread the ash around with the sole of his shoe.

"S'all right, Joe. Never short of customers. Sorry about this, mate." He lifted the hand with his cigarette balanced precariously between two fingers. "I was gasping. I've been inking for two hours non-stop."

Joey smiled, one thing he knew, was he'd picked well when he took on his crew, as he affectionately called them, they were all as good as gold. All earning him money, making a profit, and not asking for any extra this year.

"You're all right, Charlie. Everyone's entitled to a break every now 'n again. Want to keep a steady hand." He laughed as he held out his shaking hand.

"Any inspiration?" The main part of this job that used to frustrate Joey was the lack of imagination of some of his clients. Names were the worst in his book. What idiot would ask for a girlfriend or even a wife's name engraved on their skin forever? In his experience it was through drunken stupor, like his uncle, or a shiny new relationship.

At worst, it was a last-ditch attempt to prove to hold on to something unsalvageable.

"Yeah, this bloke wants Mona Lisa on his arm. I felt like saying, if I was that talented my work would be in a gallery." He tossed the cigarette butt underfoot and mashed it into the pavement. "Well, best get back to my masterpiece."

Joey went to follow him back inside, but made way for a young man dressed in a black hooded tracksuit that hung off his body and was worn around the elbows, knees, and backside. Once inside, he hovered around the till area. Joey noticed the nervous way he bounced off his heels and tapped erratically on the counter.

Joey lifted the hinged entrance and slipped behind the till. "Can I help you?"

The young man turned to face him.

"I hope so." He said, a smile lit his whole face and laughter lines etched the corners of his eyes which was unexpectedly unnerving. "A friend recommended you." Without his eyes straying from Joey's face, he pushed an image across the counter. "I understand you specialise in birds, ravens in particular."

Joey lifted a fist to his mouth to smother a cough. It had been a while since anyone had asked him to ink a raven. He inspected the image. It was an example of his early work. He'd recognise it anywhere. A special commission.

"Look, I don't know who sent you, but if you want a raven, any of the guys can work on you. Shall I book you in?"

"Oh, no. It's not for me." He retrieved the image from Joey's outstretched hand. "It's a gift."

"Right, we need to make sure the recipient actually wants your gift. Shall we book a consultation?"

"Yeah, good idea. I think you may be interested in holding this consultation yourself. You can make the booking under the name Isla Shaw. I think you were acquainted with her family when you were younger."

The young man slipped the appointment card inside his wallet, said his thanks to an emotionless Joey, walked out of the shop, and disappeared into a crowd of afternoon shoppers.

Isla sat in the pub garden snatching snippets of sun each time it pierced through the thick layers of cloud. She draped her thick Aran cardigan over her shoulders as the sun retreated. She removed the clip that kept her blonde curls tidy and fumbled to replace it, gathering the curls higher on her head. She drained her glass, checked the time, then walked inside the pub.

The bar was quiet and virtually deserted, in about fifteen minutes; she knew it would soon buzz with customers ordering lunch. Isla ordered two pints of bitter, and two pie and chips. Then she settled in a quiet corner, slipped her cardigan off her shoulders, and watched the door. A petite barmaid had just brought their meals to the table when Devon entered.

"About time." Isla grinned and raised her glass in a sarcastic toast. "I thought for a moment that I may have to eat both pies."

"Oh, I'm sure you could have managed." He thanked the barmaid, pulled his hoodie over his head and threw it on an empty chair, then took two swigs of his pint. "Needed that. Shall we eat then talk? I'm starved."

The amicable silence ended between them when Devon finished his final mouthful. He leaned back in his chair and licked his lips. "God, that was so good. I could eat that again."

Isla finished a mouthful and looked at the rest of the food on her plate, unsure whether she would finish, but determined not to give up without a fight. Devon was right, this was one tasty meal. She turned her attention to her friend. "So, how did it go? Did he bite?"

Devon pondered his answer as he picked up a beer mat, rolled its edge backwards and forwards across the table and watched the pattern of wet lines that trailed behind.

"It's hard to tell. He didn't respond to the picture and tried to palm you off on to one of the other guys. The only time I traced a difference in his demeanour was when I booked the consultation. It was when I said your name. Not a substantial change, just a flicker, but enough."

Isla took the appointment card from Devon. He'd made it for three days' time and was definitely with Joey. "Lets see how he responds to this. See who he contacts." She lifted her fork to her mouth, decided against it, and pushed her plate away. "Drink up, our guests will wonder where we've got to."

38

Fawn stood back from the incident board, an open marker pen in her hand. For the first time she'd moved both boards together. If they were working across-cases, the links had to be discussed and the boards updated. She smiled, a wild self-important smile that lit her up from the inside out. Pleased with the reorganisation of faces, speculative jottings and facts, she had added her thick red arrow to show links between people in the cases a decade apart that stared down at her and gave nothing away.

"Fawn?" Albie's voice echoed from the walls, even with the extensive activity of their colleagues. "Quick meeting in the canteen." He looked at his watch, "In about ten minutes?"

"Where have you been? You didn't call..."

"Don't tell me I worried you, dear."

She lowered her head to hide her grin, "I hope you've got something we can work with. The boards are updated, but we need more leads."

He stood back and admired her work. "I just might have some additions for you." He lifted the A4 envelope and its contents in the air and shook it. "I'll get the drinks in and you gather the troops."

Albie looked at the selection of cakes on show behind the counter and added a Chelsea bun to the two chicken and salad rolls and a cup of milky coffee already on his tray. He patted the spare tyre that had taken up residence around his midriff and made a mental note to find time for the gym. Albie wandered to the back of the canteen where there were more vacant seats and a fluorescent light that had finally given up the ghost and flickered its last. Lack of lighting gave the area an ambience. It also camouflaged the chipped paintwork.

Albie had taken a mouthful of coffee to wash down the first roll when he heard the others enter the canteen. He waved a twenty pound note in the air. "For drinks," He said to Tanya. "How many of you are there? Did Fawn tell the whole office that drinks were on me?"

She laughed, shook her head, and relieved him of his money.

He had polished off his second roll as the first few joined him. They planted themselves with workmates on nearby tables, knowing the spaces on his table were reserved. The smell of bacon drifted his way. It always happened. Someone else's food smelt more appetising than his own. Perhaps he'd made the wrong choice of savoury, but he smiled down at his Chelsea bun.

Tanya slipped into the seat next to him. "So, this is a novel idea a meeting in the canteen." She leant across him and helped herself to the salt and vinegar and gave her fish and chips a liberal scattering of both.

Albie watched her take the first mouthful and had to draw his gaze away from her mouth. It reminded him of a pet dog he had grown up with whom not only watched every mouthful you ate, but sat and salivated until he had eaten the meal.

Before he could reply Fawn joined them, followed closely by Frank. Jana made to join them, realised that the table was full, and asked to join the table on the opposite aisle.

"So what's in the envelope?" Fawn asked Albie as she sat down.

"Eat and I'll explain." For once she didn't argue and cut through a sausage, dipped it into a fried egg, and got it into her mouth without dribbling yolk down her chin.

"The information in the envelope is from a reliable source."

"So, you're confident that this dude knows what they're talking about?" Frank shook the brown sauce over his sausages for the second time and Albie grinned at the thought of Freddie being referred to as a dude.

"In a nutshell. The information is from someone who was around and high profile on the other side of the law at the time of the murders."

"So, how can you be sure the information he's fed you is up front?" Fawn dabbed the corners of her mouth with a paper napkin and pushed her plate away.

"Look, Rachel, do you really think I'd waste time if I didn't think this was kosher?" Without waiting for a reply, he opened the envelope and slid the contents onto the table in front of him while the others piled the empty plates to make room. "Right, if we are working these cases together we have to share all that we've gathered throughout the case. If any of this does not resonate with you speak up. My aim is that by the time we've ploughed through this lot, we'll have a clear idea of how to advance and solve both cases. Who's making notes?" All heads lowered, Albie slid a vacant chair to the corner of the table. "Kolska... come and join us and bring your notebook and pen."

Jana Kolska sipped from a can of lemonade, stood, and silently joined the table. She unbuttoned her top pocket, flipped her notebook open, and licked the lead of her pencil. Finally, she sat forward on the edge of her chair.

"Where do you want to begin in the present or the past?"

"Let's look at what we've got from the kidnaping case first." Rachel Fawn sipped a cup of tea, then continued. "We have five kidnap victims between the ages of twenty-five and thirty. Each kidnaping took place close to the A2/M2 stretch of road apart from the most recent which was an abduction outside a busy club and in another car."

"So one line of enquiry is the different abductions. Is it the same person or people? Why change tactics on victim five especially when the other attempts were successful?" Tanya spoke while Jana concentrated on recording the conversation.

"Yeah," Frank added "And there are also differences in each victims personal circumstances. Perhaps we need to remind ourselves of these and then try to find a link between them again. We could have overlooked something significant."

"We've got the personal information on the incident board, I can share the basic info again to refresh your memories." Rachel thought for a moment then reeled off from memory factual information of each victim while Jana continued to make notes.

"Victim one: Claire Lance is a thirty-year-old air hostess. She is single and lives at home with her father in Greenwich.

Victim two: Adele Soul is a thirty-year-old and is a cashier by day and Samaritan by night. She is married to Paul; they do not have children and live in Blackheath.

Victim three: Nina Anderson is a twenty-six-year-old exotic dancer. She is in a relationship with Libby Mann and they live in Canary Wharf.

Victim four: Esther MacDonald is twenty-nine and a cleaner at a school. She lives at home with mother Isabel and son Dillon at Greenwich.

Victim five: Delilah Grange is twenty-eight and a market researcher. She is single and lives alone at London Bridge.

""Got all that?" Jana nodded her head but remained silent.

"Right. Tanya, what have we dug up on the victims and how can we move forward with the investigation?"

Tanya's eye-id twitched and her face paled as if she'd just picked up scraps of the conversation. "Well, just let me get my thoughts in order. One second." Chat outside of their silent circle sounded muffled and distant as everyone focused on the question.

"Right, I will take a victim at a time, please butt in if I leave anything out. Our first victim, Claire disappeared into thin air and we were unaware of when she went missing because of the time between when she left for work and the airline alerted her father that she had missed her connection. Also, her father Geoff Lance has become increasingly hostile and believes his daughter is not a victim of the kidnapper." Tanya scanned the circle, "Anything to add or shall I continue?"

"Make a note to consider the order the victims went missing. Tanya has a point. It is possible they went missing in a different order to them being reported missing." Jana glanced at Albie as he spoke ,then turned to the rear of her notebook and continued writing.

"Adele Soul, supposedly our second victim, worked for several hours a day. She'd rowed with her husband a few days before and it was her husband who reported her missing. He admitted that he'd been caught sleeping around and she'd walked out. He thought she had gone to her parents, but apparently this was not the case. Apart from the fact that her husband Paul was unhelpful and seemed to lack any sympathy for his wife, I have no more to add."

Rachel took a packet of soft mints from her handbag and offered them around before taking one herself. "I think we need to look further into the victim's backgrounds. I wonder why their nearest and dearest are in denial. Could it be more about the people close to the victims than the victims themselves?"

"Have you got that, Jana, as something to follow up?" Jana glanced at Albie and nodded, but this time he thought he caught a half-smile. "We are onto number three. Who wants to take this one?"

Tanya was the first to speak. "Nina Anderson, this is complex because after we spoke to her partner, Libby, we realised that this abduction is probably a case of mistaken identity." She paused and it had the effect she expected. All eyes were on her as she continued. "Albie first linked the two cases after a discussion about tattoos with Libby. We'd noticed in a photo that Esther had a raven just under her collarbone. Libby also had a raven tattoo, and explained that Nina had driven Libby's car to work because Libby was unwell. Now we believe Libby was the kidnapper's target.

The problem is that she couldn't remember how she ended up with the artwork. Apparently, she woke up with it after a night out with a girlfriend who ended up being the murder victim Kayleigh Lambert. She was a few years younger than Kayleigh and agreed to meet a blind date with her at Lee. Green The blokes seemed harmless enough and she remembers having fun up to a certain part of the evening, but then her memory is hazy at best ,non-existent at worst. This was our break through."

Rachel nodded in Jana's direction, "We need to note that the two cases link and we have to look at all persons we believe were involved with the girls that night."

Albie prodded the paperwork in front of him with all the fingers of his right hand. "This is where the cases overlap and this information should be useful. As we know the murder of four young ladies over the period of a year where solved. Liam MacDonald murdered the killer Robson Shaw before they discovered his guilt. I recently went to speak to him in prison He is also the brother of our next kidnap victim, Esther MacDonald."

"Another link between cases?" Frank had taken his own notes.

"It is the final victim that confuses me." Albie shook his head as he spat out her name. "Delilah Grange, I'm not sure of any connection and as this abduction is so raw we need to investigate any links we can."

"Any other information to share from that envelope?" Fawn tapped her foot on the floor in an upbeat rhythm, a sign that they'd sat there long enough.

"I've been given a list of names of men in a gang. They were small-time dealers paid to pick up underage girls for other men. Plus other types of jobs that only a lowlife can pursue. Some of them you have interviewed already. We need to talk to all of them from a different perspective. I want you to believe the murders from fifteen years ago went unsolved and that they connected with the kidnappings. Your job is to find the abductor and a murderer."

Within ten minutes, Albie and Jana were the only ones left in the canteen.

"Come on. We'll make a start on this list?"

Jana tucked her notebook and pencil into her buttoned pocket, but remained in her chair and looked Albie in the eye. "I've just had a thought. Shouldn't someone delve into Robson Shaw and his killers past? If they wrongly accused the dead man of murder, surely he took the hit for someone else"

Albie smiled and without reacting to her comments turned his back and walked through the door, holding it open as if an afterthought. Jana sighed, stood up, threw her bag over her shoulder, and rushed to follow.

39

Joey finished his lock up routine twice before taking one last look and switching the shop's lights off. Silence was never a trigger of fear for Joey, but this evening it seeped into his skin and energised nerve endings that prickled in his fingertips and down his spine. Unheard sounds sped up his actions as he locked and bolted the external door. He stepped into the alleyway and jammed a blood-red crash helmet with a demonised black raven in full flight on his head. He fiddled with the keys in shaky hands and it took his complete concentration to start the engine.

He straddled the seat and roared away from the silence around him but battled still with questions he had fought to keep out of his head since he'd seen the raven tattoo earlier that afternoon. Afterwards three customers had enjoyed his skills and each left exhorting his praises and promising to send him new customers. Not that he was too worried about his business. It had been different when he first started out, tattoos were an acquired taste which meant he attracted a certain clientele. Although the interest from that quarter was as profitable as ever, in recent years inks attracted a very different kind of animal. Joey understood the footballer phenomenon. If a famous footballer invests in a sleeve, fans copy him a multitude of times. It was as easy as that tattoos came into fashion. Your average bloke or girl on the street wanted one, inks had become a status symbol. Joey wasn't complaining, it would set him up for life.

Still, he felt unsettled. He pulled into his drive, cut the engine, and studied the front of the house. One dim light shone in the hall. He checked his phone; it was six-thirty and he was reluctant to enter an empty house, so instead he made his way back to the road. His house would probably be empty for at least an hour. It was always the same when Lynne visited her sister. She took the kids for the day, lost track of the time, and was full of false apologies when she returned.

Tonight it suited Joey down to the ground. He'd have a few beers with his mates, then he'd pick up a take-away on the way home. He leaned forward, pulled in his paunch, and moved his belt down a notch to make room for his planned meal.

Joey had a spring in his step as he strode to the end of the road. He acknowledged any neighbours he passed as they pottered in front gardens and tidied flower beds or trimmed overgrown hedges. As he turned the corner, he inhaled the smell of freshly cut grass which reminded him of childhood and the strip of grass his father cut to within an inch of its life so they could play cricket together in the summer months.

"All right, Joey? Not seen you for a while."

Joey's first inclination was to fain deafness and continue towards the pub. He recognised the voice. Martin Piper was not someone he had warmed to at the best of times. Joey wondered whether it was a coincidence that Martin Piper should turn up on the same day Robson Shaw's name was mentioned.

Joey moved his mouth into a false smile and turned towards the voice, "Martin, you're right it's been a while. I've been busy, what with the shop and family. No rest for the wicked." He swallowed his laugh. "You been up to much?"

"Well, since mum passed... it's been tough. But there are always jobs to do."

Joey cursed under his breath. "Your mum. Oh yeah, I was sorry to hear about that. A bit of a shock, was it?"

"She'd not been herself for a few months. I put it down to old age. She was never one to complain." Martin stared past Joey's shoulder, "It's been six months now, and some mornings I still take her up a cuppa. I know, mad, isn't it?"

"Yeah, well, they say life goes on. Don't they? Sorry, Martin, I've gotta go. I'm late." Joey stared at the screen of his phone as if reading a message.

Martin carried on as if Joey hadn't spoken. "What about all those women who've been kidnapped?"

Martin had taken a few steps towards him and Joey was so close to Martin's face when he turned back that the stale smell of rot from his middle-aged mouth mingled with the smell of cut grass in the air he inhaled. Joey nodded his head, "Awful for the families not knowing. Why, d'you know any of them?"

"No, nothing like that." Martin took another step until their noses were intimate. Joey shuffled back on his heels, but Martin didn't seem to notice. "It's just, I've had the old bill at mine asking questions."

Joey shuffled from one foot to the other and glanced at his phone. "Look, are you free now for a pint? I'm meeting the guys in the Tiger's. I think it might interest them in what you've got to say."

Matin drew back his shoulders and smiled, then gestured to the garden tools strewn over the grass. "Help us with this lot will you, mate? Just put it round the back, it'll be all right till I get back. I'll only stay for a couple."

Joey grabbed a rake, spade and fork then reluctantly followed Martin as he pushed the lawnmower through a side gate and into the back garden which was just as well kept as the front. Rather than dumping the tools on the lawn, Joey continued to the open shed at the back, half-hidden behind the thick trunk of an apple tree in the corner. "Might as well put it all away, mate. Knowing your luck, it'll rain while you're having a pint."

Martin didn't need telling twice. He followed Joey towards the shed and passed the equipment over. It had been a long time since they had treated him like one of the lads. In fact, he couldn't really remember ever being accepted. He was the one that always tagged along and was used to do the dirty work—all the dirty work. Joey had always been all right. It was the others that could be a problem, but tonight it didn't matter, he wasn't tagging along; Joey had invited him.

A kind of hush settled as they entered the pub as if someone had pressed pause on a giant remote control. The door slammed shut behind them and cut out the growl of car engines on the road outside. Anthony Locke sat in the corner of the room furthest from the bar. He had an excellent view of the door from his position and watched Joey stroll to the bar and order drinks for himself and a companion. It was only at a second glance that he recognised the slight hunch of the shoulders and weasel features of Martin Piper, the idiot who they couldn't shake off as youngsters.

"Look who's with Joey." All eyes turned towards the bar.

Dodge frowned as he stared at the man. "Isn't that Piper? He lost his mum, didn't he? Not that long ago."

Anthony rose from the stall and picked up his glass, "Suppose I should get the next round. Same again?" He was halfway to the bar before anyone replied.

"Tony, you remember Martin, right? He used to run errands for us when he was a kid."

Anthony glanced at Martin and ignored his outstretched hand. He waved his cash in the air to catch the barman's attention.

Martin brushed his hand down his jumper and took a gulp of his pint.

"Bumped into him on the way here and I asked him to join us. He was saying he'd had a visit from the pigs, something to do with those kidnappings."

"So what, you've got something you'd like to share with us have you, Piper?" Anthony held his stare and waited like a predator stalks his prey.

"I..I don't know why you'd be interested. It's nothing."

"It must be important or Joey wouldn't have suggested you join him. Would you Joey?"

Joey picked up his and Martin's pint. "Tell you what, let's sit down shall we will have more privacy." He led the way and pulled a couple of stalls to the table with the others.

"How's it going? All okay, I hope. Long time no see Dodge." After high fives, shaking hands, and nods in Martin's direction, Martin joined the table. Anthony sat on the other side of Martin, who shifted his stall further away.

"So what's this all about, Joey? I got your text asking to meet. What's so important we needed this gathering? Pleasant as it is, I'm sure most of us have other arrangements."

If eyes were lasers, they'd have disintegrated Joey on the pub floor, a pile of ashes like Martin's mum. It seemed ridiculous when he repeated the conversation he'd had with the bloke in the shop that afternoon.

Dodge's face contorted, unsure of the problem let alone a solution.

"So what's up? Is it the fact that the woman who wants the tattoo, her name's Shaw?"

"Yeah, partly. But there's more. I mean that photo of the raven, I was associated with that type of work at the time of the murders," he lowered his voice, aware of the odd stare from blokes outside their circle. "It was inked onto skin. Yellowish skin. Dead skin."

"Bullshit," Anthony laughed into his glass and watched bubbles grow in response. "You've got an overactive imagination. It's all that creative crap you produce all day."

"Don't take the piss, I wouldn't have contacted you if I wasn't bothered. And now to top it all they've asked Martin questions. They're creeping closer. It's catching up with us all and if you don't believe me, perhaps that Dominic bloke will. Freddie Hurst's son."

Anthony leaned closer to Joey and placed a hand on his arm. "All right, calm down, Joey. I don't know if contact with gangsters is the best move. Let's discuss this together."

"Oh, you wanna talk now. Okay, start talking." One elbow on the table, Joey leaned forward and mimicked his friend, "We might finally have some questions answered."

Anthony picked at the top layer of a bar mat and ripped a thin strip of paper between his fingers like a hangnail.

"Come on Tone, get on with it," Dodge glanced at the time on his phone. "My missus ain't gonna believe that I've worked this late."

"I don't know where to start. I mean... what do you want me to say? Someone killed three girls, Robson took the rap for the murders..."

"Yeah, he was dead though. No one knows for sure he did it. I mean, it's not like he had anyone to argue his innocence."

"So what ya saying? You think someone else killed them?" Warm flat liquid hit the back of his throat and he struggled to keep it down. "You understand that if you really believe it wasn't Robson then it had to be one of us, don't you? Is that what you think?" Joey asked.

Tony stood and slammed the empty glass onto the table. It shattered silence.

"I'm not calling anyone out, Tony, but I'm telling you now, Robson didn't have anyone to talk up for him back then, but he could have now."

"Well, ya know what I say? Bring it on. Wait till this Shaw woman turns up at your tattoo parlour, that's if she does. We'll know more then." He scanned the others faces for a response.

"Agreed?" without waiting for an answer, he opened the door behind him and walked into the cool night air.

40

A game. Esther stared ahead in disbelief. Frown lines were the last of her problems but she felt them etched on her forehead as she tried, but failed, to relax the muscles in her body. A circle of faces mimicked her own. It took just two words to cause information overload. So many questions danced on the tip of her tongue. Each wrestled for pole position then fell at the finish line, leaving her speechless and inept. Kidnapped, deceived and played. Tears sparkled on the cheeks of the woman opposite as she lifted the back of her hand and wiped a drip where they merged under her chin, then used it to silence a sob.

Devon cleared his throat.

“You’ll have questions. I know. And we will answer them, but first Isla will let you in on the game and explain the parts each of you are to play to reach a satisfactory conclusion.”

Esther sprang to her feet, “What are you talking about..? You’re trying to tell us this is all a game?”

Devon grasped her arm and pushed her down. He continued to speak while he cuffed her wrists to the chair. “Don’t make this any more difficult than it has to be.” He scanned the circle. Satisfied, he nodded to Isla.

Isla looked from one face to the next, cleared her throat and strolled to a chair on the opposite side of the room. She shuffled into a cushioned chair like a storyteller ready to tell her tale.

"You must all know, before I begin, that you are playing an important part not only in a game but also in the rewriting of history." Wrinkles deepened on the ridge of her nose and she threaded her fingers through smooth curls of hair that bounced back into position like a slinky.

"I will let you in on a secret after I've given you some background. I've been subject to uncertainty and terror, so I do partially empathise with you." She measured the amount between her forefinger and thumb and squinted. "The trauma I suffered fourteen-years ago and have been fighting to overcome ever since, may seem superficial to you, but it ruined my life."

Esther struggled against the constraints.

"What's it got to do with any of us? We'll listen to you and try to understand. We're people though, and you've got us tethered like animals."

Isla intercepted Devon's raised arm and stood between them. She bent down and hissed into Esther's ear, "If you keep interrupting I'll punch you myself."

She stood again and addressed the circle.

"For me the pain started with my brother's murder." The silence intensified and the women gave her their full attention. "We took each of you for a reason. The police accused my dead brother of four murders. They said they had enough evidence to close the case and that is exactly what they did. You are all here now to catch the attention of the authorities and encourage them to reopen the case. You are here to flush out the real killer. One of you is related to the person who framed my brother and is a cold-blooded killer."

"Not got so much to say now, hey?" Devon scraped his fingers through Esther's hair and his fingers grazed her tender scalp.

"I don't get it. You're saying the kidnaps were a front. You want some kind of revenge and we're being used for that purpose?" Claire asked as she slumped in her chair.

"Justice. I want justice for an innocent man accused of murder. He had no trial because he was dead. They found evidence which he wasn't there to deny. It's easy to set up a dead man. The police had investigated the girl's murders for months with no breakthrough, and so it was convenient for everyone involved. Wrapped up nicely, too nicely."

Claire cleared her throat and looked towards Devon before she spoke, "What makes you think you're right? For all you know it happened as the police said. I mean, they wouldn't close a case without evidence."

Isla slithered closer. Her elbow extended and hand raised. Claire flinched as Isla's hand came towards her. At the last moment she pulled back and placed a finger on her lips.

"Shh, enough." She said. "We will leave you now. I think you will have much to discuss." She brushed her palm across the back of the chair and strolled towards the door. "Come on, Devon." She called him like her pet dog and he showed his obedience.

A heavy silence mingled with a cloying thickness in her restricted windpipe as Esther struggled to breathe. The nightmare engulfed her, as did the immensity of their predicament.

Esther knew why they'd chosen her. An innocent in reality, but tarred with the same brush as her brother. She'd lived with the consequences of that fatal night for several years and she'd been thankful that memories fade and people become more forgiving. She glanced toward each of her companions. If she was guilty, then they would have their own stories to tell and live in the shadow of an inherited guilt.

"I'll start then." Esther spoke with a distinct wobble in her voice. Her stomach fluttered, and an erratic tick pulsed in her eyelid. The others fidgeted with a heady mix of impatience and a pinch of relief. Esther grew in stature.

"I'm ashamed. They didn't pick me at random. They chose me because my brother is in prison. He's serving a life sentence for murder. The murder of Robson Shaw." She lowered her head and her voice. It strained to it as she continued, "Until now I could always justify his violence. He'd sacrificed his own life to rid the world of scum. The only thing about scum is, like germs, they multiply. Each more resilient, each stronger than the one before super germs and super scum."

A sob, a sniffle, and a gulp diluted the silence. Esther lifted her head and waited for the abuse to fly.

Nina shuffled her chair nearer and bent forward like she was about to share an intimate story or a well kept secret with a group of friends.

"At least they have chosen you for a reason. I don't know about the rest of you, but I don't understand why I'm here."

The clunk of mechanical latches working on revolving cogs silenced the group. Clean air was the only thing welcomed as the door creaked open.

"When you're alone have a good think about our conversation. Unpick the past. Why were you chosen?" The faint whisper from Esther were the final words spoken.

41

Joey Kohl sighed and glanced at the time on his phone. It had taken longer than he'd expected to persuade Martin that he needn't worry. Even when he'd finally shaken off his offer of another drink Martin wanted to talk, discuss his theories and fears. It was when his animated voice drew unwanted attention that Joey had sprung from his chair. It was only when he'd explained that dinner would be ruined and he was in enough trouble from his missus already that Martin quietened.

"Well, I enjoyed the catch up," Martin smiled and shook Joey's outstretched hand.

"See you around." Joey said as he backed towards the doors.

"Yeah, you've got my number now. Right?"

Joey nodded. He shouldered his way through a group by the exit and made his apologies as he left.

Joey felt his shoulders relax and the tension slip away as he stepped into the cool air. He looked both ways and wandered towards the Chinese takeaway. He ordered a meal for one and sat down to wait.

Time to think. Memories. Joey was unclear of the reliability of memories. They were often snippets of half-forgotten moments in your life that a person added to a collage and were interwoven with thoughts and comments that others recalled. As a kid, Joey had a weird belief that the day he was experiencing could be his last. So he lived understanding that he took his chances and ducked his responsibilities. The reason it was so painful to remember was that after his girlfriend, Jackie, was pulled from the Ravensbourne river. He'd erased his previous life from his mind, which included their young daughter.

Joey paid for his meal and ambled towards home. A prawn cracker sizzled on his tongue and melted to a pulp. The house was in darkness, which had become a common scenario. Joey shook his head at the thought of the last conversation he'd had with his wife. It was one thing assuring him that all was well with their marriage, but the number of times he'd come home to an empty house over the last few months suggested otherwise.

He groped deep into his pocket, fiddled with the key in the lock, and felt the solid edge of the light switch dig into his shoulder as the lights sprang into action like guards along the walls. A gallery of family photographs welcomed him, each a snapshot of a happier time. Joey moved around the kitchen, adept at preparing a meal for one. Each movement of an item sounded loud and brash in the silence and added to Joey's loneliness.

The sound of the doorbell exploded into the silence. Joey opened his mouth for the final forkful of chow mein, placed his cutlery on the empty plate, and stood heavy-limbed and full from the food.

"I told you to put your keys.." He stopped mid-flow and studied the identification held up to his face.

"Mr Kohl?"

"What is this about, is... has something happened?" A sheen of sweat beaded his forehead in the clammy, cool night air.

"I'm DS Edwards and this is my colleague, Officer Kolska. May we come in?"

Joey stood his ground. "I don't understand. What's going on? Why do you need to come into my home?"

"We are investigating the kidnappings of four women and we believe you could help us with our investigations."

He moved to one side, extended his arm and bent forward into what was almost an elaborate bow. Once in they followed him through to the living room. Both officers felt an urge to stop at each photograph and study them like a piece of artwork. Joey nodded at the settee and sat in an armchair opposite. The arms were threadbare and rounded cushion worn from years of use covered the chairs.

The intricate inking that covered most of Kohl's exposed skin mesmerised Albie. The thought of the hours spent in the chair, the pain, and expense for each piece made him squirm in his seat. It made the serpent's head on Albie's upper arm seem like a tester. The pain of the needle had stayed with him long after they finished the tattoo. In his job he could rarely show it off either. He glanced at Jana, who stared intently at the man's tattoos.

"Over the last four weeks someone has kidnapped women. They've taken them from the streets. We believe there may be a link between these kidnappings and murders of five young girls in this area twelve years ago."

Joey Kohl leaned forward, rested his elbows on his thighs, linked his fingers, and placed them under his chin. Albie watched the images on his body change shape and take on a life of their own with each movement.

"So? It's got nothing to do with me." He grinned at Jana scribbling in her notebook and gave her a wink and a light scattering of pink coloured her cheeks.

Albie mirrored his position on the settee and blocked Jana from view. "The police interviewed you in 1983 about the murders, Mr Kohl, so it has plenty to do with you."

Joey jumped to his feet, "Well I've got nothing more to say. So you're wasting your time." They stood in unison. Jana moved towards the door, but Albie stood his ground. "I told you to go. Piss off." Joey said, his biceps tensed and fists flexed.

"Sit down, Mr Kohl. We can get some answers in the seclusion of your house or I'll call for the blues and twos. Unfortunately for you they're not known for their discretion. Your choice."

Joey deflated before their eyes. He raised his palms and backed away. "All right, all right. I don't need a scene. My wife and kids will be back soon."

Jana stood in the doorway and opened her notepad.

"So the murders in '83. What do you remember?" Albie perched on the edge of the chair and waited for a reply.

"I remember little of what happened as far as details and all that. You found the killer, though. I remember that, Robson, after that bastard killed him, what's his name? He's in prison."

"You're right. We thought we'd found the killer. Convenient though, after all he was a dead man. He could hardly speak up for himself, could he? What did you know about the girls?" Albie stared at the top of Joey's head as he fiddled with his wedding ring.

"I knew who they were. Robson had shown an interest in each of them at one point or another. Liked the ladies, he did."

"I don't think that's true, is it Joey? Jackie Malone, let's talk about your relationship with her."

Joey grasped one hand with the other to stop a tremor.

"Jackie? We saw each other on and off for a bit. We were kids."

"It says here that you had a child with Jackie. It sounds like it was more than kids seeing each other. Do you know what happened to your daughter, Mr Kohl?"

He nodded. "A well off family adopted her. People who could give her everything I couldn't. I was a kid. I had nothing and when Jackie died... well, I went to pieces for a while."

"You kept her with you to begin with. You didn't put her up for adoption until she was eighteen months old. Couldn't have been easy giving her up. Why then?"

"Mum had been helping me, she had a stroke, a lively eighteen-month-old was too much for her, but she'd loved Carla. It broke her heart when I handed her over." He gripped his hands together. "It was for the best."

"Who arranged the adoption?"

For the first time he looked Albie in the eye. “Why? What’s any of this got to do with the murders?”

“Maybe nothing. We’re just trying to piece things together. After Carla’s adoption, they changed her name. Your daughter’s name is Claire Lance, Mr Kohl. She was the first woman kidnapped.” He paused and watched as Joey slammed both hands on the table and jumped to his feet.

“Well, what are you doing wasting time with me? Shouldn’t you be out there looking for her?” He clawed his hands down his face, growled, and whimpered like an animal in pain. “What the fuck are you still doing here? Find who’s got her before it’s too late.”

“We’ve got people looking as we speak. I need to know who arranged the adoption, it’s important, Mr Kohl.”

“Robson, he had contacts, or his old man did. A lawyer arranged the whole adoption. Some business man, local. He was loaded, could have whatever he wanted, but couldn’t have kids. He was all right, I met him myself and he gave me information about his family. I didn’t want to hand her over to some perv.” He sniffed up and ran his hands over his cheeks. “I couldn’t cope on my own. I never wanted to give her up.”

“Thank you Mr Kohl, if you think of anything that might help us find your daughter.” He handed over his card and gestured for Jana to get the door. “We’ll see ourselves out.”

Albie led the way. He opened the car door and leaned on the roof, “Okay, spit it out. What is it you want to say?”

She ignored him and slid into the front passenger seat.

He joined her, shut the door, wound down the window, and leant his elbow on the frame. “We’re not going anywhere until you answer me. I can’t have this silent treatment if we’re going to work together you need to speak up.”

She pulled out her notebook and tapped a rhythm with a loosely held pencil. “I thought we were there to question Mr Kohl about all the killings.”

Albie nodded, “Yeah, that’s right… and?”

She spoke quickly and would have closed her eyes if she could.

Jana had listened to the rumours. They were rife about her bosses dubious career and unpredictable character. Not that she put much faith in the rumours, but at that moment she felt like a vulnerable child near a time bomb. "I just don't understand why the emphasis veered towards his kidnapped daughter. It kind of defeats the purpose, doesn't it?"

Jana drew her shoulders back and extended her spine, still unable to turn and face Albie. She fiddled with the stitching that edged the hem of her jacket and waited for a response. She could see his body angled towards her in her peripheral vision, his gaze grazed her profile. She gave in and turned to see the amusement on his face.

"Jana." He played with her name in his mouth and relished in the surprise on her face as he used it for the first time. He thought she may protest, but she blinked a few times and held her composure. "Think carefully about the outcome and ask yourself whether he would ever open up about the murders. They were years ago and he's never once shown any sign of changing his story. What we've achieved from the direction of the interview could reap the information we need. Time will tell. Will he have a sudden epiphany now we linked the case to a loved one? That's what I'm relying on. You being innovative, Jana."

"But we don't have time, sir. That's the one thing we do not have."

"Patience, Officer Kolska." Albie's phone vibrated. He glanced at the screen and cancelled the call.

42

DS Fawn pulled up outside the gated property and scanned the high red-brick wall. She was unsure whether its role was to keep people inside or outside of the property. She wound down the car window and leant across to press the button for the intercom. To her surprise, she watched as the gates parted without the need of identification. The progress of the gates was laborious and DS Fawn had to control her need to jump from the car and give them a hand.

"Modern technology. Surely it would be easier to just open them manually."

Frank smiled.

"Here we go. About time." She pulled onto a short drive the width of the front of the house and pulled into a large space next to a worn out white van. She grabbed the crutches from the back seat and took them to the passenger door. Frank had already swung his legs from the car and swivelled his body in the same direction. He grasped the hand grips and pulled himself to standing. He nudged away Fawn's attempts of help, but thanked her with a smile.

Claire's father filled the doorway. He watched Frank bounce towards him between the metal crutches. He held his hand out without a thought, but Frank balanced expertly with one crutch up under his arm and shook his hand with a firm grip.

"PC Gibbs and DS Fawn, Mr Lance. Thank you for seeing at short notice."

Geoff Lance nodded in Fawn's direction, stepped back against the wall, and ushered them into the spacious hall. "Follow me. Tea, coffee, or perhaps a cold drink?" He asked as they entered a large open-plan kitchen and dining room. He gestured to Frank and said, "You may feel more comfortable on a breakfast stool."

Geoff Lance added water to the kettle while Fawn and Frank eased onto the stools. The backs were high and cushioned as were the seats and Frank made a mental note of asking where he could buy a similar chair for home. He placed tea in front of both police officers without asking their preference.

"DS Edwards was here a few days ago. I hope you've got good news, or some news, at least."

DS Fawn felt the hostility in the mention of her colleague's name and ignored the comment. Instead, she took a gulp of her tea, and waited for the lemon to hit the back of her throat. Tears welled in the corner of her eyes and she pulled a tissue from her sleeve and blew her nose.

"Mr Lance, we are here to ask for some information about Claire."

He leant on the breakfast bar and pushed himself to standing. Fawn mimicked him and his six foot six frame dwarfed her. "I don't believe this. You've got everything you need to know about Claire. Get out and do your job. Just get out there and find Claire." He turned to leave the room.

"That's not true, though. Is it Mr Lance?"

He froze at the sound of Frank's voice. "You want to think yourself lucky. If you wasn't on those crutches." The threat hung in the air.

Fawn stared at Frank and shook her head.

Fawn spoke to Geoff Lance in little more than a whisper. "Sit down, Mr Lance, calm down, and hear us out."

He walked back towards the breakfast bar but stood tall.

Fawn ignored the way the light deflected his shadow as it loomed over her and continued, "Mr Lance, you are correct. You gave us information about your daughter when she first disappeared, however, we believed you missed out on some vital information. Claire is not your daughter. Is she? Well, not your biological daughter, anyway."

The kitchen clock ticked in the silence and the call of a cuckoo echoed around them when the hands hit twelve.

"How do you know?" Fawn strained to hear his question.

"Let's just say we did some digging. We know it was an illegal cash transaction for a child which did not go through the correct channels. We just need you to explain."

Again, there was silence apart from the deep tick of the clock.

"By withholding information about your daughter, you have put her in unnecessary danger. And you're right, every minute we spend here with you are minutes wasted. At this moment, we could be following leads to find Claire."

"What difference does it make about her past? It's all done and dusted now. It has been for years."

Frank leaned on his crutches and tried to match him in height but was left wanting.

"It makes all the difference in the world. By not knowing who Claire's birth parents are, we were unaware of a section of her life which could help us find her."

"We need the name of her parent's and the details of how, why and when you made this transaction." Fawn waited for a moment, then caught his eye. "You do want your daughter found and the people responsible caught?"

Geoff nodded his head and took a breath. He picked at a scab on his knuckle. "We tried to have kids for years, Jude adored her nephews and nieces. She wanted to do it properly. You know, a career first. Only it didn't happen. We tried IVF and toyed with a surrogate before attempting to adopt."

"And Claire?"

"Let's just say I blessed us. The adoption agencies dug about in my past. They looked into a few of Jude's family and weren't impressed. She gave up on life, I mean. All Jude ever wanted was her own baby. A friend of ours had an acquaintance that said he could probably help us for a price. Our problem was never money. It was suitability on their tick sheets."

"Who was this acquaintance?"

"They never introduced us. He just delivered on a promise and one evening in December Claire arrived. Martin, my mate, turned up on the doorstep with her. Not a newborn. She was eighteen months old."

"So you didn't question why this little girl was exchanged for money? You didn't even want to know about her parents? How she ended up with you?" DS Fawn nodded for PC Gibbs to continue.

"Mr Lance, think carefully. Is there any information you can give us about the birth parents?"

"Her mother died after a drunken night out, she drowned. I know it devastated her father. He'd tried his best. He was grieving his wife, had to work to support them both, and with a young and demanding baby had to make some difficult choices."

"How do you know about the father's struggles?" DS Fawn glanced at her phone, at an alert.

"He told me."

"What? You know him?"

"I don't know him. I met him a few times at the park when Claire was young. I thought he was a nonce. I'd noticed him hanging around the swings and approached him. I'd threatened to call you a lot on him. That's when he told me who he was Joey, that was his name. At first I was curious, asked questions, and arranged to meet him a few times. Jude would kill me if she'd ever found out. She was ill by then herself. Cancer. She only lasted two more years. Claire was her life and probably kept her strong for a while longer than the doctors expected."

"Surely Claire's dad didn't just disappear. A distraught father who regretted selling his child."

"No, he hung around for a few years. I knew he was there, I just didn't acknowledge him, and then we nursed Jude. I'm not sure how long it was before I noticed his absence. One day he was there, the next he'd gone and our live's went on."

"Is Claire's father Joey Kohl, Mr Lance?" Frank asked as he followed DS Fawn to the front door.

"I wasn't given any information about Claire's life before. Every scrap I've told you came from Joey."

"Thank you, Mr Lance. We'll be in touch." Fawn handed him a card from the top pocket of her light jacket. "In the meantime, if you think of anything that might help us find Claire you can contact me on any of these numbers."

"Piper." He said. "That's the bloke who I gave the cash to, Martin Piper. I met him in a pub in Lee years before. He was just someone I knew, not a friend, just someone I knew."

They walked back to the car in silence, apart from the scrape of rubber as the crutches contacted paving slabs.

43

Silence shrouded officers as the video ended. Each one looked to the next, their faces etched in disbelief and astonishment.

"Frank, get on the video and pull it apart. We need any piece of information you can retrieve."

Albie glanced towards Tanya, "Help Frank. Follow up with any leads."

Fawn stared ahead, "We'll make a house call and talk to Delilah's parents. See if they have anything to add to the investigation. I just feel they might unwittingly have information to help us find the girls."

Albie nodded, turned to Jana. "Come with me." He stood and paced briskly toward the lifts. The doors shuddered open, he ushered her into the compact area, his fingertips grazed the back of her jacket. He withdrew his hand and coughed to clear his throat, "Sorry" he muttered. He pressed the ground floor button and stepped to the opposite side of the space.

Jana lowered her face, but not before he glimpsed a disguised smile. They travelled to the ground floor in silence, which continued until Albie closed the car door.

Jana stared ahead and watched people dodged around the

stationary cars to make for the exit. Albie fumbled with his keys in the ignition and started the car. The purr of the engine was so smooth it went unheard over his heavy breathing. He reversed the action and dangled the keys in his hand.

"Kolska, we've got to approach this case from a different angle. Let's face it, we're getting nowhere fast."

Jana's gaze remained steady and focused on the outside world. He tapped his ring against the steering wheel, an irritating, erratic clink. As her hand hovered over her top pocket, the rhythm increased.

"Don't tell me you need to write this discussion down." His eyes narrowed and the glimpse of a smile caught the corner of his mouth. He concentrated on her every movement as she removed her note-book expertly with one hand. Her delicate fingers wriggled the button through the tight hole and lifted the flap. She took the pencil from the tab and licked the end. She angled towards Albie, inched closer, and crossed her legs like a secretary poised to take notes.

Albie laughed, a deep guttural laugh, "I was only joking. You don't have to record any of this. I just want to discuss this with someone. You don't have to join in or answer any of my rhetorical questions, and you don't need to write anything down." A rose sheen coloured Jana's cheeks. She flipped her notebook shut, slipped the pencil in place and replaced it into her top pocket.

Albie reached across and placed his hand over hers, "It's okay. If you prefer to work that way you can write it down. Ignore me, I just forget the basics of police work is about the details. Silly really because it saves time later."

She nodded and retrieved the notebook without a word.

"So, what are your thoughts, PC Kolska?"

Jana balanced the pencil behind her ear, placed the notebook in her lap, and made eye contact with Albie for the first time. "After watching the recording, it's obvious that the cold case is the reason they took these women from their cars. We are finding new links between these women and Robson Shaw's gang. Whoever is behind this wants justice for something that happened years ago."

Albie nodded as Jana spoke, intent on listening to her words rather than the excitement on her face during her retelling of her assessment of the situation. He wondered whether people ever asked for her opinion, and if they did, whether they listened to what she had to say.

"I hear what you're saying PC Kolska, but are you working on facts or intuition?"

Jana lowered her eyes and tilted her chin towards her chest. Her silence dragged on and just as Albie went to speak she looked up again and locked his gaze with her own.

"Some from the facts and evidence gathered already. But, I would be lying if I denied that underlying the theory there wasn't a smidgen of intuition, sir." She grinned, "Gut feeling. Is that what it's called?"

The sounds of 'Hey Jude' rung out from his phone. "Keep that thought," Albie said, holding a hand palm up.

"How many involved? Okay, so who called it in? Yeah, fifteen minutes away. Tell them to keep everyone involved and witnesses at the scene."

Albie reached behind, breathed in, pulled the seatbelt across his stomach and clipped it in place. He waited until Jana had mirrored his actions.

"A fight in the Tiger's Head involving some of the old gang." Albie placed his arm on the back of her seat, look behind, and reversed out of the space. He put the car into gear and foot on the accelerator then skidded out of the car park.

Sombre mumbles welcomed them into the back bar where the regulars gathered. The majority showed signs of what would turn into swelling and nasty bruises as the evening progressed. A few cleaned blood from their faces and hands with damp paper towels. Some snarled at each other across the room while others strutted around. But one thing was obvious all their anger and energy was spent. Uniformed officers stood in between the injured on either side of the bar and went about taking statements from damaged individuals.

"I hoped they'd send you," Albie swung round. The barmaid from their first visit licked her lips as she swayed her way between tables.

"Look at them," she said, gesturing to the men. "Can you believe grown men brawling? They should know better, the lot of them."

Jana stifled a grin, and Albie cleared his throat.

"So Ms?"

The barmaid edged closer until their arms touched, then she ran her finger over his hand. "It's Miss. Miss Sloane. As I've told you before, I'm happy to help."

"Good, Miss Sloane. Are you happy to answer some questions?"

"Okay, where do you want me?"

"PC Kolska," Jana wiped the grin from her face and walked towards them, "Miss Sloane is happy to answer our questions. Upstairs may be a good idea."

The barmaid pouted and held his gaze before she slouched towards the room behind the bar. "Wes, take over for a while will you? I'll take my break now." The young man finished pulling a pint, raised his hand, and continued to talk to the customer. A young girl barely old enough to drink.

"Bloody kids. He's more trouble than he's worth," Miss Sloane made for the stairs. "This way. Mind the books."

Jana tiptoed her way around piles of books that languished on either side of each stair and left a narrow pathway in the middle. Jana was tempted to peruse the titles, but refrained. She promised herself that if the opportunity arose, she would look on the way down.

"So, what happened?" Albie asked as he dragged a spare chair from an opposite table.

"No comment." Albie surveyed the redness and swelling around Anthony Locke's left eye and cheekbone and followed his gaze to a table in the far corner where Joey Kohl leaned over an agitated Dodger.

"Like that is it? Perhaps the others will be more forthcoming."

Albie was two steps from the table when Anthony spoke again. "No. Wait, it was my fault. I started this, Dodger just caught me on a bad day."

"Okay, I'm listening." Albie retraced his steps, sat, and waited. "Now listen carefully," He moved closer and grabbed Anthony by his lapels with both hands. He studied his whitened knuckles, leaned into his face then hissed through his teeth, "I'm not known for my patience, apparently it's not a quality of mine, but guess what? When I'm working to find kidnap victims whose lives are ticking away, I'm also light on the sympathy and empathy traits."

"All right," Anthony wriggled and caught his breath. "I'll talk."

Albie eased his grip and watched as Locke slid down the wall and eased his delicate body back in the chair. He scanned the room, went through the motions of straightening his clothing, pushed his fingers through his hair, and cleared his throat.

"What do you want to know?"

"I want you to tell me what the hell this is all about." Albie slammed his hand down on the table. "Start at the beginning."

"Loads of allegations have been flying around since we had a visit from some businessmen."

"Men's names? Allegations?"

Anthony looked down at his clenched fist and opened and closed it with care. "These men came with a warning, and if I talk to you... well, it's lights out for me."

"And if you don't I'll take you in and make it known how free you are with your information. How much we value your support and what a great man you are to lay your life on the line to catch criminals. Your choice."

Locke scanned the other tables, everyone was engrossed in their own conversations.

"You can't do that."

"No? Watch me." Albie leaned forward and gripped the back of Locke's arm. "We've wasted too much time already."

Locke struggled against his hold, "It was Freddie Hurst. The businessmen were here on behalf of Freddie Hurst. He was a local gangster at the time and this was his patch when I was younger."

Albie released his grip and gestured for him to sit. "So, let me get this straight. You're saying that Freddie Hurst sent his cronies in to threaten you into silence about the murders of those young girls?"

Albie stood and paced. He felt the blood drain from his face. Each step he took was like wading through treacle. The gaggle of voices retracted into the distance as he tried to digest Locke's words.

"These businessmen. What did they have to say?"

Locke looked down and shuffled from one foot to the other.

"It was basically a warning. We're not to mention Freddie's name." He raised his eyes to meet Albie's. "To be fair, there'd be no need to. If he was involved in those murders, you'd not find any evidence. That type clean up after themselves. Some poor sod would have taken the wrap for his actions."

Albie wiped the sweat from his forehead and the back of his neck, "Take his statement." He said to an officer by the next table as he made for the bar.

"Kolska, wrap it up now we need to go." He shouted as he pushed passed the barman who'd moved onto another young customer. Albie made a mental note to send some officers in looking at IDs. He leaned across the barman and moved the vodka he'd just poured away from the girl.

"Oi, what the fuck.."

"Lovely." Albie shook his head at her, then turned to the barman. "If you want to keep your licence I'd pour her a coke."

"You can't do that I'm eighteen." She fumbled aimlessly in her handbag, moving the contents around in a never-ending circle. "It's here somewhere."

"Forget it love, I know a fake ID a mile off. Now take the coke and be grateful that you're not being thrown off the premisses. And you..." He turned his attention back on the barman, who busied himself moving glasses and bottles around and wiping the sides with a cloth. "If you want to keep your job then stop serving underage girls."

"Aww, come on... these girls, it's difficult to know whether they're over eighteen."

"Save it." He said as Kolska appeared on the bottom step with two books in her hand.

"Thanks, I'll bring them back in a few weeks." She waved the books toward Ms Sloane, who tripped as she shuffled around her on the bottom step, slid her hands over every curve of her body and followed Albie to the door. She reached forward and placed her hand over his as he gripped the door handle.

"Allow me."

Albie tried to wriggle free, but she had a solid grip. He felt heat rise from his neck and knew the blush would have reached his cheeks. He smelt a mixture of sweat and stale lavender perfume as she edged closer. There was a faint hint of garlic hidden under a peppermint haze when she spoke.

"I'll not forget you, Albie Edwards, you're mine. If you come back again, you may never get away." She giggled like an excited schoolgirl and pressed her breasts against his chest. "I hope to see you soon." With a wink and a smirk, she turned on her heels and headed towards the bar.

Albie opened the door wide and gestured with a nod for Jana to go. Even with her head lowered he could sense her amusement.

"I thought we were in a hurry." She mumbled to the ground on the way past.

"I'll pretend I didn't hear that PC Kolska and remember I'm your senior officer." He added, making sure she caught his light-hearted tone.

"Where are we going now, sir?"

"Just get in. We'll talk on the way."

44

"Tanya? Kolska and I are following up some leads connected to the cold case. We'll have to go off radio for a while. Anything we need to know?"

"When are we expecting you back?"

Albie thought for a second, he'd had to take Kolska with him and knew it was a risk to involve her. He would leave her in the car a distance away from the club. He'd be quick. All he needed to do was to convince the old man to stop involving himself in police business.

"Only two hours we're chasing up a lead."

"Well, what we've got here can wait a few hours. By the time you're back Fawn should make an appearance."

"Right, you can catch me on this number via text but the phones on mute and the radio is off." Kolska fidgeted in her seat and lowered the passenger window an inch. "Keep at it, see you soon. A coffee would be good when we get back."

"Yeah, I'm sure it would be, sir. You must take your chances. Stay safe."

Albie muted his phone with her final words ruminating in his head. Tanya's intuition had always startled him and of all the words he'd needed her to relate, they were at the bottom of the list.

"Right, that's sorted." He said aloud as he pocketed his phone and stopped at a red light. He scanned the shops to his left. The area had always looked shabby, in need of a good makeover, an injection of council money to spruce the place up. But it was no different to other local areas, except perhaps for the smell of dereliction.

Albie indicated right and manoeuvred the car into a narrow alleyway between two buildings. The car fell into an eerie darkness without the glare from the headlights. Albie opened his door and turned towards Jana as she copied.

"I've got some business to deal with." He said to the back of her head. "Just wait for me here. It shouldn't take any longer than twenty minutes. Write up some notes from your interview with the lovely Ms Sloane."

Jana fiddled with the button on her jacket and cleared her throat, "I don't feel comfortable with this, sir. I think I should partner you or at least follow from a distance."

Albie tapped his ring on the steering wheel, "I'm giving you an order, Kolska. You stay put. Do you understand?"

"But..."

"I said, do you understand?"

She lowered her head and pulled on a loose thread which held the button in place. Her nod was subtle but enough for him to leave the car and walk towards the main road without a backward glance.

Noise assaulted Albie as he turned the corner. The hum of traffic with the occasional shriek of a hooter. Loud, uninhibited voices shouted over the noise of the traffic. With a hint of music added into the mix just to keep the punters interested and wanting to investigate further, the thrill seekers and adrenaline junkies weaved between the Friday night party people and slipped into the facade of a club with near anonymity.

Albie hesitated for a moment and scanned the road both ways before he crossed and entered the club. A baseline throbbed and vibrated from the walls while lights whipped across a near empty dance floor. The clientele attracted so early in the evening were often voyeurs and weasels who hid in the shadows, camouflaged and warmed with alcohol by the time the place was heaving. They'd watch and wait, survey the crowd until their eyes came to rest on vulnerable prey. Then they'd hover, like a hummingbird ready to drain the elixir.

Whenever he was in the proximity of his father and his parallel life, Albie's senses switch to hypersensitive. He was always aware of what might have been and how he was within touching distance of his other life every time he met with Freddie Hurst. He surveyed the bar area. The barman smiled and beckoned him over. He pulled him a Guinness, straightened a row of four beer mats and placed the pint glass on the one nearest to Albie.

"I know who you came to see." He said, "but you're out of luck. Freddie's taken a turn for the worst."

Albie pushed the pint back towards the bartender, "Listen, I need to talk to him so stop pissing me about and tell him I'm here."

The barman stared at him as he pulled his phone from the tight pocket of his faded jeans. "Dom," he spoke in a whisper, head down. "Your brother's here asking for Freddie." He held the phone out to Albie. "He wants to talk to you."

Albie stared at his outstretched hand for a few seconds and couldn't help but notice his protruding veins. Each blue snake moved independently to the rhythm of his pulse.

"Yeah, it's me. Where have they taken him? Can he still talk? Don't give me that crap, I'll get there as soon as I can. Catch him before he goes down." Albie placed the phone next to his untouched pint, said cheers to the barman's back, and made for the street where he'd left Jana.

The cool night air caught his breath as he turned the corner into the alleyway and he bent forward to offset the first spots of rain that threatened to break from the group of dark clouds overhead. The figure backed against the door of the car looked around her as a silhouette of a man twice her size leaned closer. Obstructive and intimidating in his stance, he smothered her from all sides. Albie slowed and took in the scene. Within seconds, his head bowed, his arms pumped as fast as his heart and he sprinted towards the figure who loomed over Jana. Without thought, he used his momentum to knock him off balance and landed on the damp, filthy pavement next to his victim. His left arm and shoulder ached as he struggled to his feet. He ignored Jana's attempts of support.

"Shit, Albie." Albe ignored the spittle that ran down his cheek. He grabbed the lapels of his brother's jacket, dragged him to his feet, propped him against the car, and held him in place.

"Cut the crap, Dom. Keep your hands and threats off my officers and take us to Freddie." With each breath his chest burned, he leant into his brother and turned his nose up at the aroma of stale sweat, cigarette smoke, and garlic. A deadly combination to inhale.

"Kolska, are you all right?" The slight nod was enough reassurance and he made a mental note to check with her properly once they had spoken to Freddie.

Albie turned side on and leaned into Dominic while he opened the back door. "Get in." He said and took a hesitant step away from the warmth of his brother's body. Dominic bent over, one hand on his stomach and the other on his crotch while Albie listened to his breath gradually slowing. "Now. Don't piss me off. Get in now." He said and pushed him into the back seat.

Dominic lashed out. His elbow caught Albie just below the eye. "Get your fucking hands off me. Whatever you do to me, I'll enjoy replicating on your little friend over there." His smile, handsome to some, turned up at the ends into a bitter twist.

Jana shuffled back from his eye line and hid in the shadow of an overhanging arched doorway. Albie shoved Dominic inside the car, then turned his attention to Jana.

"It's okay, he's harmless. Just full of himself. Can you drive?"

Jana stood silently. She stooped as if examining her shoes.

"You either drive or you get in the back with him. Your choice." Without a word, Albie watched as she slipped the keys from her jacket pocket and headed for the driver's door. He slipped in beside his brother and waited until she was ready.

"My dear brother here will give you directions." He said as he watched for her reaction in the rear-view mirror. But if she held questions, she hid them well. All he noticed was how she held his gaze with her deep-brown eyes watery, and weary.

The journey was quick and uneventful, the traffic sparse. The digital clock on the dashboard flashed eleven-thirty pm. Albie wrestled with his conscience on the short ride. Jana was with them and unwittingly drawn into a family matter. He loosened his tie with sweaty hands and his fingers stilled when he placed them in his lap. He'd made it a rule to keep work and personal life separate. Now here he was with his darkest secrets on the verge of being revealed.

"Pull over into that space." He leant between the two front seats and talked to the side of her face as she reversed the car into a tight gap. She navigated a concrete pillar and squeezed between two other vehicles. He leant in closer until his lips grazed her ear, his voice nothing more than a low hum. "Stay put and lock the doors. I'll be back before you notice me gone."

"Sir." She answered the windscreen held her attention.

Dominic shuffled forward and spoke to the back of her head his garlic breath polluted Albie's air, "She's coming with us."

He put one hand up before Albie could protest. Albie saw the glint of silver in his other hand as Dominic grabbed Jana by the hair and whipped the knife across her neck, drawing a fine line of blood on her pale white skin.

Albie felt a pulse pound in his ear and was unsure if it was his or Jana's. He could hear his brother utter instructions like someone spoke in slow motion, deep and drawn. His breaths were pants, which reminded him of his pet dog after they'd been for a run as a child. Jana stayed unperturbed apart from a strange, almost inaudible shrill that squeezed its way from her lips. His eyes met hers in the windscreen's reflection. They pleaded with him to save her from this horror. Only one thought entered Albie's head at that moment. He would not let Jana become another Olivia Devine. That's why he found it difficult to breathe. That's why his voice wouldn't work.

"Much as I'm enjoying this little game, watching you squirm. It's time we paid the old man a visit. Funny, but when I told him you were on your way, he perked right up. So..." he said as he opened another blooded gash just below the first on Jana's neck.

Jana whimpered.

"That's enough, I'm here aren't I. If anything happens to her then Freddie will outlive one of his sons and it won't be you."

Dominic grinned again and showed an immaculate set of white teeth through which his garlic breath seeped. He relaxed his grip on the knife and Jana's hair, then eased his hand away and stroked the side of her face with the blood smudged knife.

"Get out." He whispered and she removed her seatbelt with a shaking hand, opened the driver's door, and slid between the cars on wobbly legs. Dominic followed. He grabbed her around the top of her arm and pulled her back towards his body close, so close that the point of the knife pierced the skin at the top of her right buttock. Her whole body tensed.

"Be a good girl and stay close to me. We wouldn't want you drawing the wrong sort of attention to us now. Would we?"

"Come on, Dom. Let her go. It was my decision to come and see Freddie. Let go of her, she'll do as I say. You don't need the knife."

Albie watched the tick in his brother's right eyelid spasm as he considered his request. He released the grip on her arm and slipped the knife inside his jacket pocket. Jana took a deep breath and her shoulders slumped as she moved towards Albie. He raised his arms as if to welcome her into an embrace but she stopped just outside his reach and raised her hands to her blooded streaked neck.

"Jana, it's important that you listen to any instructions I give you. Do everything I say. Nothing else. Do you understand?"

This time she spoke in a hollow whisper. "Yes, sir."

Dominic's callous laugh echoed off the concrete walls that surrounded them. "Just how you like your ladies, ay Albie. Subservient and obedient. Let's hope this one survives."

Albie stared at the twisted smile on his brother's face and the infuriating tick that played over his eye. He'd never felt such anger all he wanted to do was wipe that cocky attitude from his face. But instead, he just gestured for him to lead the way and stayed close enough for Jana to feel his presence.

45

The lift doors opened and a familiar smell of cigarette smoke lingered from the patients whose visitors had sneaked them passed the nurse's station to share an illicit puff.

Albie tapped his top pocket and felt the packet of twenty he carried around with him. He made no excuses for being prepared and he justified his actions by telling people who ask that his job is demanding job by keeping twenty unopened cigarettes on his person he had an option to light up when life gets tough. So far he could proudly declare himself a non-smoker, apart from a celebratory cigarette he always has when he solves a case. For the first time in the three years since he'd given up, he was close to giving in to temptation.

The waiting room was the source of a hum of chatter. A fluorescent strip light blinked into an erratic beat which reminded Albie of intermittent lighting just before a storm breaks. The stale air was humid and recycled. He turned his attention to his brother rather than explore his thoughts about the many germs he was inhaling.

"This way." Dominic put one large hand in the small of Jana's back and pushed her towards the stairwell. "Just keep going up to the second floor. You first bro." He took one step to the side and made way for Albie before following.

The corridor was silent. The nurse's station was deserted and the light from a desk lamp was the only evidence that someone was on duty. Albie followed Dominic and Jana into a small side room. The lights were dimmed and the room was filled with the occasional bleep which sounded over the dull buzz of machinery.

Dominic nodded to a chair in the corner, and Jana slipped into it with the movement of an unnoticed ghost. Albie stood at the end of the bed and studied the outline in the murky light. As his eyes adjusted, he held back a gasp. Freddie looked pitiful. He'd always been such a strong intimidating character and Albie couldn't relate the Freddie in the hospital bed with the image of his father.

Dominic bent his head and whispered into Freddie's ear, a mumble too soft to interpret. Freddie opened his eyes and scanned his surroundings until he spotted Albie.

"Albie, you came." He patted the bed on the opposite side to Dominic. "Come closer, son, it's difficult to talk with you so far away."

Albie hesitated and glanced at Jana. He needed to gage her reaction, needed a chance to explain, needed her not to freak out. But whatever was going through her mind, he could not read it on her face. Even though she kept her expression blank, he knew she would want answers later. He had put her in danger and broken so many rules, but he'd worry about that later.

Albie took a few tentative steps, near enough for Freddie to grab his hand. His hand jolted from under Freddie's unexpectedly cold grip.

"Listen, You've gotta promise me you'll look after your brother if I don't come out of this with a cohesive mind."

Albie tried to answer, to laugh at his suggestion, but he continued to meet his father's persistent stare with silence. Any words of response lodged in the back of his throat. Instead, Dominic's moan of disbelief echoed around the sterile room.

"You've got to be kidding me, Freddie. I'm never gonna accept help from the filth, brother or not. After you've had your operation you're gonna be just fine, and if you're not? Well..."

"Dominic, just stop right there." Freddie shifted his body upright on the pillows that supported his tired frame and growled at his youngest son. "Unless you're ready to see the ugly side of your father, you'd better listen. Albie is the oldest. Now I know what you think about this. You've made it quite clear, but he's your big brother and is entitled to take over the family business."

"No, you listen to Dom, Freddie. If anything happens to you, which I doubt very much we'd be so lucky to witness, I'm the last person you should trust with your business." He shook his head in disbelief. "Why would you even consider me as a benefactor? I might be your son but never make the mistake of thinking I believe blood is thicker than water."

"You've got no choice, they're my wishes. I've left it all to you, Albie... my firstborn."

The muscles in Dominic's jaw contracted and red blotches highlighted his cheeks like an off duty clown who'd neglected to remove all of his makeup. He looked from one to the other, his arms hung loosely at his side with the only trace of tension in his balled fists.

"Don't I get a say in this? It's not like Albie works in the business. He's a bastard pig... you can't trust him. What about me?"

Albie took another step closer and leaned closer to Freddie, "Dominic's right, it's a stupid idea and it'll never happen," he leant the patient forward and puffed his pillows before releasing him back to the mound of support. "This is how bad a son I am. I haven't come to visit you because of your illness or because I think you'll die. I'm here to find out what else you know about this cold case I'm investigating."

His father just stared ahead. Waited.

"What is it you don't want me to know? Obviously, it's something that can show you involved in underhand business, ruin your reputation or put you inside again. Well? Don't go quiet on me now, Freddie. From the way you're talking, no one knows whether you'll survive this operation. So now's the time to spill, to clear your conscience."

"That's enough. Dad needs rest. He's said what he needed to say. You can bugger off now and take your new piece of skirt with you." Dominic sneered, his eyes focused on Jana, his tongue traced his bottom lip. "Or you can leave her here, if you want. Introduce her to a real man."

Albie ignored his brother and turned his attention back to Freddie. "Look Freddie, just tell me. It must be important for you to send Dom and the gang to the Tiger's Head. Scared the shit out of the locals."

Freddie smiled. "How's whatever I say going to help? It all happened a lifetime ago."

"Well then, you've got nothing to lose. If you die, you'll have a clear conscience and if you survive, you could be the soul person commended for saving the young kidnap victims. A win-win situation."

"It was me," Freddie said matter-of-factly, "It was supply and demand. I didn't ask questions. I just ensured the girls arrived. The young gang who found the girls would groom them, and when they were ready, they'd brand them. But the murders..." He shook his head, "that was not part of the deal. One of those men got a taste for killing."

"So what are you saying? You know who killed those girls?"

"No, what I'm saying is it wasn't Robson, even though he took the rap. He was the scapegoat. It came together nicely, really. Him being attacked by that young girl's brother. It happened just after the girls started to turn up dead. He was the murderer. The evidence I had planted made sure of that, and it meant my business could continue."

Albie waited in case he had anything to add, but he'd closed his eyes as if to dismiss him.

"So, you planted the evidence. But who killed the girls and why did you protect them?"

Freddie kept his eyes closed and shrugged. "Never found out. It could have been any of the gang. My focus was on the business. We needed to continue to supply girls who were more cautious. Every business goes through lows at various times. We'd lost assets, but we had to decide the quickest way to move forward and Robson was the way."

Albie studied the grey, worn face of the man he'd avoided calling dad for most of his life. A fierce man, feared and admired in the same measure by several notorious people. He was vulnerable at that moment. His eyes were closed. His body pierced with needles and covered in monitor pads with the attached machines registering his life. He was alive while death touched many others because of him. Albie smarted at Freddie's cold-hearted description of the murdered girls. They were assets in his business. Products lined up and branded to sell to the highest bidder. Albie felt his face colour, just like Dominic's. It was possibly the only physical trait they had in common. The images of the dead girls played through his head and the girls who were missing because of Freddie's arrogance and lack of 'business ethics'.

His pulse quickened, he ran his hands through his hair as his breathing responded to his heartbeat.

This was his Father. Scum. Still unwilling to save victims of his underground empire. This was the man he'd spent his whole life desperate to escape. But no matter how he distanced himself, Freddie kept interfering in his life. Here he was vulnerable, accessible, and alone with only Dominic, the son who truly cares.

The deep disgruntled bass of a laugh regurgitating from the depths of his stomach fractured the silence, interspersed with the beat of the monitor and hiss of breathing equipment that kept in time with his own pulse. Albie's animalistic response startled the others. He lunged at the old man and wrapped his hands easily around his fragile throat. Thoughts flashed through his mind, his mother lying in a bed similar to the one his father lay in now. Her beautiful face unrecognisable, mounds of swollen flesh, gashed and disfigured by the unrepentant monster of his youth. He dug his fingernails deeper into the back of Freddie's neck, then plunged his thumbs into either side of his windpipe and squeezed. He forced himself to watch as his father's pupils dilate and marvelled in the patterns the pinpricks of blood made in the yellowy white of his eyes as his blood vessels burst.

The old man thrashed his hands, unable to make much impact other than scratches to Albie's arms like a cat battling to escape. Albie's body worked instinctively. The more his father struggled, the tighter his grip. His own breath whooshed from him as two strong arms grabbed him from behind like a boa constrictor crushing his prey. He fought to breathe, break away from the grip. Dominic held on tight. Just as Albie felt his father's defeated body collapse under his force, Jana slipped under his arm her back to him she worked on releasing his hands from his father's neck, she dug her nails into his wrists and when there was no response tried to jam her fingers under his to release the pressure. She then spun to face him and without warning pressed both thumbs against his closed eyelids until a piercing pain shot through his jaw. Albie tweaked his grip and fell forward under the weight of Dominic.

His brother scrambled for the knife in his pocket and pressed the tip into the right side of Albie's lower back. The hostility of the tone in his brothers near silent whisper hissed on his garlic breath as the steel nipped his skin.

"I should finish you now for what you've done to the old man."

A hollow laugh caught at the back of his throat as he released Albie from under his hefty body and after one deliberate surface slice of the knife stood to full height. "But you know what I think? You just may have done it yourself."

Albie pushed himself to standing with the help of Jana. He looked to his father, struggling to put the oxygen mask over his nose and mouth, but pushing away Dominic's help. His neck was marked and sweat dripped down the side of one temple, but apart from disheveled hair there was no sign of the vicious attack. His father's eyes met his and were void of emotion. For the first time Albie saw himself in the man that lie before him. Frustration mounted as he realised that his reaction had given his father the satisfaction he'd craved. Albie was his son and no amount of effort on his part would ever change that fact.

. . .

Albie bent over the curb and threw up. He dry heaved again and again until tears streamed from his eyes and his gut burned. His body was on fire even though the air was cool. It could not placate his body's response to his actions in the hospital room. Jana rubbed his back with a firm hand. Yet it did nothing to ease his shaking or the despair he felt about his actions. His thoughts of cowardice and disappointment that he did not complete Freddie's termination conflicted with the confusion and guilt of his actions as a police officer. He wondered what Jana made of the situation while she stood by his side and continued to rub his back. She'd been a silent spectator, for now. But Albie knew that eventually she'd want to know more. Just like Olivia... and she'd just been buried. Jana would be different. He would protect her from his life. Do what he needed to keep her safe.

46

DS Rachel Fawn took the stone steps to the double-fronted door of the elaborate detached house two at a time. She had expected an expansive home, but this property and surrounding land screamed decadence. From the individual statues lining the entrance to the marble columns, which she had to stop from using to prop herself upright. Frank gave her a reassuring smile as she knocked on the door which she ignored.

Inspector Masters had asked Frank to tag along at the last minute. She wasn't sure why and had to admit the request unnerved her. Silly as it sounded, she couldn't shake off the fact that it was like sleeping with the enemy. There was no doubt in her mind that Frank Gibbs would be expected to report back and she would not give either him or Edwards the satisfaction of messing up.

Rachel Fawn studied the windows on either side of the royal blue doors and glimpse through the distorted glass for movement or shadows. She stepped forward and knocked once more, conscious to put an extra force into the movement. Frank backed down the steps on unsteady feet. It's the first time he'd ventured out without his crutches, and Fawn watched him waver, unsteady on his feet. That was Masters' reason for Frank's attendance today—a nice easy job to whet his appetite and check out his physical capabilities. Well, it appeared they'd had a wasted journey.

"Did you phone ahead?" Fawn ignored Frank's question, half listening for footsteps behind the door. "What I mean is are they expecting us?" She nodded then reached to knock once more, amazed that there was no doorbell for such a large house.

"I'll look around the back. You never know they may be in the garden. That's where my parents spend most of their time as soon as there's a hint of sunshine."

Without a word, Fawn followed him through an arched gate which he shoulder barged open. The side entrance was difficult to negotiate and Frank warned her about the thorn-covered branches as he forced a pathway. She avoided the thorns but not the water droplets that splattered her suit and hair.

She brushed her hands down her damp jacket, trouser legs and through her hair, dislodging some debris before they entered the back garden.

A walled patio stretched across the width of the house, dotted with pots of new-bloom daffodils and the ends of snowdrops. Clean whites and yellows sparkled in the tepid sunshine. A rectangular wrought-iron table surrounded by six cushioned chairs was the centrepiece and looked out on the lush, newly cut grass, and trimmed bushes. The focal point was a prominent fountain. Water streamed from dolphins mouths that surround Zeus adorned with a fair coating of moss.

"Can I help you?" A man lowered the broadsheet to the table and removed his reading glasses as he stood.

"DS Fawn and PC Gibbs. We rang ahead, sir. Sorry about the intrusion, but we were knocking for sometime."

The man rubbed his hands down his casual trousers, then offered it to both officers before gesturing to the table.

"Malcolm Grange. Please, sit. Can we get you anything? Tea or coffee?"

"A coffee, DS Fawn?"

Fawn nodded her agreement and watched Malcolm Grange jog into the house.

"So, what do you think? He doesn't seem to have any idea why we are here. I wonder how close he is to his daughter?"

Fawn surveyed the garden and thought how three of her back gardens could nestle comfortably within this one.

"Remember, we are unsure if Delilah is a victim of the same people. The execution was different, from the others. If the parents only keep in touch with her twice a week, they may not be aware." She watched Malcolm Grange carry an overloaded tray. An elegant grey-haired woman strolled behind him. Her slim build reminded Fawn of Twiggy and her large mouth stretched into a horsey grin that showcased a perfect set of white teeth.

Fawn copied Frank and stood and introduced herself to Patricia Grange as the couple reached the table and handed out refreshments.

"So sorry about earlier, I had the doorbell removed recently, when the front of the house was last painted. It's one of those jobs I keep forgetting to get done. I must say how brave you were to attempt the side before we've let the gardener loose on it this year." Patricia smiled and it lit up her face.

"So what's this about officers?"

Fawn took a sip of coffee, placed the flower-patterned cup on the saucer and pushed some stray hair away from her face.

"When was the last time you heard from Delilah, Mr Grange?"

"What sort of question's that?" Humour etched his face as if he was part of a bad joke.

Patricia rested a tiny hand on her husband's arm. "What Malcolm meant to ask is why do you want to know? Has something happened?" Fawn watched the muscles in Patricia's cheeks tense before her mouth drooped and the smile that greeted them earlier fell into a slump to match her frown.

"The reason we're asking is we've had some footage sent to us that shows your daughter approached by two people as she unlocks her car. They then forced her into another car with an unknown driver."

A low-flying crow headed for the grass in front of them, interrupting the silence and pillaging in the moist soil.

"So you're saying they have taken her?" Pricilla shook her head as she spoke. "There must be some mistake, she was here this time yesterday, sitting just where you are now. I mean, Malcolm was at work, but she was here."

Malcolm jumped to his feet, swiped his hand out in disbelief and forced a laugh. "Listen to yourselves. I've never heard anything as ridiculous in my life. Delilah kidnapped? Why would anybody want to kidnap Lilah?"

"How did she seem to you? Mrs Grange?" Fawn asked while Malcolm Grange sat back in his chair and picked up another scone.

Patricia didn't hesitate with her reply, "Excited, she was full of the joys... always. That's just Delilah, she lives life to the full, and loves every minute." Patricia Grange slid her fingers inside the arm of her thick sweater and eased a tissue into her hand. She dabbed an errant tear that sat on her cheek, clasped both hands together, and lowered them into her lap with a sigh. "Why on earth would this happen to Lilah? I don't understand."

Fawn turned her attention to Malcolm Grange. He sat upright with legs crossed watched his wife, but he did not once move to comfort her or give her support. Instead, he stared at her as if in a trance.

"Mr Grange, have you been following car kidnappings that have taken place recently? All the women are in their late twenties to early thirties."

Both Mr and Mrs Grange gave her their attention.

"Yes." Malcolm Grange said, "you would have to live on another planet not to be aware of the investigation."

"And in your profession, Mr Grange, I'm sure you have your own theories about why these women were kidnapped?"

"Well yes. I suppose I do, but what has this got to do with Delilah?"

Frank cleared his throat and placed a file on the table. He nodded to Fawn before she continued.

"Well, Mr Grange, the thing is we have kept some specific information out of the news."

"I see, and how does this specific news related to the 'so called' abduction of our daughter?"

Frank coughed and took a mouthful of coffee while Fawn cleared her throat. She realised Malcolm Grange had gone into lawyer mode and would question everything she said unless she explained it in detail.

"Fifteen years ago there were a string of murders in South London, young girls were exploited. They were groomed by young men then handed over to entertain at, shall we say, unorthodox parties. I think you'd agree this is shocking." Neither of Delilah's parents responded so Fawn continued, "Four young ladies were less fortunate than the others and turned up drowned in the Ravensbourne river. Do you recall these murders, Mr Grange?"

Fawn watched him tilt his head as if in thought. She wondered if he was unsure of whether to come clean. He was obviously unsure how much she already knew and what would happen if he denied or understated his connection with the crimes that later came out.

"The Raven murders. Yes, as I'm sure you are already aware, I was the lawyer for the defence. It was cut and dry really, Robson Shaw was found guilty of the deaths of all four girls. The evidence against the defendant was undeniable and his defence... well, let's just say it was lacking. Robson Shaw was no longer around to plead his innocence."

"And what about the allegations he groomed young girls for parties attended by wealthy businessmen who paid well for their company?"

"I will stop you there." Patricia Grange said, fidgeting in her chair, "I still do not understand what any of this has to do with Delilah. From your own admission, this happened over a decade ago. I want us to stay in the here and now. What are you doing to find Delilah?"

Malcolm smiled at his wife and laid his hand on her arm. From his expression he appeared relieved for the timely interruption. "My wife is right. If this has happened to Delilah how can we help?"

Frank moved his chair closer to the table and leaned forward as if to share a secret. "Have you any idea of her whereabouts, Mr Grange? Did she share her plans with either of you?"

"Only that she was meeting a client for a meal that evening. She was in two minds whether to go." Patricia fiddled with the sleeve of her jumper.

"Go on." Frank said when she lifted her head and palmed a tear from her cheek.

"She went, after all business is important even if the client is a bit of a creep, that was what she'd said just before she left."

"Did she mention the client's name?"

Patricia Grange thought for a minute then nodded, "Mr Soul, that's what she said. I remember because I made a joke about David Soul in Starsky and Hutch, but it went right over Lilah's head."

Unsure of the reference, Frank glimpsed at Fawn to see if she had a response. When she shrugged her shoulders he waited, straight-face to see if Mrs Grange had anything else to add, before he gave his attention to Malcolm Grange.

"What about you, Mr Grange? Have you anything to add? Do either of you know of people who would want to harm Delilah?"

They both shook their heads and Mrs Grange picked at the tissue between her fingers.

"Apart from the obvious fact that your daughter has been abducted, it surprise us that you were unaware until we visited. We would have expected kidnappers to have been in touch." Frank looked around and gestured to the house. "Why haven't you heard from her kidnappers asking for a ransom?"

Mrs Grange shifted her gaze to her husband but remained silent and continued to shred the tissue.

Fawn interjected, "The concern my colleague has, and I believe I'm right in saying." She gave Frank a tight smile then continued, "He thinks the kidnappers have contacted you and told you not to involve the police. Now is he correct, or this is the first you have heard of Delilah's disappearance?"

Mr Grange pushed his chair from the table and charged at Fawn before she could move. Frank, quick to see the threat, was on his feet to cut him off. Malcolm Grange wagged a finger at Frank as he yelled. "How dare you come into my house, tell me this traumatic news, and then accuse us of lying about our daughter's disappearance. You need to leave, both of you, now."

Fawn stood and nodded to Mrs Grange, who watched her leave through tear-stained eyes. Then followed Frank along the side of the house, careful to dodge the prickly branches.

"Well, what do you think?" Frank asked as he opened the driver's door and watched Fawn slip behind the wheel.

"I think their reaction was farcical. Well, Malcolm Grange's was at least. Get in and we'll contact Edwards. I think he'll find the links between the two cases important."

Fawn slipped her phone from her jacket pocket and within a few minutes had sent a text and had manoeuvred the car out of the drive and into the quiet back road which skirted the Grange's property.

47

"Ladies, we've added a new member to our elite group." Isla said standing at the front of the group like the leader of a recruitment drive. "The final piece to the puzzle."

"The final player in the Game." Devon added as he entered the room arm in arm with a tall slim woman her purple low cut dress ripped and stained. Her hands were manacled and her makeup smudged into a grotesque mask.

"Meet Delilah Grange." Isla took her other arm and guided her to an empty seat. Esther, in the seat next to her, stared off into the distance. "This is where it gets interesting, ladies. Some of you have been with us longer than others. I know the unfairness of life."

"Life's what you make it that's what I say. Isn't that right, Esther?" Devon dragged a chair from the side of the room and sidled up to her. He looped his arm over her shoulder like teenagers in the back row of the cinema.

Isla pressed on. "I've already hinted that you are all linked. The kidnappings weren't random as the press seem to think. They took a lot of forethought, planning, and nerve."

She took a step to one side and turned on a projector.

"This is cosy, isn't it?" Devon lowered his voice and edged closer to

Esther, who remained still under his touch. Isla lowered the lights. On screen, a young man smiled out at them. He held the hand of a little girl who mirrored his smile and stared up at him in adoration.

The background was familiar, but it could have been one of several parks. There were a few children in the background playing on a roundabout. It was the equipment that aged the picture, especially the cheese cutter.

Isla watched the faces of the women as they waited for her to speak. She'd loved the cheese cutter. It was so dangerous, especially when the older boys made it go high, but she loved the thrill of danger even at such a young age. She'd just loved to spend her time with Robson.

"Does anyone recognise the man in the photo?" She waited and looked from one to the other.

"No? What about this one?" The next image drew a murmur from her audience. It was a photograph of an official police print. The same man lay in the shadow of an alleyway. His features concealed, his body lay twisted on the grimy pavement, and a rubbish bag split open behind him. What was clear to see was a pool of blood that seeped from a wound in his chest and another gash to his stomach?

Esther tried to hide her face in Devon's chest as silent tears ran down her face. Devon gripped her jaw and forced her to face the front and look at the body. "Take a good look, Esther. He's why you're here."

"Esther, you may be the only one who recognises Robson, my brother, but you are all connected to his death."

"This is ridiculous, I've never seen him before in my life." Delilah stood and wobbled unsteadily on her heels. She scanned the faces behind her no one spoke. "What's wrong with you all. Say something. Scream or shout." Delilah turned her attention to Isla. "What have you done to them?"

"Sit down, Delilah. Let's just say they've been with us for a while. It's easy to lose track of who was last medicated. They know what can happen if they misbehave."

The next slide revealed a grainy image taken from a distance. Two police officers manoeuvred a prisoner into the back of a police van. Even though the photograph was long ranged and taken without the officers knowledge, Esther would recognise her brother Liam anywhere. She lifted her hand in front of her face and lengthened her fingertips towards the screen. Her brother actions had saved her from a monster, that's what she'd been told, and that was how she lived with his incarceration.

"This is the man they imprisoned for murdering Robson. So you see there are two grieving sisters here today, both filled with unprecedented emotion."

Devon stroked Esther's arm, then held her in an embrace and rocked her subdued body.

"I understand that some of you are frustrated, still unsure of your connection with the murder of my brother. But it's not just his murder I'm concerned with. You're all here to help me clear his name."

Delilah laughed. A snort that gained Esther's attention. "So you expect help from us when you have us trussed up like pigs."

Isla smiled in her direction but let her continue her rant. "I have this theory. Perhaps I'm old-fashioned, but if you want people to help your cause, whatever that may be, surely you'd at least treat them like human beings?"

Devon rose from his chair and moved between victims like a panther. "Now where would be the fun in that?" He caught Delilah under the chin with the ball of his hand and shoved her jaw closed. His fingers encompassed her nose and forced her mouth shut. She struggled to disengage from his grip.

"Release her, Devon. Ms Grange has a valid point and to be fair she is our newest participant. She isn't aware of recent events. The loss that some players have suffered, and like the others she doesn't know the consequences for not playing."

Esther stirred from her sedated state. "And if we help you?"

"My brother's freedom for yours." Isla bent before Esther and whispered in her ear. "I'm not a monster you have my word."

"You forget we've seen you break your word. Adele remember."

Isla shook her head and rose, an amused grin on her face. "We'll get to that shortly. Devon is excited to see your reaction. But first let's discuss the murders of four young girls fifteen years ago and my brother's conviction for their murders. He was an innocent man accused and found guilty of murders he did not commit. And you?" She said addressing all the women in the room. "You will flush out the real killer and clear Robson's name."

As Isla had hoped the sleeping tablets administered the previous evening had worn off. The women looked from one to the other at their bemused faces.

"So you're saying that anyone of us could be related to a killer? I just don't buy that. What I also don't understand is why you've gone to all this trouble and not just partitioned government or asked the police to reopen the case or whatever else they entitle you to do as his family?"

As Isla aimed her answer at Claire, she noticed the effect incarceration had had on the first woman taken. She'd not given up exactly, but had quietened. The fight had drained from her with each new victim added.

"That is precisely why you are all our guests Claire. We exhausted all avenues before we resorted to the Game. We have planned it in great detail. I persuaded Devon to go along with the idea. At first he wasn't keen, but I had no choice. The law stinks and because no one will listen, I've had to resort to this. Those girls who died their killer is still at large and at least one of you unwittingly knows him."

"So is this about your brother or the murdered girls?" Delilah's question hung in the air unanswered.

Devon joined Isla at the front of the room and wound an arm around her shoulder, "We're going around in circles. Let's discuss connections."

Isla nodded and showed the next slide. The screen was split in two, a photograph of Claire Lance with her father, Geoff. Next to one with a smiling young man who stared down at a blanket-wrapped baby in his arms. The brownish colour of the print aged the picture.

The gasp from Claire was audible. She rubbed the back of her hand against her face to eradicate errant tears that escaped her eyes.

"Obviously the first image is of Claire and Geoff, your father I believe?"

Claire nodded but remained silent.

"Would it surprise you if I told you that the other image is you as a newborn baby?"

Claire cleared her throat, "That's impossible. We had a fire in the house when I was little and all of my baby photos burned, none survived."

"That's just one of several untruths you've been told. The man holding you in the baby photograph is your real father. His name is Joey Kohl."

Isla watched as the information shared had time to sink in while Claire, open-mouthed, shook her head in denial.

Isla continued, "I know it's hard to believe but Geoff Lance paid extortionate amounts of money to adopt you. It was illegal, but we have no way to prove it. Geoff has a very good lawyer. Joey is the link he was in my brother's gang. He was an amateur tattooist who branded the young girls chosen for the parties."

All eyes were on Claire Lance. There was a low buzz in the room, and a sweet excrement of adrenaline.

Nina wept when she was told that she was a mistake, taken instead of her partner Libby. She nodded in anticipation when asked if she wanted to know the connection with the murders and Libby.

"Libby Mann was a tomboy who used to run errands for the gang. She'd help lure the girls. Befriend them. They used her as a pawn and took the girls to be branded. She has her own Raven tattoo but because she was a distant relative of ours they kept away her from the parties. She had a relationship with a gang member, but we're still unsure who."

"You know I'm in a relationship with Libby. She's a Lesbian. I think you've got it wrong, you know about this relationship." Nina said, disillusionment clear in her eyes as she tracked Isla's movement.

Isla dismissed her comment with a brush of the hand and moved on to Esther.

"Esther, you are kind of special. Everyone knows you're the sister of the man who murdered my brother. But that's not the only reason. Do you want to tell everyone your brother's motive for the murder?"

Esther lowered her head for a moment as if in prayer before attempting to turn in her chair. She stared at the hungry eyes facing her, took a deep breath, then began.

"Robson had taken a liking to me. I was fourteen and my older brother Liam was an acquaintance of his. I'd dress up when Robson came round. You know, put some make-up on and short skirts. The thing was, I didn't realise how dangerous my behaviour was, it was my vulnerability. Robson invited me out, just to the youth club. We messed about, nothing heavy. Kissing and touching."

She smoothed her hair and tucked a few stray hairs behind her ear, cleared her throat, then continued.

"After a few weeks, he introduced me to his friends, they were friendly enough. They were a few years older than Robson. He fixated me. It was cool having this older guy pick me up from school on a Harley Davidson. Arguments started between me and my parents. Robson got inside my head. I couldn't stay away. I slept with him on my fifteenth birthday and we celebrated with this. It was a present from Robson. Joey's masterpiece." Esther undid the top three buttons of her dress and let it fall open to reveal a full span raven hovering on the mound of her left breast.

Nina strained to see the tattoo, "Libby has one identical. It's just below her collarbone, but it's the same."

Devon walked towards Esther, eyes fixed on her breast. "Beautiful." He whispered so only Esther could hear. "They also found raven tattoos on the four dead girls."

Esther stared at the smirk on Devon's face as he spoke, "Robson's job to supply the girls. He gained their trust and acted like a loyal boyfriend. But once he'd arranged for them to be branded, it meant he planned to introduce them to the party scene."

Esther blushed at the matter-of-fact description of her abuse. She ignored Devon's flippant remarks and sought to scan over the details. "Liam realised I was in some kind of danger when he glimpsed the tattoo one evening. He went berserk. He forbid me to contact Robson. He tried to warn me about the danger I was walking into, but I wouldn't listen. We had a massive row and I walked out on Liam. Two hours later Robson was dead and Liam was in police custody. He's refused to see me in prison. He saved me from… well, I don't like to think… death."

She stared at Isla, "So don't talk to me about your poor hard done by brother. He may not have killed those girls, but he set them up to go to hell and back."

She held up her arm to protect her face from the sharp slap that rattled her cheekbone. Then another from the back of Isla's hand, a large crystal ring cracked into her eye socket. Devon grabbed Isla around her waist and caught one of her arms in his grip, the other flayed around in Esther's direction. Esther swung her foot as high as she could and it caught Isla in her stomach. The full momentum sent her clattering to the floor in a pile of chains.

The rattle of chains rang through the room, at a methodical pace to begin with, the clink of an old man dragging his feet. The noise built, a gradual ascent until it echoed in a frenzied mishmash accompanied by flaying limbs ecstatic with Esther's fight back.

Devon scanned the room and lowered his stance, face taut, teeth bared, ready to pounce. His sudden movement stalled the heated voices and clank of chains. Once again he fisted a handful of her auburn hair and Esther's shriek added to the cacophony of noise. Devon hoisted her to her feet with a forceful yank which exposed the angry-pink of her scalp. With his free hand he retrieved a handful of chain attached to the wrist irons that held her hands in place, and in one swift action wrapped the iron licks around her neck. He released her hair and pulled the chains like a boa constrictor readying its next meal. Esther contorted her body against the unexpected attack. She dug her fingers under the chains to elevate the constriction on her windpipe. Her eyes bulged and her arms flailed as she struggled to breathe. The chains continued to rattle, an incoherent distortion that hammered in her head and announced her demise.

"Enough," Devon hollered over the mayhem. "Unless you're okay with witnessing a death."

For a fraction of a second Esther panicked, her legs gave up the fight to keep her upright. The noise deafened her and her chest heaved as if frantic to catch its last breath.

The raucous subsided. A gradual radiant of descent until Esther's whimpers were all she could hear reverberating in her head. He loosened his hold and she collapsed on the floor in a heap.

As Isla regained her composure and addressed the women once more, Devon sank to his knees and stroked Esther's hair. He wiped her tears and exonerated her for her previous actions.

Isla smoothed her suit with steady hands, ran her fingers through her tousled curls, and sat on Esther's chair. Her legs outstretched in front of her, she leaned back and rested against the back of the chair. She took her time. Once she had the attention of all the women, she broke the silence.

"Delilah, I suppose you're wondering why we took you?"

Claire spoke up, "Yes, why are you here?"

Delilah pushed her shoulders back, then turned and answered Claire, who had slumped forward in her chair. Raw welts from the chains indented her wrists.

"I've been wracking my brains, and there are so many reasons for me to be here. You probably could think of reasons if you scourer your conscience." Her laugh pierced through the heavy atmosphere. "I mean come on. You haven't lived into your thirties without pissing a few people off, and you're cuckoo if you think otherwise."

"I said I don't know why the fuck I'm here, not that I hadn't pissed anybody off." She threw her body forward against the restraints, sinews stretched in her neck and eyes bulged in her taut face like an alien's attempt to burst into the room.

Delilah remained stock still. The ghost of a grin etched her face. She was used to being attacked and she always stood her ground. Her only telltale tick was a nervous laugh brought under control with age and experience.

"Wow. You are one angry beast."

"That's enough. You've been here five minutes and I've been through hell. I was the first one taken. What's the betting that they're probably watching us now and loving the show. We should work together. We've all got the same purpose: to walk out of here alive."

Isla intervened and addressed Delilah. "Well, you were hand-picked. We bided our time, messed up your kidnap on purpose. You've got one person to thank for your demise. Malcolm Grange."

Delilah watched her mouth form a lopsided circle as she spat out her father's name in a pucker of distaste.

48

Albie awoke to a loud banging. Unsure of whether it was inside his head, he flung his left arm over his eyes, too fragile to move but aware that it was inevitable. He counted to ten with each pound of his head turned on his side, dragged the duvet from his waist, and over his head. This worked, dulled the sound, but did nothing for his full bladder. He swore as he swung back the duvet and edged to the side of the bed. Albie sat up gingerly and placed his feet flat on the carpet. Before he stood, he waited for his vision to adjust to his surroundings and the room to justify.

His journey to the bathroom was fraught, but worthwhile and once he'd splashed water on his face, he knew the only cure for his head was plenty of water, two tablets and if he could face it, breakfast. He navigated the darkened bedroom again, still unable to face opening the blinds, slipped on a pair of boxer shorts from a chair in the corner and rubbed the palm of his hand over his stubbled chin.

Darkness followed him from the bedroom to the living room, in fact it seemed to be a theme throughout his flat, unusual for Albie, he barely ever shut the blinds in his flat, he was so far up that no-one could see into his home.

After negotiating the living room obstacles with just a knock with the coffee table, which would probably leave a nasty bruise, he'd reached his destination. It was then that before he laughed at the stupidity of not opening the living room blinds. Kettle filled and heating, toast in the toaster, and eggs in the microwave, Albie made his way back to the blinds and pulled.

"Aargh. What are you doing?"

Albie's heart jumped and he fell over his feet. Spread on his settee, barely covered by the bedding, Jana flopped an arm over her eyes in a half-hearted bid to keep the stream of sunlight at bay. She tugged the quilt over her body with her other hand, but not before Albie glimpsed her damaged skin. His brother had left his mark on her the night before. He lowered his eyes and swallowed a dry, sore gulp that echoed in his head. Images flashed in front of his eyes like a disjointed movie of the night before. He'd diluted his memories with the quantities of whiskey he'd drunk when they'd reached the safety of home. This was a usual reoccurrence for Albie, his way of dealing with guilt. He swallowed once more, this time saliva basted his throat and made speaking easier.

"Breakfast?"

Jana stretched, slid her arm from her eyes and squeezed them shut tight against the sun. Dominic had marked as well her face. Not as badly as he'd expected, although the worst of the bruising would form around her neck. Her skin was mottled and blotchy from the indents of his brother's fingers.

She croaked rather than spoke. Her face flushed and her hand reached for her throat, "I am hungry. Perhaps something soft?"

Albie watched as Jana ran her fingers over the surface of her swollen neck. She flinched when they reach her throat. Next they travelled to her left eye and she dabbed her swollen, crusted eyelid with another flinch.

"The bathroom?" she asked, shirking the quilt to the floor. She stood on unsteady feet and followed where Albie pointed. He watched her leave the room and smiled for a shy, introverted woman she had no qualms about walking around in just her panties in her bosses house.

They ate in virtual silence, except for the sounds of Jana as she struggled to swallow. She'd found an oversized t-shirt Albie had left out for her on his bed after she'd attempted to make herself at least appear presentable.

Albie's anger heated his blood as he watched Jana nibble a small mouthful of egg, and he clenched his fists and frowned at the tension in her face as she swallowed.

"I'll run you home in a minute." Albie said when Jana pushed her plate to one side. She raised her face to his and attempted a lopsided smile. "And I suggest you stay there for the rest of the day. That looks nasty." He held his fingertips millimetres from her face before lowering his hand and reaching for his phone.

"A lift home would be good. I need to change." She smiled and pulled at the hem of the t-shirt. "But I'm fine to work."

Albie cursed under his breath when his phone didn't respond and hunted around the kitchen for his charger.

"Look, you had a nasty experience last night and..."

"And how is having time on my own going to help?" She coughed and held her throat.

Albie waited for her coughing to subside. He plugged in the charger hidden under a week old newspaper he still hadn't got round to reading and shrugged. "If that's what you want. For the record, it's against my advice"

Jana nodded the smile faded from her face. She rose from the table and gathered her belongings without another word. She struggled out of his t-shirt and he got a glimpse of her firm breasts before averting his gaze.

"Shit." He watched as a ton of messages and missed calls pinged onto his phone.

Jana stopped buttoning her shirt and waited for him to elaborate. Instead, he darted passed her into his bedroom. How had he let this happen? He readied himself and in extra quick time patted his pockets and recited his mantra: wallet, keys, cigarettes, and lighter. Ready, he grabbed his jacket off the back of a chair and joined Jana, who waited patiently by the front door. He'd locked the door and had called the lift before he realised he'd left his phone on charge. He cursed, ran back to the flat and fiddled with the errant lock, which proved tricky because he was in a hurry.

The corridor was empty when he reemerged; he jogged to the lifts, stomping from foot to foot as he watched it ambled up to his floor. He chewed on the skin around the nail of his thumb and pushed his way into the lift before an unsuspecting woman and her two youngsters had the chance to leave. The woman eyed Albie in distaste, kept one finger on the open button and ushered her children out.

Outside, the sun was trying to break through the clouds. Jana wasn't in the entrance hall, so he scanned the street before he noticed a piece of paper folded under his windscreen wiper.

Making my own way home. I thought it was for the best. See you at work.

Albie screwed the paper up and shoved it in his jacket pocket. Relieved, he opened the car door and slid inside. He hadn't relished the thought of explaining to his colleagues why he'd given Jana a lift to work. He'd have made up some story, but he knew people would have made up their own, which would be juicier and probably closer to the truth.

Albie pulled out his phone and took a few minutes to read the messages from Fawn and listen to her gradually escalating voicemail messages. Just for a second, she reminded him of some of his exes when their relationships had become stale. He was thinking he wasn't a relationship kind of guy. Even though his mother and Eva always blamed his choice of woman rather than his incapability of holding down a successful relationship.

The texts and voicemail messages boiled down to a few questions: *Where the hell was he? Did he not care that they were in the middle of a time sensitive investigation? Why was he such a selfish dick?* And *How would he feel when she ended his career for him. That's if he didn't already have a hand in it himself?*

Albie sighed, his mind worked overtime. He'd messed up when he'd visited Freddie. He'd got sidetracked and he would have to have a bloody good reason for going A.W.O.L last night.

On the drive to work, he racked his brains for a believable solution but pulled into a parking space with nothing.

The incident room buzzed with the sound of telephone conversations colleagues engaged in conversations. Albie caught Jana's eye across the room. From a distance and probably with the help of a layer of makeup, her face showed little of the damage so obvious at his flat that morning. She didn't acknowledge him or even return his smile. She looked intently at Frank who was engaged in deep conversation with herself and Tanya.

"So you decided to show your face, I'm surprised you bothered."

He'd recognise that voice anywhere, especially with the added layer of sarcasm. Fawn walked up behind him and spoke to his back. "Well?"

Only a few people looked their way and quickly went back to their discussions..

Albie lifted his hands in surrender, pivoted around to face Fawn and shrugged. "What can I say? The battery went on my phone."

Rachel Fawn crossed her arms over her chest, frowned, and tapped her foot. "So you're telling me from eight last night you never thought to check your phone or contact me."

A grin tugged at the corners of Albie's mouth and he had to make a conscious effort not to give her some wisecrack answer. The room had quietened and he knew Frank and Tanya would listen. He made an attempt to keep a straight face.

"Look, there's nothing I can do about last night. I'm here now, so what did you need to discuss?"

A twitch in the corner of Albie's right eye irritated him. He raised his hand, used his index finger to massage his eyelid. Fawn said nothing, just studied him further as if trying to catch him out on a lie.

"This way." She said and the whole room let out a breath in unison. No showdown today.

"Malcolm Grange. My gut tells me he is our link between the two cases." Fawn leant back against her tidy desk in the corner of their shared office. It was just about big enough for two people if they didn't mind intimacy. That was the main reason Albie preferred to desk hop in the main office. Too much Fawn was bad for his health, but too much Fawn in such close proximity was toxic.

"And you've come to this conclusion because of your gut. Any actual evidence to tie the man to either case? Let's face it, I couldn't see him being involved in the kidnapping of his own daughter."

"I'm not suggesting he's involved in the kidnappings. I'm suggesting he's a target because of his involvement in the cold cases."

"Go no."

Fawn sighed, stood on tiptoes, stretched up, and felt about blindly on the top shelf. She pulled on a pile of files that teetered on the edge of the shelf. Albie watched her struggle for a few more seconds before he reluctantly offered his help. He'd got a sadistic kick from her defiant struggle and he knew he was the last person she'd ever ask for help. His extra foot in height made the task easier.

Fawn prodded the pile of files piled neatly on her desk, "it's interesting when you delve deeper into the cold case files, the number of times Malcolm Grange turns up as their defence lawyer. It appears he worked for not only Robson Shaw's family but also for several associates, including Robson's gang members. Don't you think it's interesting that young yobs had the same defence as a corporate businessman?"

Albie pondered her words. "If that's the case, if Delilah was taken because of her father and we can find links between the other kidnap victims and this case, no matter how tenuous, it's another connection. Great work, Fawn."

"I'll get the team to look for links then? You're a condescending bastard, Edwards. You know that though, don't you?" She grinned, picked up the files, and made towards the office.

Albie held up the palms of his hands, "What? Do you doubt that it's a genuine compliment on your aptitude at closing cases? You never could take a complement." He smirked at her hand gesture and watched her prance from the room, head held high. He let out a long breath, relieved at how the meeting went, and knowing it could have been so much worse.

49

A clean-cut young man grimaced as Joey shaded the final part of a serpent's head on his bicep. He shuddered in time with the repetitive movement of the needle over the same patch of skin. When it was over he unclenched his teeth and studied the finished work. A grin emerged on his face with the same slow precision as each detail on his arm. Joey took a photo of his latest piece of work and pinned it to the board behind him—a trophy board of achievements. Another satisfied customer. He watched him leave and shoved the extra cash in his pocket to sort out later.

Joey was situated at the back of the shop. A position he earned over the years, during periods of time when he was an employee. He took a moment to stop and observe in wonder, satisfied customers, handpicked staff, and an apprentice out front. He had achieved so much more than he expected from his business. They were never short of custom and reaped the profits from the early years when he lived hand to mouth.

Joey Kohl was definitely at the height of his career and no matter what happened at home he'd fight to keep this place. Decision made, he looked at his phone. He had a half-hour break before his next appointment. Time enough to eat and put together a contingency plan. He strolled up the high street and snaked through crowds. The buzz in the pub at lunchtime gave him an injection of adrenaline. The thought of being alone in a crowded place gave him the anonymity he craved, with the added benefit of companionship if he felt the urge to interact. He ordered pie and chips, then found a table in the corner and nursed his pint of bitter as he contemplated the forthcoming appointment.

"There you go, mate. How's it going Joe? Business good is it?" The barman slid the steaming pie in his direction, followed by cutlery.

"Thanks, Harry. Yeah, all's good." Joey unwrapped the knife and fork from a paper napkin and cut into the crusty pastry. Steam swirled into the air and a creamy sauce erupted over his chips. Joey raised his head and opened his mouth to speak, but Harry had already excused himself to serve another customer. He scooped a lump of chicken onto his fork, blew, and watched little waves form in the gloop of sauce then stabbed the prongs into a chip raised it to his wide-open mouth. He used the back of his hand to catch sauce escaping down his chin, then licked it off once he'd swallowed his mouthful.

For the next fifteen minutes, Joey concentrated on his meal. He collected the last of the sauce and pastry crumbs on the knife, wiped it expertly against the edge of his fork and savoured the final mouthful. He pushed the plate towards the centre of the table, drew the pint of bitter towards him, leant back and stroked his stretched but rounded midriff. In that moment, Joey realised there was no master plan. In his contented frame of mind he was sure of only a few things. The first was that he had to meet her. This Isla Shaw. If not now, she would find him and he'd rather it was at work than at home. He also thought that she may have nothing to do with Robson. It was probably a coincidence. The tattoo and the girls would turn out not to be on her agenda. Joey had, however, decided that questions would go unanswered if he was wrong. After all, what could this young girl hope to achieve?

'Sweet child o'mine' echoed around the shop when he opened the door and it relieved him to find it was business as usual.

"Joe, some girl came in, said you had a meeting. She's gotta put a ticket on her car. She'll be five minutes."

He felt his smile slip. He strolled to the back of the shop and prepared his area.

Her entrance raised some eyebrows. He glanced in her direction, caught by the shock of silver blonde hair, and delicate pale skin tone. Even from his position at the back of the shop, Joey knew there was a connection between this girl and Robson. If only he could remember Robson's sister's name.

"He's at the back love," His young pretender nodded in Joey's direction as he moved towards her.

"Miss.." He flicked through his appointment book "Shaw, right?"

Isla perched on a chair at the back of his area. "Yes, but please call me Isla." She smiled. Under any other circumstances, he'd have been as intrigued with this woman as other men in the room. She wasn't petite, but proportioned in a way that drew a man's attention.

"Okay, Isla. So your friend booked this appointment. He wants you to have a tattoo. Is this your choice? The reason I ask is that you must be sure you want this permanent marking."

Her smile broadened, "An interesting choice of word... marking..." She paused and Joey waited for her to continue. Isla stood and shimmied through a gap and twisted at the waist to reach his board of honour.

"Is this all your work?" She traced the images with the tip of her fingernail. He felt warmth drift from her body as he leaned over and removed a few of his favourite examples.

"I know you're interested in a bird tattoo." He spread out a handful of examples like a hand of cards. "These are some examples of recent work that may interest you."

"Oh no, Mr Kohl. I know what I want, a raven. I thought my friend had shown you a copy of the image I was after."

Joey leant back against the draw where the picture was hidden. "Yeah, now you mention it, he did show me something."

"It was a photo of a tattoo you inked."

"I don't think so. This is my resumé..." He raised his arm and gestured to the pictures on the wall. "The best examples. Birds aren't my forte. I prefer people, angels, that kinda work. If you must have a bird though I'd recommend the snowy owl or what about a magpie? They're very popular."

"Joey." she held out a replica of the photo her friend left. He ignored the personal use of his given name. "That's what I want. Just the same as the girl's you say my brother murdered."

The shop was quiet, apart from Fleetwood Mac's Dreams escaped from the speakers. Thankfully, everyone appeared too engrossed in their work to have heard her last comment. "I think you should leave."

"You don't mean that, Joey. Claire would like me to stay."

Joey sunk inwards, his shoulders curved to protect his heart. He outstretched his right arm and grasped the counter. His fingers itched, the skin across his knuckles stretched and pale. He wondered what her porcelain skin would look like adorned with a red handprint.

"Yes, Joey, you heard right. I know what has happened to Claire and I'll share that with you if you will share your part in the murder of the Raven girls." Isla rose from her chair. "I would like to book an appointment for tomorrow at the same time. You can think about your options. Oh, and I would still rather have a raven tattoo." Isla took a few steps towards the door, shuffled through the contents of her handbag and handed a card towards Joey. "Here's my number if you need to contact me before tomorrow. Goodbye for now, Mr Kohl."

Every head turned and followed her retreating figure. "Nice one, Joe." The apprentice next to the door shouted. A few of the clientele waited for a response but were sidetracked by the buzz of needles.

Joey cleared his area, grabbed his jacket, and slipped the spare keys onto the counter. "Zip, I'm off. Lock up tonight, will you?"

"Right mate."

"Do us a favour, Zip. try to get a hold of my four o'clock. Either you can finish him or he can sort out another appointment."

The buzz ceased and for the first time Zip looked up, "You all right, Joey?"

"Yeah, something's come up. Will you just do it for me?"

The air was cool and the rumble of traffic drowned out any response from inside. He leant against the window, lit a cigarette, and took a drag. An unfamiliar sea of faces shimmied in the dance of life around each other, each one intent on their own destinations and needs. Joey made his way down the side alley that led to the back of the shop. She wasn't there, but she was watching. He felt her eyes on him, the back of his neck prickled, and his sixth-sense was in overdrive.

Joey threw his leg over the thick leather seat of his Harley and tensed his thighs. By the time he'd turned the key in the ignition, tightened the strap of his helmet, and revved the throttle, his whole body was alight. The thrill of the ride was just a fragment of why Joey kept the bike. He'd heard the underhand sniggers and whispering of a midlife crisis. If he should believe his missus, his choice of transport amounted to nothing but a desperate bid to cling to his youth. What she didn't understand was the pleasure he gained from his bike. Not just the physical thrill but the mental high, pheromone. As soon as he felt the exhilaration as he cut through the air, and the gasps to catch his breath pheromone exploded his brain and to every nerve in his body. He couldn't remember the last time he'd felt that way in bed with his wife. No, she would never understand.

Joey knew where he was heading. The traffic wasn't an issue at this time of day. He headed for a place where he could order his thoughts and consider his options. The Kent countryside spread before him. London was never the answer, not during times of dilemma. He weaved in and out of cars on the M20 until he reached the Brands Hatch turn off and headed towards Vigo. He parked outside the George Inn. There were only a few other vehicles parked in the dimly lit car park. Thankful to hit the pub between the lunchtime and evening rush, he wandered in and ducked his head to avoid the timber beams on the already low ceilings. He reserved a table for later and left his helmet behind the bar with a strikingly attractive barmaid who seemed to show a particular interest in his tattoos.

"Perhaps we can discuss them later," He'd given her his most seductive wink then left to replace the nostalgic sounds of Black Sabbath with the musically superior calls of the surrounding countryside.

Joey grew at least three inches in stature as he took in the deserted fields. He felt his lungs expand to twice their size and anticipated the pleasure of light-headedness that always followed. He revelled in how the village saw little change. The path he walked although trodden by many others was in the most part deserted. Whenever he'd walked to the Doldrums and Pilgrim's Way, he'd meet a sprinkling of fellow travellers along the route, but they were often ramblers or dog walkers all prepared to keep to themselves.

He raised his head and thanked whoever was listening for a cloudless sky and smiled at the memory of the bombardment of rain he'd endured on a previous visit.

Today the haze of the late afternoon sun tickled the back of his neck cooled by a light breeze, fresh and clean, he scanned the downs, filled his lungs with clean air, turned, and began the steep ascent through the woods. The chirps of birds, scattering squirrels, and other unseen creatures were his only companions.

Joey jumped a fence which encircled the iconic stones. Offerings swayed in the breeze. Each tied to the outstretched branches of the overhanging tree. Each one bore an individual message to the burial ground. Each one a gift to the unsettled spirits.

The ground was solid and he wriggled to find a comfortable spot. He closed his eyes and cast his mind back to his early twenties. He was a bit of a Jack-the-lad. It was true, he'd loved the ladies but knew when enough was enough. If a girl said 'no' that was good enough for him. He'd move on until he found one who'd say yes. Someone like Julie Malone, his Julie, who'd died so young and left him with baby Carla. The past wasn't somewhere he ventured often. For every good memory he had, there was always a sinister part of his youth he wished to forget.

Although in reality, he could never be sure whether he'd had embellished memories. Joey Kohl knew he didn't relish the connection he had with the dead girls at the forefront of his mind again and that was the impact the appearance of Isla Shaw had caused.

The Shaw girl reminded him of her brother, the silver blonde hair and and bow lips, although she didn't have Robson's Mediterranean blue eyes. Girls had loved Robson, they flocked for his attention, and he could have had his pick. In fact, he often did.

That's why it made little sense. Once he was dead all the evidence that surfaced connected him to the girl's murders. Joey remembered questioning Anthony at the time, "It just goes to show. We don't really know people." Anthony had shrugged his shoulders and ordered another pint. It was never discussed. Just accepted. For the first time in twenty years, Joey wondered about Robson's innocence. If it was true, he'd played his part in harbouring a killer.

Joey checked his phone for a signal and rang the number on the card.

"It's me, Joey." He listened to the reply on the other end of the phone. "I know you want to know the killer's identity. Well, it's me." There was a long silence on the other end of the phone and for a moment he thought she'd hung up. "I'm not listening to what you have to say. I can prove I'm the killer, but I will only cooperate if you release the girls unharmed. A trade off. You get the real killer and the innocent go free. Text me an address and we can trade."

Joey hung up and dialled 999. All he cared about was Claire and he knew that the police were the only chance he had now to ensure her safety.

50

Isla cancelled the call. "Devon, we need to get ready for a pickup. Joey Kohl has just confessed to killing the girls." Isla had been expecting him to be in touch but not to confess. A rumble of doubt bubbled in the pit of her stomach. This wasn't right, it was too quick.

Devon walked into the room, adjusting his flies.

"Remember what we talked about if the plan went wrong?"

Devon nodded.

"Are you still all in? I need to know because I've a feeling that this may not work out in our favour."

"I said at the beginning that I would not go to prison... I still feel the same."

Isla unlocked a musical box on the dressing table and handed him a plastic bag which held two blue tablets. She put a replica bag into her pocket.

"So, what's the plan?"

"I've messaged the meeting place to Joey Kohl. You get Claire ready for the handover and I'll call the police with the information. I'll meet you in the car."

Devon bent down and kissed the top of Isla's head. "It may not have to end this way." He said as he tucked the tablets into his own pocket and left the room.

Isla stared at her reflection in the mirror and traced her face with her fingers. She'd always known she would die young, just like Robson. They were destined to live life to the full and die hard.

"I know you can hear me, Robson. Wherever you are. It's nearly over and it feels good to tell you we found the murderer. I'll be with you soon and I can tell you what you deserve to know. Just one more task and we'll be together again."

Isla lifted the phone and called the police. "I have the name of the Ravensbourne murderer. No, I won't leave my name. Listen, I need you to tell DS Edwards that the murderer is Joey Kohl. He can find the missing girls at Crocken Farmhouse." She cancelled the call and picked up her bag. At the door she surveyed the room one last time and walked to the top of the stairs.

"Where are you taking me? No, stop it, that hurts." Devon clung to Claire. He ignored her screams and dug his fingers deeper into her skin.

"Looks like your real daddy came through for you, Claire. Now settle down and we'll take you to meet him."

Claire stopped struggling and looked into Devon's eyes. "Is that true? I'm I really getting out of here?"

Devon nodded and opened the back door of the car. "Now in you get like a good girl." She bent down and slid across the back seat and he shuffled in next to her.

Claire tried to relax, but Devon could feel the racing of her pulse and the rush of energy she exhumed.

Lights glared from all the front windows in the house as Isla slipped into the driver's seat. She smiled at Devon, "They should be able to find the girls with the light show. If they struggle, then we really need to rethink our police force."

Devon laughed, "So, this is really the end?"

"We'll see. If it is though, it's been a fun ride." She started the ignition and drove to the end of the drive. "Remember, any sign of police at the drop off area then we put the plan into place."

Claire sat forward in her seat and placed her hands on the back of Isla's. "We'll die. That's your plan, isn't it? You'll kill us all. Why? How will it help your brother now?"

Isla shifted gear, "Not all of us will die, Claire. Only those who deserve to die. If your conscience is clear, then you have nothing to worry about."

"And, Joey? Is he going to die?"

"Sit back in your seat, Claire. I need to concentrate. I don't want to miss our turning."

"It's second on your right." Devon said as they headed towards country lanes. "Half a mile on and it's the first left. The Anchor pub, it's in the middle of the village."

Isla sighed, "I used to love the village when I was a little girl. I'd play tag with Robson and his friends and we'd have picnics. It seemed like the sun always shined when I was young." She smiled, "The sun always shined when Robson was alive."

Claire shuffled in the back seat of the car. "Robson wasn't all good though, was he? He was human. They involved him in selling those young girls to older men. He may as well have murdered them."

The car skidded from side to side and Isla glared in the rearview mirror. "Don't speak about my brother. You didn't know him. What right do you have to throw accusations? We're ready to die, are you?" Isla yanked the steering wheel to the left, then right, and Claire screamed.

In the distance a light flickered over the Anchor pub. Across the road Isla could just make out a roadblock.

"Joey called the police." She said and pulled up the handbrake. "Plan A or B?" She asked Devon, who sat with his eyes closed in the back of the car.

For a moment, Isla thought she'd lost his bond, until he opened his eyes and smiled. "Plan B." He stepped from the car and rounded to the passenger door. "Get out."

Claire looked up at him in disbelief, "What?" she stayed put and glanced at Isla, who didn't speak.

Devon gripped her upper arms and dragged her from the car and threw her into the bushes that edged the road. "You should really do what I say. It's for your own good." He bent down and grabbed her face then leaned in for a painful kiss. "I'll see you in another life." He said, as she scampered backwards to break his hold.

Isla opened the plastic bag and held the tablets in her hand. She waited until Devon settled in the front seat and held his too. "Okay?" She asked and they both threw their heads back and swallowed. Isla passed a bottle of water to Devon and revved the engine.

"Are you ready?" Isla stroked Devon's cheek and smiled.

Devon kissed her hand. "As I'll ever be."

Isla put the car into drive, pushed her foot down on the accelerator, and closed her eyes.

51

A woman tapped her fingers on the front desk while the police officer on duty attempted to complete information on an official looking form.

"Excuse me," she said, tapping harder.

The officer took her time and filed the documentation before acknowledging the woman.

She slipped her pen behind her ear and took a sip of water. "How may I help you, madam?"

"I've got to see DS Edwards."

"About?"

"Look, I just need to see him. I've some information he'll find useful."

The officer smiled at the woman, who had her thick bottle-blonde hair piled onto the top of her head and held in place with a giant clip. She had a delicate pattern of butterflies tattooed on the inside of her arm at the elbow and travelling the length of her upper arm to finish just under her collarbone.

The officer placed her pen on the desk and straightened to her full height. "I need to know what it's concerning before I contact the detective, Ms..."

"It's Mrs. Mrs Kohl." The woman slammed her palm on the desk and studied the officer's poker face. "I know you've got my husband in one of your cells, and that's why I'm here." She glared at the officer who still hadn't moved. "Well, are you going to call Edwards or not?"

"There's no need to call Edwards," Albie said as the front door to the reception closed behind him. "I'm DS Edwards. What can I do for you?"

Mrs Kohl turned and stared at Albie's outstretched hand for a moment before shaking it with the firmest grip she could muster.

"Lynne Kohl... I'm Joey's wife."

Albie leaned his back against the reception desk, and the officer on the other side picked up her pen and continued to fill in the forms. He was tempted to speak, but waited until Lynne Kohl's breathing steadied and the dark pink blotches that covered her cheeks showed signs of fading with her aggression.

"I've come to drop off some papers that Joseph asked me to bring to the police station if they ever arrested him." Lynne Kohl pushed the envelope towards Albie's chest and took a step back. Albie grabbed at the envelope before it fell to the floor and lifted his head as she strode towards the door.

"Just one moment, Mrs Kohl." Albie raised his hand and voice at the same time. "It would be helpful if you stayed while we went through the contents." He shook the envelope in his raised hand. "We may need some clarification."

Lynne Kohl placed her hand on the doorknob and hesitated before facing Albie.

"Look, let me be clear so there are no misunderstandings. I know nothing about my husband's past, and that suits me just fine. I've got two kids to collect from school in thirty minutes." She gestured towards the clock on the wall. "If you need clarification of anything, ask the person in the know, Joseph."

Without another word, she opened the door and slipped out onto the street.

Albie smiled at the officer behind the desk. "Well, at least we know where Mrs Kohl lives when we need a statement from her. Not that I can see her adding anymore information to what we already have."

Albie raised his hand and wriggled his fingers as he nudged the double doors to his right open with his side. "Later," he said to the bent figure of the officer who was still engrossed in the forms on the desk.

Albie took the stairs at the end of the corridor, two at a time, until he reached the offices at the hub of the investigation. He wound his way between desks and gestured to his colleagues to follow towards the boards. At the front table, he fanned out the contents of the file while the others gathered around.

Fawn cocked her head to the side and examined the paperwork from a distance. "So what delights do we have here, Edwards?"

Albie scoured the information, grinned, and ran his fingers through his hair as he replied, "I have a feeling we may have hit the jackpot."

Gibbs, Watts and Kolska followed the interaction with interest.

Fawn picked up an A5 envelope and scattered the contents on top of the documents. "Because?" she asked, picking up a dog-eared photograph of a baby.

Albie ignored Fawn's question and instead turned to Tanya. "Get the interview room ready. We need to have another chat with Joey Kohl." Then he turned his attention to the others. "Lynne Kohl has just handed us Joey's life insurance. I have a feeling that the killer's identity is amongst this paperwork."

Seconds passed in silence as the officers absorbed his words.

"Come on, sharpish. The first one to find the links will have drinks on the house when this is all over. My treat."

Albie stared at the four neat piles of paperwork his team had organised. One pile unconnected to the case. Another associated with the baby girl he'd sold. The third was work related, and the final pile, compiled of photographs, notes, audiotapes, and a small bag of earrings, was the most relevant.

He placed the final three piles in a tray and marched towards the corridor where Tanya paced back and forth outside of an interview room. She stopped, raised her head, and mirrored his smile. "You've got something useful then, sir?"

"Let's just say, Kolska pieced together most of the links we needed. I'm sure we'll find more the deeper we dig, but for what we need now, I'm happy with what we've got. It will be a cheap night for me too. Kolska isn't really a drinker, so I'd say it's a win all round." He winked at Tanya and a smile lit up his face. He placed his hand on the door handle. "Ready?"

Tanya nodded and followed her boss into the room.

Joey stared at the images placed in front of him, and his face blanched. Albie noticed an intermittent twitch pulse in his right eyelid. With each piece of paperwork he scanned, he rubbed his hands together to remove an invisible stain, and sweat beads dotted his hairline.

"What have you got to say about these, Joey?" Albie pushed forward a small bunch of photographs. Although they were blurry and taken at night, they came in pairs, and each pair reminded Albie of a before and after picture. The same boy smiled out from every photograph. The difference between each pair was that the girls in the pictures only smiled out from one, in the other, they laid still as if asleep in a river, the smile then snatched from them with their life.

Joey lowered his head to his hands and breathed deeply. He shook his head. "I don't believe it, I told her to hand the package to the cops if they arrested me."

"You've kept this under wraps for years, Joey. You didn't even speak up when Robson was put in the frame for the murders." Albie paused and shuffled through the papers before he continued. "This," he said, pushing an old employer form across the table, "was an eye-opening document. It wasn't you tattooing the girls, that job fell to Liam MacDonald. Was that how he got to know the girls well enough for them to trust him? Did he know you'd taken the pictures of him and the bodies? Was that why Robson ordered you to put a raven tattoo on his sister, Esther?"

Both Edwards and Watts waited while Joey gnawed on his bottom lip and stared into space.

"Well, I don't think I should say any more. I want to speak to my lawyer."

Edwards and Watts stood at the same time. "We thought you'd need to talk to him. We have some questions for the man who signed these legal documents. You'll be pleased to know that Malcolm Grange is on his way, but whether he'll be representing you in this matter is doubtful."

Joey Kohl bent his head, straightened his fingers, and examined his fingernails as the officers shut the door behind them and left him in the care of a young uniformed officer who stared over his head at the wall behind.

52

The building looked bleak all year round. Today the sunshine lit up its faults, all the cracks and crevices that a Victorian build portrays. Dank, dark and gloomy like the prisoners it homes.

Albie reversed into a parking space and looked at the fragile woman sat beside him in the car.

"Are you sure you want this?" He asked his companion. "Just because your brother has asked to see you doesn't mean you have to turn up."

Esther raised her head and answered, her voice as fragile as her body. "It's the first time he's asked to see me since the court case. He'll have a reason for this visit and I doubt it will be about my wellbeing. If he cared about me he'd have wanted to see me before now."

Albie nodded. "PC Watts will be with you at all times and the team will hear every word he says to you. You are completely safe." He motioned to the wire strategically placed under her clothing. "The slightest problem and they'll pull you out. Try to stay on script, but if he seems suspicious, it's all right if you improvise."

"What if I can't worm a confession out of him? I mean, he's not necessarily going to fess up to his little sister after all these years."

"Don't you worry about that, it's not your problem. That's why we get paid the big bucks, leave it to the police."

Esther smiled. It was the first time he'd seen her smile since they rescued the girls from the farmhouse four days earlier. That day she had sobbed along with the others. Not a violent cry but an eerie drone, a sob the disturbed even the hardest heart. The team were treading softly with the girls, but Albie knew the victims horrifying stories would come out. He also knew the suffering they will relieve in their dreams and daydreams for many years.

"Right. I'll leave you with Tanya. You'll nail it."

Albie stepped from the car and made his way through the prison gates by foot. He had wanted to remain with the team, but Esther had received a request to visit her brother, and Albie's instructions were to support her.

Albie lowered his head, rubbed the sole of his shoe over the concrete and called out to the woman. "I'll meet you back here in an hour. I have to deal with some family business of my own."

Esther flattened wayward strands of auburn hair to her head, slung a bag over her shoulder and followed Tanya Watts, her head held high.

The hospital wasn't too far from the prison. The walk suited Albie, a chance to clear his head after the previous night. Questions had mingled in his head and this was his opportunity to weed his thought of redundant reasoning.

Freddie sat up in bed. His face wore a healthy flush. They'd tidied him up, washed and dressed him in a clean pair of pyjamas. He motioned Albie into the room with a wide smile on his face, "Come in, son. It's good to see you. Sit down, sit down."

Albie faltered by the door for a second, surprised by Freddie's active delight in seeing him after their previous meeting.

"Sit down." Freddie said again and pointed to the highjack chair by the side of his bed.

"This isn't a social call, Freddie." Albie said as he crossed the room to the chair.

Freddie smirked, "I'm not that naïve to have thought otherwise. It's just good to see you, anyway."

"I'm here about the case. We have found the women who were kidnapped."

Freddie's expression didn't change. So Albie continued. "The thing is, Freddie. I believe you know more than you're letting on. You had your fingers in every pie back then, no-one would get away with anything on your turf that you didn't know about and survive."

Freddie's grin widened, "So, you want me to hand over the real murderer, do you? Ha, I thought you would have figured out who it was by now."

Albie's grin mimicked Freddie's, "Oh, I have. I'd just like your confirmation. I'm also flummoxed why you'd frame Robson Shaw."

"How about you get us both a cup of coffee and I'll tell you a story. Just like old times."

Albie didn't argue, he walked to the door, looked up and down the corridor and made his way to the coffee machine.

Esther sat across the room from her brother. Liam was not how she remembered him. In fifteen years he'd changed beyond recognition. He was a large man, like their father. Every part of his body that she could see was muscular, even his large hands looked dangerous.

"Liam." She said, unable to look him in the eye.

"You came. I wasn't sure whether you would after all this time."

Esther felt like reminding him it had been his choice to break all communication, but remembered Albie had spoken to her about avoiding hostility.

"So, how have you been?" She kept her eyes on her hands and fiddled with a tissue between her fingers.

"It's not the Ritz, but I'm used to it, in here now. Let's face it, this is my home for a few more years yet."

Esther couldn't help herself, she looked into his eyes and asked, "Why did you ask to see me, Liam."

He stared at her for a few moments, "Just to make sure you are all right. I heard what happened. We hear everything that goes on in here."

"Why? What could you do anyway?"

Liam leaned back, "I worry about you. No matter what you think. I worry about you. You'd be surprised what I could orchestrate from in prison. I have my contacts."

Esther jumped to her feet and lunged at her brother. "What the same contacts that helped you with the girls?" Two prison officers pulled her away from the table and towards the door.

Liam stood shackled. "Wait." The prison officers stopped but tightened their grip on Esther. "What are you talking about, Esther? What do you know about the girls?"

"Did you kill them all, Liam? Was that how you got your thrills, you bastard?" The prison guards dragged Esther from the room without an answer. But she didn't need an answer. His guilt lit up his face with the grin that formed on his lips.

Freddie drank the dregs of his coffee and licked his lips like it was the best he'd ever tasted. Albie had barely touched his. One sip of the bitter brew had been enough.

"So, what do you want to know?" Freddie dabbed his mouth with a tissue and squeezed it in his hand, then waited for Albie's response.

"Why? That's what I want to know."

"Why what? Be clearer than that. I'll not discriminate myself by answering the wrong why."

Albie laughed. "You're definitely feeling better, old man."

Freddie laughed too and fought off a cough. "Don't make me laugh." He said in between coughs, "It hurts."

"Why did you fit up Robson with the murders? You knew it was Liam and he was in prison, anyway. So why fit up Robson Shaw?"

Freddie placed both hands by his side, "It's simple, son. It was about territory. That's all I've ever been concerned about, territory."

"Meaning?"

"Robson Shaw was mouthing off to anyone who'd listen that his father was knuckling in on my territory and it probably would have happened. But son, no-one will do business with a family caught up with murder while they're under the police radar."

"What about Liam? He hasn't paid for the murder of those young girls."

"He's in prison, anyway. The parent's of the girls think their murderer is dead. No harm done." Freddie took Albie's coffee off to the side and gulped it down.

"No harm done? What about the kidnapped girls? Another woman was murdered and two people are dead because of a pact killing. And you say no harm done."

Freddie raised his voice, "Well how was I to know Robson Shaw had a psycho sister? You can't pin that on me. Here, take this, you'll need it at some point. Talk to my solicitor, he may help you."

Albie glanced at the card and laughed, "Thanks, Freddie, I will. This just gets better and better."

Freddie shut his eyes, "I'm tired now. You can go, son. Dom will be here soon and I don't think he's ready to see you again, not yet anyway."

Albie walked down the hospital steps and found an empty bench. He read the card he still held in his hand. Malcolm Grange solicitor. He slipped the card into his pocket. He'd enjoy contacting Mr Grange, but not today. Today he would celebrate another solved case.

He put a cigarette between his lips, lit, and inhaled. As he blew the smoke into the air he pulled out his phone and messaged home.

ACKNOWLEDGMENTS

I want to thank the wonderful people who have provided invaluable input and kept me sane through this process. To my husband, Roy, and my children, Dan, Lee, Samantha, Ben, Steven and Luke who have listened to me ramble on incoherently as I tried to think through story ideas.

Beth and Tom, thanks for asking the awkward questions. Thank you to both my editor, Josiah, you are a saint and to my daughter, Samantha, who proofread the final draft.

Finally, I would like to thank you, the reader, for taking time out of your day to read 'Isla'sGame'.

Please consider leaving a review at the online store where you purchased this book and/or telling a friend about the story.

You can find the link here: Amazon Kindle

ABOUT THE AUTHOR

Kimberley Shead is an emerging author of crime fiction. She lives in London with her husband, Roy, two of her children, and Rex, the family's German Shepherd.

Kimberley loves to write as near to the sea as possible. She is inspired by music and part of her writing process involves building playlists to evoke the emotions of the characters in her books.

For more information please check out:
www.kimberleyshead.com

ALSO BY KIMBERLEY SHEAD

DS Albie Edwards Series

Buried Memories

The Voyeur

www.ingramcontent.com/pod-product-compliance
Lightning Source LLC
Chambersburg PA
CBHW020500310726
48979CB00016B/2739/J
9781838243135